HIS FOUND LYCAN

LYCAN SERIES
BOOK TWO

JESSICA HALL

BLURB

Haunted by the shadows of their pasts, King Kyson and Ivy stand on the precipice of a future darkened by secrets and bloodshed. Ivy, once a rogue condemned to death, now stands as the mate to the last Lycan royal, King Kyson.

Yet, just as Ivy starts to trust Kyson and learns of their bond, King Kyson learns her mother is responsible for the brutal massacre of the Landeena Kingdom and the death of his sister.

King Kyson is torn between his fierce love for Ivy and the overwhelming desire for retribution. When he punishes her for the sins of her mother, all the trust he had built up with her shatters.

Feeling betrayed, Ivy tries to escape with her best friend Abbie, but soon learns that running from a mate bond, and Kyson's wrath, isn't as easy as she hoped.

Just when she thought she would finally be free, Ivy finds herself condemned to fate worse than death, and this time at the hands of her mate.

CHAPTER
ONE

K YSON

    I had an entire speech thought out in my head, I even went so far as to think of what I would say to her, but that went out the window the moment I laid eyes on her; I lost it. I know it's ridiculous - because she doesn't even resemble her mother in any way, Marissa's face was all I could see the moment my eyes landed on her.

She is their child. And I can't see past what they did. I couldn't see her, see my mate, instead I saw the enemy and reacted. The moment I looked at her, I could only see that bitch that mutilated my sister and killed her and her child. For years, we hunted down the wolves that helped the hunters, we wasted years trying to find out who the ringleader was, only to learn she was dead all this time.

I just can't fathom how she could do it; she had a child herself, and yet she killed a pregnant woman and her unborn baby—killed the Landeena's and Queen Tatiana's baby. The same woman helped wipe out an entire village of children before sending them down the river to me in a warning. She was a mother herself and did that to another mother, killing all those innocent children.

There was no one I hated more than Marissa Talbot. She took

1

everything from me. Everything and everyone I cared about. Pacing my bed chambers, I try to think, try to see past my rage. Her scent is everywhere in this room, lingering on my sheets, her essence filling my sacred space, and it is driving me insane.

Grabbing the chair, I fling it across the room, watching the wood splinter and crack against the wall with a loud creaking thud. Despite my hatred and fury, the bond calls for Ivy, and I want her. However, I am not safe to be around her. My mind is warped with uncontrollable anger.

The door opens, and Gannon walks in; my eyes take him in briefly, noticing the damage I had caused him, before they dart away guiltily. Gannon's black eyes are cold, hard, and unforgiving. His lips are lifted in a snarl, and his hair is disheveled. He's shirtless, his muscled chest covered in blood from the various wounds he sustained from our fight.

"Where is Ivy?" Gannon demands, his tone clipped and holds a warning as he looks around the room. "Well Kyson? I swear to God if you..."

"If I what?" I snarl angrily as I fist my hands. My hand throbs painfully, and I know it is because the bond has awakened after being so near her and is in full swing. I can feel her pain as if it were my own, feel her anguish and confusion. But I have to shake off the look she had given me when I tossed open the door or I'll be sick. Gannon growls and stalks toward me. Before I can react, I find myself slammed against the wall.

"Where is my fucking Queen?" Gannon roars, his hands fisting my shirt as he glares at me. Before I can respond, the door flings open and I punch him. He grunts, stumbling back before I kick him, sending him flying backward into the bookshelf. A few books tumble off the shelf, spilling onto the floor. With a snarl, I move toward him, but Damian gets between us as we charge at each other. Damian and shoves Gannon back.

"Stand down, Gannon!" Damian snaps, his tone telling him he is in serious danger of breaching the pledge he swore to uphold.

Gannon glares at me, pointing an accusing finger. "You have made a fucking mistake, King or not; I won't stand by this. Now where is our Queen?" Gannon bellows. Damian is caught between us, looking at us both, trying to figure out what the hell happened. We still hadn't had a chance to tell him, and I was in the process of telling him when Ivy had walked up earlier, making me lose my trail of thought as I became consumed by rage.

"Will someone tell me what has happened and why you just made me put your fucking mate in the damn stables like some wild animal?" Damian demands, looking at a complete loss for words.

"The stables?" Gannon gapes at him, then glares at me.

They both hate me. I hate myself for what I did. I just lost control, and if she was near me, I may have killed her.

The stables, for some reason, were what came to mind, being the furthermost place from the castle itself while still being somewhat covered from the elements.

"You fucking bastard, you fucking promised. She isn't her mother, you can't punish her for something she had no part in," Gannon snarls. If he were anyone else, I would have killed him for daring to talk back to me, let alone touching me. But Gannon and I grew up together, he is considered family, more than a guard.

"Who," Damian shakes his head, looking between us. "What in the world happened when you were gone, and who are you talking about?" Damian demands to know. But Gannon and I are too busy glaring at each other to answer.

"Fix it! I swear, Kyson, I have stuck by you for fucking decades, opposed nothing you have asked of me, but if you don't fix this. I am walking, King or not. I am fucking done," Gannon spits at me, then stomps to the door.

"Where are you going?" Damian asks, trying to figure out what is going on.

"To find my Queen," Gannon snaps as he rips open the door to my growl.

"Wait, just fucking wait until I know what's going on," Damian snarls at us both. Gannon growls, but closes the door and folds his arms across his chest.

"Now, explain," Damian says.

"Marissa Talbot is Ivy's mother," I tell him.

"What?" he asks, shocked.

"The werewolf hunter, the one that killed my sister and the other Lycan bloodlines. Her mother was the insider, she was the one that killed them," I growl. Just speaking that vile woman's name was like ingesting poison.

"What? How is Ivy connected to this?"

"She's not. Her mother killed them," Gannon growls. "Not Ivy, she didn't kill them, you bloody twat!" he snaps, turning his attention to me, and I press my lips in a line.

"That's what Alpha Dean had to tell you?" Damian gasps, looking between us, while I wander over to the bar to drown my sorrows and my guilt.

"Wait, that is why you sent her to the fucking stables, Kyson? For something her mother did?" Damian asks, outraged.

"He fucking said he would leave it, forget it. He agreed she was innocent. She didn't fucking kill your sister, Kyson," Gannon snarls.

"You think I don't know that?" I roar. This is so fucked up; I don't think I can be around her, not without the risk of hurting her.

"What about her father?" Damian asks.

"They are trying to find his link to all this. We also think he was not aware of the crimes bestowed on his wife, we found nothing on him, that's why we are late," Gannon explains.

"And you're sure it's her parents?" Damian asks, sitting down on the edge of my armchair and rubbing both hands down his face. He looks just as defeated as I feel, dark circles under his eyes and his overall demeanor is drained of life.

"Kyson was supposed to show her a picture to make sure, but instead, I come up here and find out she has been taken to the fucking stables like some farm animal!" Gannon growls. "You're going to have a *very* hard time walking this back, Kyson."

"Gannon enough, it may not be right what he did, but stop. Just let me think," Damian says. He knows better than anyone how much that woman haunts me. The horrors of finding my sister like that and what that woman did to her. How she could do that to another mother sickened me.

"Go, take a photo to Ivy, verify it is her mother while he calms down," Damian says to Gannon, who nods and walks out. He is livid, understandably, but I had kicked Ivy out long before my brain processed what I had done.

"Kyson, you could ruin her by not accepting her, ruin your only chance, bonds are easily damaged," Damian says, and I look away from him, not able to stand seeing him angry at me. His disappoint-ment is palpable.

"I know," I tell him, feeling sick to my stomach and looking down at my hand that seems to have grown its own pulse. I flex my fingers, which are still throbbing.

"Maybe you should go for a few days, get away for a bit. I can bring Ivy back up here and watch over her until you get your head around this," Damian suggests, and I growl.

Yet, all I can think about is her intruding in the very place her mother slaughtered my sister mercilessly. "I do not want her in this room," I snap at him, and he growls, shaking his head at me.

"Well, move fucking rooms, Kyson. It's depressing as fuck that you use your sister's old room and that shrine of a room. This is not healthy, especially the room you have across the hall full of all Azalea things. You need to get over it, move on and stop living in the past. Ivy is your chance to do that. She is not her parents, not our past, she's your fucking future, and you're about to ruin it!" Damian snaps at me.

How could he say that? Marissa Talbot took everything from me, and now I am supposed to love her spawn, accept her like her mother did no wrong? What cruel fucking fate made me mates with the spawn of Marissa Talbot; it's a fucking cruel joke, that is!

"What's done is done. Ivy has paid enough for her parents' sins.

5

You don't need to punish her for them, too," Damian says, standing up.

I know the horrors she has suffered very well, and now I am another one to inflict more pain. Logically, I know this, but the burning hatred of what her parents did overshadows the bond. I can't let this go. So the safest place for her right now is far away from me. I sip my drink, not bothering to give an answer to his words, it would only end with more arguing.

"I get Kyson, I do. But you need to find a way to look past who her parents are because if you hurt her?" I glance over at him, and he looks away for a second before sighing heavily. He turns his face back, meeting my gaze.

"I am with Gannon. I won't stand to see you destroy her. I will walk. I know everyone else in this castle will walk for her too. You are not the only person that has waited for your Queen." He pauses for a second, glancing at the glass in my hand.

"This place has been a shrine for too long. We won't watch it go back to being a prison of your depression. Fix it, or you are on your own, my King," he tells me. She has been here five minutes, and they've turned on me!

"She isn't of royal blood," I tell him.

"No, but she is our rightful Queen. The person destined to rule alongside you. You are our King, and we all took the same pact when you appointed us as your guard."

"We swore that when the time came, we would protect our Queen over you, if that means choosing her over you..." Damian says to my growl as he continues giving me a hard look. "... then so be it.," he finishes before storming out.

The moment the door closes, my legs give out. I collapse on the floor. My feet go from under me and I lean against the small bar. I know they are right. And I know I've fucked up, yet I can't control my anger.

I promised to hurt the people responsible the same way they broke me, but I had no idea that the person that would be taking that

punishment would be my mate. Feeling for the mindlink, I search for Gannon. He should be with Ivy by now and hopefully have some answers.

He allows the mindlink but growls at me when it is opened. However, he doesn't try to shove me out.

'How is she?' I ask, trying to keep the frustration I feel from my voice.

'How do you think? She is confused, and you broke her fucking hand,' he tells me and I glance at mine, that explains the throbbing sensation I feel.

'It will heal when she shifts. Did you show her the photo?' I ask and Gannon growls. I can tell he doesn't want to answer me.

'Gannon?' I snarl.

'Yes, Marissa Talbot is her mother, but that doesn't mean she needs to pay for what her parents did, Kyson,' Gannon finally answers. I kinda hoped she wouldn't recognize them, yet I knew that was wishful thinking.

'Just stay with her,' I tell him.

'I was planning to. Do you think I will leave my queen unguarded?' he retorts.

I growl at his words. She wasn't even marked yet, and my royal elite guard is already choosing her over me, the pact isn't in full swing until I mark her, I can still force them against her until then!

'Are you really going to make her shift on her own?' Gannon asks me, making me remember she will shift tonight.

'You're there,' I tell him.

'Kyson, that is not the same. She is petrified, and you fucking promised her,' Gannon growls. I really need to remember not to tell them so much because now he is using it against me.

'Kyson! You gave her your word!'

Guilt gnaws at me, and I reach up, grabbing the bottle off the shelf above my head and cracking the lid. I take a swig while trying to decide what to do before answering.

'Tell me when she starts to shift, and I will come down,' I sigh, cutting

off the link before he can protest. I pull my lips between my teeth before getting up and grabbing a few bottles from the bar. If I am going to keep this promise, it would be best if I am too drunk to shift if I am going down there. At least until I figure out what it is I am doing with her.

TWO

I VY

I'm taken to the stables, which is by a huge man made dam. As we approach the stable, I notice a few guards coming out having unlocked it, watching me with curious and awkward eyes. The porch front has a roof that overhangs and a few old rickety rocking chairs that overlook the dam and pier. It's surrounded by a wide array of plants, flowers, and herbs. The air is moist here and the smell of fresh hay lingers in the air.

Inside the stable, several horses are standing in their stalls. The smell of hay and leather fills the air, and the wooden stalls creak as the horses shift in their shelter. A few of the horses whine in greeting as I walk by. I stop, looking at the huge white one. I reach out my hand to stroke the velvety muzzle of it. The horse pushes its head into my palm as if it wants more when Dustin nudges me forward.

I am mesmerized by the beauty of the horses, yet glancing around, I never pictured that I'd be living with them. Yet, I guess I can't truly escape the fact that I am a rogue, and this is far more than I deserve. I should be grateful he didn't kill me because it was clear he wanted to.

"Quick, sit down while I try to take care of your hand," Dustin urges, dragging a cut in half a wine barrel over. He flips it over, so I can sit on it. The other guard growls at him before gripping his shoulder, and Dustin glares at the man's hand touching him. Staring up at the man, he glares at me with so much venom, that I instinctively drop my gaze.

"We were told to bring her here, that is all," he snaps at Dustin. He is only trying to help fix my hand? I steal another peek at the man, who stares back at me like I am the scum of the earth, and I quickly avert my gaze again.

"Remove your hand, Trey, or you'll fucking lose it," Dustin snaps at him.

"I'm following orders, the King said. Bring her here, and that is it, not fucking help her. She doesn't deserve help after what she did," he spits, yet no one has told me what it is I did yet? If I know, maybe, I can correct it or make amends. Did I forget one of my chores?

"Fuck the King," Dustin snaps, and the man's grip tightens on Dustin's shirt, who goes to turn when Gannon walks in.

"Yes, fuck the King. Remember where your loyalties lie, Trey," Gannon warns him.

"They are with my King. Not with a traitor!" Trey answers.

"That so-called traitor is your Queen and the King's mate," Gannon snarls at him, and the man whimpers before his eyes go to me.

"You haven't been here as long as the rest of us, but the King swore us all to choose his Queen over him."

"If so, why is she down here, then?" the man demands.

"Because the King is an idiot. Move Dustin. I will wrap her hand. Go fix up the old King's quarters for me," Gannon says, crouching down in front of me.

"He's letting her back inside the castle?" Dustin says, looking relieved.

"Hopefully, Damian can convince him. This is no place for a Queen," Gannon tells him.

"Just get it ready for me, the moment I can take her back safely, I want it ready," Gannon explains.

"Yes, Sir," Dustin says, while Trey growls and Gannon glances over his shoulder at him.

"You're off guard, get out of my face," Gannon orders him, and I feel his aura rush out and Trey doubles over before rushing out.

Gannon sets to work on cleaning my hand and wrapping it. "It will heal once you shift. Do you think you can hold off a couple of hours?" he asks kindly. Yet, my hand is throbbing. Can't he give me his blood or heal it like the King did my back? Right now, I will try anything if it means the pain will stop.

"Can't you heal it?" I ask, hopefully. My hand is throbbing to its own beat, my fingers are black and purple, and fragmented bones are pushing beneath my skin like splinters when the frame broke them.

Gannon chews his lip nervously and then sighs.

"I would if I could, but only the King can heal you. My saliva or blood won't work on you since you aren't mine," Gannon tells me, cupping my face with his huge hand. What does he mean? I thought all Lycans can heal.

"Did the King refuse you to?" I ask him and he frowns. "No, Ivy. But Lycans can only heal their mates," he tells me.

He pulls his phone out of his pocket. "Once the moon is at its highest peak, I will take you outside, so you can shift, my Queen," Gannon says.

"Please don't call me that," I murmur, looking away from him. As he said, this is no place for a Queen, a slave maybe, but not a Queen, and clearly Kyson doesn't want me to be his.

"I need to ask you something," Gannon says, unlocking his phone and scrolling through the pictures. He stops before turning his phone to me.

"Do you know this woman?" he asks, and I take the phone from him. A whimper escapes from my lips when I realize it is my mother. I nod, tears trekking down my face.

"She's my mom," I smile, brushing my thumb over the picture of her. She looks a little younger than I remember in this picture, but I know it is her. Gannon hangs his head and shakes it. He sighs heavily before looking up at me.

"He will come around, Ivy. You just need to give him space," Gannon tells me.

Come around to what? I think. How does everyone seem to know what's going on except for me?

"What do you mean? I don't get it. What did I do wrong?" I ask. Gannon frowns when I see his eyes glaze over, and I can tell he is mindlinking. I wait for him to finish, and his eyes flicker before falling back on me.

"You did nothing. It's what your mother did. She killed the Landeena King and Queen; she also killed the King's sister."

I blink, astonished, unable to believe what I am hearing. That would be impossible. She couldn't have.

"Just try to get some rest. After your shift, I will take you to Kyson's old quarters, he can't keep you down here forever, it will drive his Lycan side mad."

"But my birthday isn't for another couple of weeks," I tell him.

"The fact you recognized the King as your mate, Ivy, shows your birthday is today," he says, just as I hear someone curse.

The stable door opens, and hope bubbles in me at the thought of it being Kyson to tell me this was some sick joke, but it is just Clarice and Abbie. They stop by the door and glance at Gannon, who nods to them before standing up and walking out. He stops by Clarice at the door.

"Don't be long; I don't want to be dragging you to the cells for disobeying the King," Gannon tells them. Clarice nods before rushing in with Abbie close behind her. Abbie embraces me, hugging me then checking me over, while Clarice stands with a frosted cupcake in her hand, a deep look of concern on her face.

"You've been baking," I tell Abbie, whose uniform is covered in flour. She shakes her head.

"No, I just spilled the bag on the counter before I came down here. Clarice made a cake for you," she tells me, dusting herself off.

"Well, I had a cake made, but I couldn't carry it down," Clarice says sadly.

Abbie falls to her knees beside me, her eyes wide with excitement. Excitement that quickly dims. "You should have seen it, Ivy. Clarice did a good job. She spent all day making it. It's so pretty, better than the ones we used to make at the orphanage, it..." Abbie trails off before frowning.

"You enjoy it then," I tell her, knowing just how much we always wished to celebrate our birthdays but were never allowed. We had been strictly forbidden to make ourselves birthday treats or sample the other treats we made in the kitchen. Abbie and I would stare longingly at them.. We never knew if they tasted alright, but the delight on the kids' faces told us they must have, or maybe they were just being polite.

Clarice nervously glances at the stable doors. "We can't stay long; Gannon is right; the King is on the warpath, but I couldn't let you go without wishing you happy birthday," Clarice says, placing the blue cupcake in my hand. She stabs a candle in it and lights it with a match, while I stare at the flickering flame.

This was never how I pictured my birthday to be, not that I ever saw myself actually celebrating one, the one chance I might have was now stolen from me once again, yet this one hurts most. Maybe because for a second, I thought it was going to be a good day.

"Blow it out and make a wish," Clarice says, and to humor her, I do. Abbie smiles sadly and kisses my knee where she is crouched beside me, her green eyes filled with tears.

"What did you wish for?" Clarice asks, a teary smile on her face.

"I wished to be free," I whisper, and Abbie sobs.

"Don't," she chokes the word as if it strangles her. "Don't say that" Abbie cries.

"I think it's a good wish," Clarice says, looking confused at Abbie.

"Not where we come from. The only freedom rogues get is in

death," Abbie chokes out, and Clarice looks at me, bewildered, before grabbing my face in her shaking hands.

"You wish for anything but that. Do you hear me? I will not watch my Queen die. I have buried enough of them," she chokes as before letting me go, then walking out. Abbie watches her go before looking back at me.

"I wish I could stay to see you shift," she says, and I nod, terrified of the thought of shifting with no one here, in a stable of all places, surrounded by hay and horses. I think I would have preferred being locked in my room at the orphanage, at least I'd have had Abbie.

"It's not too bad. We have slept in worse places," Abbie says, glancing around, trying to uplift my mood.

"I will speak to Beta Damian. Maybe he can convince the King to let me stay here with you, or I can try to sneak down," Abbie says, and I shake my head.

"No, stay in the castle; you don't need to be punished too," I tell her. Abbie looks at me confused, while chewing her lip.

She sighs heavily and glances around at the horses. "This isn't how I pictured today being," she admits.

"Well, I never pictured making it to this day at all?" I remind her and her eyes dart to me.

"More than my life," she whispers, and I swallow.

"More than my life," I return to her, and she lets out a relieved breath.

"Abbie, love, you need to go," Gannon tells her, and I see her cheeks turn a little pink. I chuckle at Abbie, a silly smile tugging at my lips. She didn't get flustered much, but just that one endearing word sent her crimson. She nods before standing and kissing my forehead.

"I will try to come back. If I don't, I will tomorrow," Abbie says, rushing back to the door. She looks up at Gannon as she passes him.

"I won't leave her alone. Once she shifts, I will sneak her back into the castle," Gannon tells her before reaching for a lock of her auburn hair. He twirls it around his finger and then clears his throat before nodding and letting her rush off. I raise an eyebrow at him.

"What, she is pretty," Gannon says, shaking his head like he just got caught doing something he shouldn't.

"Yes, she is," I tell him with a smile, and he blushes slightly, clearing his throat.

CHAPTER
THREE

ABBIE

The stable door groans open, and our steps are hesitant, our shadows flitting against the wooden walls of the stables when I find Ivy sitting on top of an old wine barrel that has been turned upside down.

The room, dense with the smell of hay and horses, suddenly feels tighter, more constricted when I see the saddened look on her face. They hadn't told us what happened, only that we could go spend a few minutes with her and wish her happy birthday. I'm so confused... I thought we were safe here.

Gannon, whose gaze remains hardened, acknowledges our presence with a brief nod. He stands, his tall figure casting a long shadow, and murmurs a warning, "Don't be long; I don't want to be dragging you to the cells for disobeying the King." His voice is cold, and filled with anger. I have never seen him look angry.

Clarice, her fingers trembling slightly, is the first to approach Ivy. She holds a frosted cupcake as if it's a lifeline. Yet, it's Ivy's gutted expression that draws me in. Her ebony hair, usually vibrant and full of life, lies limp against her pale skin. Her cerulean blue eyes, usually shimmering with excitement at seeing me, are shadowed with despair and confusion.

"We can't stay long; Gannon is right; the King is on the warpath, but I couldn't let you go without wishing you happy birthday," Clarice tells Ivy, placing the blue cupcake in her hand. Clarice lights it with a match, and I stare at the flickering flame.

"You've been baking," Ivy asks me, and I glance down at my uniform.

Shaking my head, the weight of our predicament hits me anew. "No, I just spilled the bag on the counter before I came down here. Clarice made a cake for you," I admit, my voice shaking. A cake, such a simple pleasure, feels out of place amidst the palpable tension.

It's not just the cake or the stable, it's the unspoken reality that binds us. The chains of servitude, of being mere pawns in a kingdom that's never truly been ours. Yet, for a split second, we both had hope we'd find home here. Ivy, despite being the king's mate, is now condemned to these stables, away from the luxury of status she barely had a chance to grasp. Now if a Queen has been placed here, what chance do I have, we have. We might have been better off with our fate decided by our old Alpha.

"Well, I had a cake made, but I couldn't carry it down," Clarice tells her sadly.

"You should have seen it, Ivy. Clarice did a good job. She spent all day making it. It's so pretty, better than the ones we used to make at the orphanage, it..." I trail off before frowning.

"You enjoy it then," Ivy smiles encouragingly, but that wouldn't be the same thing without her, it was made for her. Ivy's longing gaze drifts towards the blue cupcake as Clarice places a candle on it, its tiny flame flickering brightly.

"Blow it out and make a wish," Clarice tells her. Ivy blows the candle out without excitement or light in her eyes. I know she only does to please Clarice. I was so excited to help Clarice, and it was all for nothing. I smile sadly and kiss her knee, giving her hand a squeeze from where I sit beside her.

"What did you wish for?" Clarice asks, a teary smile on her face.

"I wished to be free," Ivy tells her, and a choking whimper leaves my lips.

Such a simple wish, laden with so many complex emotions. The pain of our shared history as slaves, the injustice of it all, wells up. "Don't," I choke out, tears threatening hearing her speak those words.

"Don't say that," I whisper. Anything but that, she can't wish for that. This was supposed to be a fresh start.

"I think it's a good wish," Clarice says, looking at me, startled.

"Not where we come from. The only freedom rogues get is in death," I tell her. I knew precisely what Ivy meant by those words. Clarice looked at her, shocked before grabbing her face in her hands.

"You wish for anything but that. Do you hear me? I will not watch my Queen die. I have buried enough of them," Clarice says before walking out. I watch her go before turning back to Ivy.

"I wish I could stay to see you shift," I tell her, and she nods. Glancing around, I see that this place is cold and lonely. Ivy stayed with me, not that she had a choice about being locked in the room with me, but I at least still had her by my side. I wonder if maybe I can convince Gannon to let me come down when her shift starts, so she wouldn't be alone.

"It's not too bad. We have slept in worse places," I tell her, glancing around, trying to uplift her mood, but I might as well have been trying to grasp air with how useless my attempts to cheer her were. Maybe if I ask the King, he will allow it, or I could deliberately get myself in trouble and hope he kicks me out here with her.

"I will speak to Beta Damian. Perhaps he can convince the King to let me stay here with you," I tell her, although my chances of even getting close to the King's quarters to ask Beta Damian are slim. Ivy shakes her head.

"No, stay in the castle; you don't need to be punished too," she tells me.

"Abbie, love, you need to go," Gannon calls out softly, and

embarrassment courses through me at his endearment, and I know my cheeks turn a little pink when Ivy looks at me questionably.

Leaning forward, I kiss her forehead and cheek. I don't want to go. She doesn't deserve to be out here with farm animals, but I would rather not ruin my chances at being allowed back.

"I will try to come back. If I don't, I will tomorrow," I tell her, rushing back to the door. I look up at Gannon as I pass him.

"I won't leave her alone. Once she shifts, I will sneak her back into the castle," Gannon tells me before reaching for a lock of my auburn hair. He twirls it around his finger and then clears his throat before nodding, and I rush out before he does anything else that I would have to explain to Ivy.

Liam is waiting for me when I return to the castle, and I head for the guard's quarters, hoping to find Damian to see if he will grant me permission to stay with Ivy for the night. The thought of her shifting with no one but Gannon upsets me.

Climbing the stairs, it's not long before I hear Liam's footsteps rushing to keep up with me. Reaching the second-floor landing, I see Damian in the hall talking to one of the guards before he turns and heads toward the King's chambers. Turning on my heel, I go to head down there, only for an arm to wrap around my waist and turn me in the opposite direction.

"Uh ah, can't let you do that?" Liam tells me, and I grit my teeth as he walks me toward the guards quarters.

I peer up over my shoulder at him as he keeps forcing me in the opposite direction. "Then can you ask Damian if I can stay with Ivy?" I ask him, and he sighs, steering me down the next corridor.

"Gannon is with her. She will be fine," he says, and I stop.

"Abbie?" he says, and I shake my head, but he rolls his eyes, grips my wrist, dragging me along with him. I try to pull out of his grip, only for it to tighten.

"Abbie, if you go barging in there, you will only make things worse. Leave it be and trust that Gannon will look after her," Liam scolds me as if I am some disobedient child. Truth be told, I don't mind him. He seems okay, a little eccentric, but I know he cares deeply for Gannon and, unfortunately, the King, who currently is on my hate list.

"What if she gets cold down there?" I wonder aloud.

"Gannon sent guards to get firewood. Dustin will take her blankets. For now, you need to go to bed," he says, stopping at my door. He opens it and motions for me to go inside. "In ya go, don't make me tuck you in," he warns me. Tears prick my eyes as I step toward my door.

"And don't think of trying to sneak out. Gannon asked me to watch you. I will be right outside this door, Abbie. Trust me, you won't get far," he tells me, and I glare at him.

"But by all means try, I loves me a game of cat and mouse, and I could use the entertainment," he chuckles, shutting the door, and I sigh, moving toward my bed.

CHAPTER

FOUR

I VY

After everyone leaves, I'm left alone inside the stables. My stomach sinks somewhere deep. And without Abbie here to take my mind away from this life of mind that always seems to fall on me in tatters. I feel nothing but grief. I grieve the happiness I felt momentarily, only to lose it just as quickly as I found it.

Peering around, I notice that this place feels lonelier than the orphanage, lonelier than when I first came here, and was petrified about spending my first night away without Abbie. Rubbing my arms, a cold settles into my bones, and I pick at the cupcake that was brought down for me. I stare at the frosting, trying to imagine what the cake would have looked like. Yet, doing that saddens me further, and I lose my appetite to finish it.

Instead, I drag a bale of hay from one of the stalls when I hear the stable doors open. "What are you doing?" Dustin asks me, quickly rushing over to help me. "Where do you want it?"

I point to the small fire, and he grabs it, placing it close but not too close that it risks catching on fire. He steps aside, waiting for me to sit down, but when I don't, he watches me as I try to break the thick strings holding it together. He sighs heavily, leaning over me, and using his claws, he slices it. The strings fall away, and I grab a handful, spreading it out on the floor to try to make a bed.

"This is some bullshit," Dustin mutters, and I wonder if I am about to get in trouble for ruining the bale that is obviously for the horses when he growls, shrugging off his jacket and his shirt.

"What are you doing?" I ask him when he grabs one of the horse blankets from the wall too. He lays the blanket on top of the hay before rolling his shirt into a pillow for me. He then holds his jacket open for me. I step closer, and he slides it up one arm before I slip my other into the other hole.

"Unfortunately, I don't smell like the King. But it will keep you a little warmer," he tells me.

"Now, I need to find another shirt, despite the King sending you here. He won't be pleased to learn I am walking around barely clothed in front of you." He smiles at me sadly before turning.

"I will bring you back a blanket," he says before walking toward the doors and leaving. A few moments after he leaves, Gannon enters, also stripping his jacket and shirt off, and giving them to me. He nods once at me.

"Dustin will bring me another," he tells me when I try to hand it back, already having Dustin's.

"Thank you," I tell him and leaves, shutting the door behind him.

Sinking down on my makeshift bed, I try to get comfortable while waiting to shift. One part of me is curious about what my wolf form will look like, while another part of me fears the pain of my first shift.

Yet as the night goes on, the flames in the fire flicker, I feel myself becoming increasingly restless, my bones ache, my ass has gone numb from the hard floor. Despite the hay, it does nothing more than give a little cushioning.

Despite the pain in my body, every part of me is yearning for Kyson, yearning for his touch, his scent through the bond. I sniff Dustin's shirt, but it offers nothing more than a little warmth. My legs, arms, and even my scalp all ache. How did Abbie endure this torment before shifting, or is it merely the bond? Yet, getting up and stumbling toward the window, I see the moon is high in the sky already.

Shouldn't I have shifted by now? I wonder when I hear the door open and see Gannon checking on me. He cautiously steps into the stables, peering in all the stalls before spotting me in the far one looking out the window.

He lets out a breath, yet worry crosses his features. "You sounded like you were in pain," he tells me, and my brows furrow. "You haven't shifted yet?" he seems just as confused.

"Apparently, I am a dud in that department, too," I tell him, and he swallows thickly.

"You're not a dud, Ivy. The king will come to his senses. Just come away from the window. You're shivering," he tells me, and I glance down to see my skin laced in goosebumps. "There is still time for you to shift," he tells me, glancing at his watch.

Gannon leads me back to the fire. When I sit back down in my straw bed, Gannon stokes the fire. "I will grab you some more wood," he tells me.

"He promised," I whisper, thinking of when he said I wouldn't have to do this alone. Gannon stops, and I don't think he heard me when he turns to face me. He looks like he wants to say something but then closes his mouth.

"I didn't think he'd break a promise, but he's just like everyone else. I am still Ivy, the rogue girl. You. No one, I liked being someone," I tell myself more than him.

"You're still my Queen," Gannon tells me, and I look at him sadly and smile.

"No, I am the daughter of the woman who kills Queens," I remind him of how unworthy I am. He presses his lips in a line and glances away.

"You're not your mother."

"He doesn't seem to think so. Maybe this payback for what she did? I'm her punishment, but the goddess didn't need to punish Abbie alongside me all these years," I tell him.

"The King will come to his senses. The guard won't allow you to remain down here forever. It will drive us mad," Gannon says.

"Why would you betray your King for a lowly rogue?" I chuckle.

"You stopped being rogue the day the king laid eyes on you. From that moment on, you became our Queen. You just didn't know it. As your guard, I promise I will not let you rot here forever. Give him a few days to calm down; I am happy to remain with you," he tells me.

"And if he doesn't come to his senses?"

"Then the guard will challenge him for you," he says without further explanation. He then leaves to collect more wood.

As I sit there in the flickering light of the fire, my body continues to ache, and my mind races with thoughts of Kyson. I can't help but wonder where he is, and what he's doing. Is he worried about me?

Suddenly, a sharp pain shoots through my body, and I let out a low growl as I feel my bones begin to shift and change. It's unlike anything I've ever felt before, and for a moment, I feared that something had gone wrong. But then the pain begins to subside, only to return with a vengeance, yet no matter how many times the agony rolls through me, I don't shift.

K YSON

    Gannon never returned all night. I waited for the mindlink to open and tell me she had started shifting. Once midnight came and went, and the sun started to rise, I get to my feet and peered out toward the stables in the distance through my window. I see Gannon standing out front, and what's more, I notice Abbie rushing down the dirt path toward the stables.

It angers me that Abbie would defy orders and go to her. I told everyone to steer clear of the stables. She clearly has no issue disobeying what she has been told.

Opening the mindlink, I feel for Gannon's tether when my door opens, and Damian walks in, making me lose concentration. "She never shifted," he says, anger still on his face.

"I figured that much out already," I tell him, my tone clipped in warning. Damian glances around the room and growls at the littering of bottles covering every surface. He shakes his head before grabbing my bin.

"You're drunk and clearly haven't slept," he snaps disapprovingly.

"I was waiting for her to shift." I fold my arms across my chest, feeling a headache coming on. Must he be so loud?

"And the bottles?" he asks, picking up an empty one and tossing it at the fireplace. It shatters, making me growl. Yet, he doesn't seem bothered by my fury as he starts tossing bottles in the bin. I hate it when he does this... cleans up after me like I'm a toddler.

"I don't need your scolding, Damian," I answer, walking over to my bed and lying down.

"She never shifted," Damian states again.

"I am aware."

"Gannon said all night she was fretting, trying to nest with the damn horses. You are delaying her," Damian yells, his face turning red in his frustration.

"I am doing no such thing; I had her put outside where the damn moon is, so don't blame me for her not shifting. She is probably the oddity that gets the traits and does not shift." I snarl back angrily.

Damian growls at my words. Though deep down, I know it was because of me. I could feel her distress, I just couldn't bring myself to go to her.

"At least fucking heal her hand and stop being a jerk," he snarls, storming off to my closet. He comes out with some of my clothes in his arms.

"We are moving her to the east wing, your old room. That's where she will be when you get over yourself."

"I don't want her in the castle," I growl.

"Too bad I am not having my Queen in the fucking stables like some farm animal. You will regret how you are treating her, Kyson, so I'm stepping in before you cause irrevocable damage if you haven't already," Damian snaps before walking out and slamming the door behind him.

I sigh and turn over, glaring at the picture of my sister on top of the bedside table drawer.

Maybe he is right, and I am being irrational. Yet, I can't get the picture of her mother from my head, the state of my sister, the way her stomach was torn into, and my nephew mutilated in her womb. That day didn't just destroy me, it destroyed all of us, yet everyone else seems to have forgotten the pain her mother caused us.

Feeling the mindlink stir, I let it open, briefly I believed it would be Damian or Gannon wanting to scold me some more, so I am shocked when I learn it is Trey.

'*They found more bodies,*' Trey says through the pack link.

'*Where?*' I ask him, needing a good distraction. Perhaps leaving this place will help me clear my head and get myself back in order.

'*Two days from here,*' he answers.

'*Get a car ready,*' I tell him.

Getting to my feet, I move to my closet and pull on some clothes. I change quickly, stumbling around the room. Maybe I overdid it last night because now I am up and moving, I still feel hazy and tipsy. Walking out, Dustin stares vacantly ahead. "When did you get here? Shouldn't you be down with...." I stop, not wanting to mention her name.

"Gannon sent me up late last night," he answers in a clipped tone. He, too, is mad at me? Is anyone not mad at me?

"Fine, then tell Gannon and Damian to meet me at the cars. You are to remain with me. Send Trey to watch over the mate for me," I tell him. He nods, and I stumble down the steps, trying to find my feet.

Dustin grips my arm as I lose my footing. "My King, I don't think Trey is a good choice to watch the Queen," he says, and I look at him. He drops his head, and I notice him swallow as I glare at him.

"He is part of my guard; he will do the job he is asked," I tell him, continuing down the steps.

Losing my footing again, I stumble on the bottom step and nearly hit the ground. Guards rush toward me when I collide with someone. They prevent my fall, and I shake my head as I grip the person's shoulder to remain steady.

"Are you okay, my King?" Ester asks. I internally groan. Great. It's Ester. I wave the other men off.

"Fine, just help me to my office."

"Of course," she says a little too willingly. I held back my swear, letting her steer me to my office. Once inside, I flop into my chair.

"I will retrieve some water," she says, and I wave her off.

"My King, I am not leaving my Queen in the care of Trey," Dustin states, more boldly this time, and I growl.

"Whatever. I don't care. Just leave me, and tell Damian to get me when he is ready to leave," I snap at him, dismissing him and allowing Ester to steer me toward my office. Once inside, I fall onto my chair behind my desk while Ester lingers, and I close my eyes, trying to catch a little sleep before leaving, which no doubt would be soon when the mind link opens up.

"Roads are closed over the bridge. We need to wait," Damian tells me.

"Wake me when it opens," I tell him.

"Yes, my King. What about Ivy?"

I press my lips together before sighing and pinching the bridge of my nose. "Put her in my old quarters, ensure she has what she needs."

"She needs you, my King," Damian tells me.

"And I can't be near her right now," I reply with a growl.

"Kyson, if you leave. What will happen if she shifts?"

"What do you expect me to do?" I ask, slightly annoyed.

"I expect you to stay."

I growl at his words. "We will talk about it when you wake me," I tell him, cutting him off before he can say more.

Forcing myself to my feet, I notice Ester is still there. "Leave, I want to rest."

"I'll be outside if you need me," she answers, and I wave her off as I stagger over to my chair, falling heavily into it and welcoming oblivion when sleep finally takes me.

However, I toss and turn from the bond, calling me to go to her, her distress waking me constantly. Trying to get comfortable, I block everyone out. Damian would find me when it was time to leave, and eventually, I slowly drift off. Though, I don't remain asleep for long when I feel someone touch me.

The feeling of someone tugging on my belt makes me stir and move in my sleep, only to feel my zipper undone. I blink up at the ceiling, confused. Wondering if I dreamt it, I close my eyes again before feeling a hand reach into my pants. I jump at the feel of fingers wrapping around my cock, and I lurch upright, only to come face-to-face with the intruder. A vile scent wafts into my nose.

"I didn't mean to startle you, my King," Ester's faux seductive voice reaches me like someone is drilling into my ears.

I instantly slap her hands away while barely containing my rage at her actions. I want to slap her for daring to think that she can touch me.

"What do you think you're doing?" I growl at her before rubbing my eyes and peering down at her. I blink again when I see she is naked, feeling like I must be dreaming.

She leans forward, placing her hands on my knees, her tits squeezing together as she smiles seductively.

"And where are your goddamn clothes?" I ask her, averting my gaze to anything apart from her. The woman's desperation repulses me.

"You were having trouble sleeping; I have been watching you. Let me help," she says while reaching down and tugging at my pants. I grip her hand and growl at her.

"I don't need your help, Ester; I suggest you leave while you still can," I warn her. She jerks her hand from my grip, and her eyes well with tears.

"My King?" she cries.

"I am not yours, nor will you ever be mine. Now get out before I have you whipped," I snarl at her.

"Oh, my King, you must be tired; it's me, Ester," she says, now trying to climb onto my lap. I grip her throat, disgusted that she even dared to think she could touch what does not belong to her.

"I said get out; you are not Ivy. You do not touch me," I tell her before realizing what I said. She stumbles backward when I let her go. I watch as she snatches up her clothes before looking at me. I growl at her, and she runs out the door, opening it just as Damian is about to walk in.

Great!

"Have you completely lost your damn mind?" Damian snarls, entering and slamming the door behind him.

"I woke up to her touching me," I tell him, rubbing my eyes again.

"Please tell me you didn't," he snarls.

"What, of course not. What do you take me for?" I demand, outraged, that he would assume I would cheat on my mate, no matter how disgraced she is.

He sighs, and I re-button my pants before sniffing my clothes. Her stench is all over me.

I tug my shirt off and toss it in the trash with a growl.

"I want her away from my side of the castle. I don't want to see Ester's face here again."

"I will have it arranged. What about what Dustin told us about her?"

I had completely forgotten about that.

"Good, banish her then."

"My King, she is a Lycan. Where would she go? We are the only Lycan pack left?"

"Then banish her from the castle," I tell him. I may not be able to be near Ivy, but not even I would do that to my mate. Cheating in my eyes, is unforgivable.

CHAPTER
SIX

ABBIE
I am up early before the sun has even risen fully. I am anxious and want to sneak down and see Ivy, so I can bring her something to eat. I wonder how her first shift went. Getting dressed quickly in my maid's uniform, I open the door to find Liam standing next to my door, playing a game on his phone. His fingers jab hard at the screen while he curses at it. *He must be losing,* I think, rolling my eyes.

Shaking my head, I step past him, and he follows with his head down, focused on his game.

"Stupid game," he growls as he follows me downstairs to the kitchens.

"What are you playing?" I ask, not really caring, but if I have to listen to him curse his phone out, it would be nice to know what he is cursing about. I wait for him to answer as he starts stabbing his phone viciously with his finger.

"A cake-building game," he tells me, and I pull a face at that. With the crazy finger poking and cursing, I assumed he was playing some killing or shooting game.

"A cake-building game, cake like you eat?" I ask, wondering if it is code for something else.

"Yep, making this stupid pink unicorn thing, but the sprinkles are going too fast, and the placement is wrong. It deducted more bloody points," he snaps before looking at me, and he grabs my arm, making me stop. He looks me over from head to toe, and I step back from him, not liking how he is eyeing me.

"Have you got a phone?" he asks, and I roll my eyes as I continue walking into the kitchens. "Of course you don't," he mutters as I shake my head and step into the kitchen. "Ah, she has one," he states as he turns to Clarice.

"Momsy, oh dear, Momsy?" he calls in a sugary sweet voice as he moves toward Clarice's station with a practiced, boyish energy. She lifts her gaze and raises an eyebrow at him as he skips over to her.

"Yes, Liam?" Clarice yawns tiredly, looking like she had no sleep at all.

He stops next to her bench, drops an elbow onto it, and places his chin on his hand, batting his lashes at her.

"Can I borrow your phone?" he asks, and she sighs, giving him a pointed look.

"What's wrong with yours?" she asks, pointing to it in his hand.

"Nothing, but I need to download a game on yours so that you can send me your coins."

"You want my phone for a game?" she repeats, pulling it from her apron pocket. She eyes him suspiciously while he giggles like a schoolgirl. She hands it to him, and he lights up as if all his Christmases come at once.

"You better not be using it for porn like last time. Damn near gave me a heart attack when I opened my browser to see what you're into," she scolds.

"I promise." He offers her his pinky. She smiles and chuckles before grabbing his face and squeezing his cheeks, making him have fish lips.

"I'm serious, I want my phone back."

He wiggles his squashed lips at her, and she laughs, letting him go. "I am just downloading a game so that I can send myself some sprinkles," Liam tells her, unlocking her phone as if he had done it a million times before. Clarice raises an eyebrow at him.

"Sprinkles?" she asks him, and he nods, focused on her phone. Clarice looks at me, and I shrug. It is so weird seeing how carefree she is with Liam like he is her ray of sunshine. She messes his hair lovingly, returning to her duties.

Liam sits on a stool by the counter, and I set to work making Ivy and Gannon some breakfast so that I can take it down to them. It is the perfect excuse to go there. The King surely doesn't intend for her to starve.

When I am done, Clarice finds me a picnic basket, and I leave Liam with Clarice, rushing out the doors toward the main foyer area to see a commotion.

A loud roar rings out from down the corridor, and I see Ester running stark naked from the King's office. My stomach sinks as she rushes toward me, clutching her clothes in her hands, just as Damian steps out from the stairwell further up. He grabs Ester by the arm and shakes the woman with a sneer on his face.

His eyes run up the length of her, making him growl loudly at her state of undress. He shoves her away before both his hands hit the door of the King's office, he then slams the door shut with a loud bang. I gasp as Ester runs out the castle doors. And I turn to find Dustin glaring toward the doors she ran through, along with half the kitchen staff who had rushed out to see what the commotion was.

"He wouldn't have, would he? Ivy, she's..." I stutter, tears burn my eyes on behalf of my best friend. Surely, the King didn't kick his mate out to be with the likes of her. If he has done so, then boy have I misjudged the King. Dustin growls before storming off, and I turn to find Clarice with a murderous glare on her face.

She presses her lips in a line before her eyes go to mine. They soften a little before she gasps. "Come on, you go down there like that, and Ivy will know something is wrong," she tells me. I look down at the picnic basket in my hands, and nod my head.

Ivy is hurting enough, and she can read me like a book. It will only hurt her more if I go down there crying about what I saw. Plus, I'm sure she'll find a way to make me tell her. So reluctantly, I follow Clarice, knowing she is right.

Liam is waiting by the kitchen doors when she walks toward them, and Clarice stops beside him.

"Find out what happened for me; I swear if the King..." she doesn't finish.

"He did, and I will whip him myself," she growls, striding past him. Liam watches her go before gripping my shoulder when I go to pass him.

"Chin up, Love. I know the King. He is being a dickhead, but he isn't unfaithful. It is nearly impossible for one to cheat on their mate. At least for us Lycans anyway," he tells me before walking off toward the guards at the end of the hall.

Stepping into the kitchen, I find the staff are all murmuring about the King. I listen, trying to calm my racing heart.

"She is always all over him, though I thought he learned after the last time," a cook named Sheri tells Amanda, who sighs heavily.

"Enough, ladies, we will find out. You know the King is on edge after the news he received last night," Clarice says, cutting the ladies off.

"What news?" I ask Clarice curiously, but it is Sheri who answers.

"Another family was found, and more children by the river," she explains with a grim expression on her face.

"How old were they?" I ask, horrified that more rogues were killed.

"A few around our Queen's age, and some young ones, about five or six years old, and an elderly woman," Clarice answers before she sniffles.

CHAPTER
SEVEN

ABBIE

    "What a waste of life." Clarice states. Silence falls over the room, and I am shocked to see so much heartache on the woman's face. They are Lycans, yet they mourn for those killed by the hunters, despite them only being lowly rogues and werewolves. Growing up, Ivy and I were constantly reminded of what scum we were for being rogue. Werewolves hate rogues. Yet here, everyone considers us as people, not the dirt beneath their toes. It is odd and hard to get used to, and I wasn't sure if I would ever get used to it. But Lycans don't seem to be prejudice of what we are.

    Everyone turns back to their tasks and Liam returns moments later, and Clarice looks up at him. Everyone stops what they are doing, waiting for him to answer the unspoken question from Clarice.

    "The King woke up to Ester touching him. He tossed her out and had Damian order her off the castle grounds," he says, and Clarice lets out a breath. The tension in the room dissipates significantly at his answer. Clarice nods her head while Liam climbs up on the bench beside me, helping himself to some fruit salad that Clarice is making.

She slaps his digging fingers only for him to pout at her, and she clicks her tongue before relenting and giving him the bowl of fruit.

"I didn't think he would, but with how drunk he was, you can never be certain," she says, looking relieved as she eyes Liam devouring the freshly cut fruit salad.

He watches eagerly as she retrieves another bowl and starts making more, and I turn my attention back to Clarice. He stole one of her puddings earlier, yet she didn't seem bothered by Liam. They actually seemed quite close and Clarice seems to adore the psycho.

"He'd have copped a beat down if he had by not only me but I think the entire guard," Liam chuckles.

"You'd really fight the King?" I ask, shocked. Liam raises an eyebrow at me.

"We'd lay our lives down for our Queen. And that is what Ivy is, even if dumbass doesn't see that at the moment," he explains.

"You all really care for Ivy, don't you?" I blurt, shocked at their disgust of their King's hypothetical infidelity. I certainly didn't think they would care since he is a King and can technically do as he pleases.

"This castle has been the prison of the King's depression for far too long. Since he found Ivy, we can all suddenly breathe. No one wants to go back to the way things were," Clarice tells me.

"Plus, none of us want to hurt him. He is a good King; despite current behavior, he is a good man just troubled by the demons that lurk in him," Clarice adds before telling the servants to tend to their chores, and I watch them all rush off.

"What do you mean that none of you want to hurt him?" I ask. Could they really hurt the King?

"Some of us have a blood pact with our future Queen. If he were to physically hurt her or try to kill her, we would have no choice," Liam says behind me, and I peer over my shoulder at him. He shrugs, yet still, I am confused by his words. It is Clarice who answers, causing me to turn around and face her.

"The King's guard was originally made of 12 men. After his sister

36

died, we lost a few guards, but those that remained and some of the staff were tied by a pact. The King asked us to swear to protect his future Queen no matter the cost, even his over his life," Clarice explains.

"That was the worst week of my life," Liam growls, and whatever happened back then, I can see haunts him just as much.

"But I would do it again," Clarice shrugs.

"You're part of the guard's pact?" I asked her, and she nods.

"I am one of the few servants here that is."

"Yeah, a week full of the King forcing his blood down our throats and us breaking his command," Liam explains.

"Huh?"

"For the pact to work, the King can't be able to command us to harm his Queen. It's a safety thing. When it comes to the King, she is the only one we can override his command on. He could tell us to kill her, but we would do the opposite. We would kill the King for her," Clarice answers.

"But I have seen him command his guard before," I answer.

"It only works if he asks us to threaten her life. We can't. The King can still command us, though it is more painful when he does. We can resist it to a sense, but if he pushes us too hard, we would relent."

"Unless it comes to the Queen," Liam says, that bond can't be broken.

"I still don't understand," I admit. Though I didn't know much about Lycans, so maybe that is why.

"The King's blood was infused by witch magic," Liam shrugs.

"Witches still exist?" I ask, a little shocked.

"Yes, of course, just not in plain sight," Liam answers.

"So no matter what, you will keep Ivy safe even from the King?"

"Yes, assuming he doesn't kill us to get to her," Clarice answers.

"So you and twelve guards?"

"It was twelve; some have lost their lives since the pact," Clarice states.

"Whose left?" I asked curiously.

"Myself, Liam, Dustin, Damian, and of course, Gannon. A couple of others, but we are the main ones you will find guarding the Queen," Clarice answers.

Clarice picks up a tray and turns to me. "Now Ivy must be starving, so we better get you on your way to her," she says, repacking and checking the picnic basket.

"Also, Abbie, I need to send you to town a little later, we have guests coming this afternoon," Clarice adds.

"Who?" I ask.

"Alpha Kade, one of the packs with allegiance to the King. He is helping with the rogue childrens' deaths." I nod, wondering If Gannon can come since I still can't read.

Chewing my lip, I am about to tell her that is why Gannon came with me when she speaks again.

"I have already called ahead. You just need to pick up the order. Though I am a little upset, you didn't tell me you can't read," Clarice says, and I look at the floor.

"Had to find out from Damian when he told me the Queen couldn't," she says with a shake of her head. "Now come on, let's get a wriggle on," Clarice says moving toward the door.

EIGHT

IVY

My night in the stables was horrendous, and the following morning I had woken in the makeshift nest I had built. It became obvious I wouldn't be shifting. Gannon tried to tell me it was because I was fretting for my mate. It made no sense to me. I had just seen him the day before, even if only briefly, but it was enough for him to rip my heart out.

I would have preferred if he had because last night was one of the worst nights I have endured. More so than when he was gone because I knew he was here, he was just out of my reach.

The King didn't even come down when I should have shifted last night, not that I did, but he had promised. For some reason, I thought he would keep it, though it wasn't the first and probably wouldn't be the last promise he'd break.

The fact that I can't shift is just something else for him to hate me for. He has a dud for a mate. It's bad enough I am a traitor in his eyes, yet the Moon Goddess had to do one better and make me a failure.

"Ivy, Abbie will be here soon with breakfast. Do you want to shower?" Gannon asks me and I peer up at him from where I sit in the hay.

"Am I allowed?" I ask him and he purses his lips. I smell terrible, having slept in a stable with the horses.

"I'll sneak you into the maid's quarters," Gannon tells me. "You can shower in my room." He holds his hand out to me, and hesitantly I take it. He pulls me to my feet and I dust off my clothes that are filthy.

Gannon leads me up to the castle, but instead of going through the main doors, he leads me around the side to where the doors lead into the huge ballroom. Grabbing my hand, he pulls me along, leading me through the halls, then stops at a door. He pushes it open and looks around inside.

Once he is sure no one is in there, he motions for me to enter. Only before I can, I freeze when I hear the King's voice, my heart races in my chest when I hear his growl up the long corridor. Instinctively, I turn to find him storming towards me, and I am about to run when his aura rolls over me and pins me where I stand.

"You are not welcome in here," he snarls, and my eyes drop to the floor. My breath comes in small rasps, while my chest constricts, and sweat beads on my neck. His footsteps grow nearer when suddenly Gannon steps out of the bathroom directly into his path.

"What is the issue, my King?" Gannon asks, though his body stands like a wall between us, and Kyson drops the command his aura had over me. I stumble forward into Gannon's back, his hand gripping my hip to steady me, only for Kyson's snarl to echo off the glass windows and throughout the corridor.

Gannon pushes me behind him, and I clutch the back of his shirt to remain upright while I regather myself. "Did you expect me to let her fall, my King? If you don't want me touching what's yours, maybe you shouldn't have discarded her so easily," Gannon snaps at him, making my brows furrow.

Peering around Gannon, I see that King Kyson has a hold of Gannon forearm, the same arm that Gannon used when he pushed me behind him. "Why is she in here, she is forbidden from stepping inside the castle walls," Kyson sneers and his eyes move to me peeking out from behind Gannon, his eyes then dart to my hand clutching Gannon's shirt and I notice his claws slip from his fingertips, making me gasp.

I let his shirt go quickly, not wanting to anger him more, yet why would he be upset with me touching one of his guard when he doesn't want me?

"She wants to shower," Gannon snaps at him.

"I don't care what she wants, now get her out of my castle!" Kyson yells, making me flinch.

"Well, didn't you wake up on the wrong side of the bed," comes Liam's voice. Looking under Gannon's arm, I notice Liam has come up behind Kyson and Damian too.

Kyson looks back at them and growls. "Get her out, she is not welcome here."

"Exactly where is she supposed to wash then, my King, because last I checked there are no bathrooms outside."

"In a trough for all I care," he snarls. Tears spring in my eyes at his words and silence falls, yet that silence is almost deafening as they stare at him. "Fine, you won't remove her, I will," Kyson threatens.

"One step, my King, and you'll find my blade in your back," Liam threatens, emerging from out of the darkness. I gulp, noticing Liam now has a knife which he twists between his fingers. Kyson grits his teeth and turns toward him, within seconds Liam is against the wall, the King's hand wrapped around his throat, but Liam smiles sadistically. There is seriously something wrong with that man to challenge the King so openly and *enjoy* it in the process.

"You dare threaten me?"

"It wasn't a threat, my King, I warned you," Liam tells him, and I see Kyson's brows furrow. Yet when Kyson straightens, I notice the knife in his shoulder blade. My eyes widen in horror at what Liam did.

Kyson, noticing it, pulls it out. "Seems I'm faster," Liam tells him. Kyson presses the blade to his throat.

"I should kill you for that," Kyson tells him, a shade of red slowly creeping all over his face.

"But you won't. You don't want to hurt Kyson, you know that, just as you don't want to hurt me," Liam tells him.

"Have you forgotten who she has taken from us all!"

"Ivy has taken nothing. And the sooner you see that, the sooner you can move on from this. You can't keep punishing her for something that wasn't her fault," Damian's voice cuts in, and Kyson spins to face him.

Kyson's eyes flick to Damian and then to me, and I feel a sickening fear in the pit of my stomach as he takes a step towards me. Gannon steps forward again, shielding me from Kyson's wrath. "You need to leave, my King. Now is not the time," Gannon tells him firmly.

Kyson's eyes narrow and for a moment, I think he is going to attack us all when I speak up. "It's fine, I will go," I tell Gannon.

CHAPTER
NINE

I VY

"Ivy?" says Gannon, turning to grab me. But I quickly rush off the way we came in. I don't want anyone getting hurt over me having a shower. It's fine, I can wash in the lake. At least then, I won't have to worry about him storming in and dragging me out by my hair.

"Ivy, wait," Damian's voice calls out behind me. I ignore him and I rush out the doors before Kyson can witness how much he hurt me. As I'm walking back down the path toward the stables, I hear Abbie call out to me. Peering over my shoulder, I see Abbie carrying a picnic basket.

"Hey, what's happened?" she asks, taking in my tear stricken face.

"Nothing, I am fine. I just ran into Kyson is all," I tell her, and she stops, looking up toward the castle where I see Kyson still arguing with Damian and Gannon.

"Come on, I have food. Are you hungry?" she asks and the moment she mentions eating, my belly rumbles. She chuckles, looping her arm through mine and leading me toward the pier that overlooks the lake.

Abbie sits with me on the pier that allows us to walk out across the man-made lake that is in front of the stables. She had brought me over here to have breakfast, though I had no appetite and couldn't bring myself to eat. Although we found peace in the morning sun and enjoyed the rays heating my cold skin, I felt cold all over deep into my bones.

It is like I had never known warmth and won't again. The ache is horrible. Abbie tries to cheer me up. She tells me of everything that had happened in the castle last night. Though it mainly falls on deaf ears, my thoughts fixating on how Kyson glared at me in the corridor.

Apparently, she heard the word from one guard that more children were found in riverbeds in neighboring towns. She also said all night, the castle was on edge and that the King had been insufferable. He even attacked two of the night guards. I stare longingly at the castle, knowing he is there. Despite him just casting me back out moments ago, I still long to be close to him. He is close, yet so far away, too. Pulling my gaze from my thoughts, Abbie moves closer to the edge of the pier, and I grip her arm.

"Abbie!" I hiss as she tosses her legs over the side and into the water.

"Gannon is right there," she points him out, and I notice he has returned from arguing with Kyson, and I let her go with a sigh. I know he won't let her drown; fear still bubbles in me. Abbie continues dangling her feet over the edge. But I am not daring enough.

I can't even see the bottom of the still lake. It must be quite deep. Watching her so close to the edge makes my nauseous stomach feel worse. If she falls in, I would be of no use to her and would drown myself trying to save her. However, Abbie is right, and I know I am being foolish. Gannon won't let her drown if she falls in. He would come to her aid if needed.

"I have to head back soon. I have to go into town for Clarice to grab some supplies," Abbie says. My eyes blur with more tears at hearing she would have to leave me, knowing I will be on my own all day, but I nod sadly, knowing it can't be helped.

Honestly, with the way Kyson acted earlier, I am surprised he let her come see me. Now I will have to go back to my prison, stuck in the stables where he placed me.

Abbie pulls her lip between her teeth and clutches my fingers gently. "Maybe I can ask if you can come?" she says, hopefully. I know it will never be allowed. However, I never have a chance to answer when I hear screaming coming from the castle's direction.

My head whips toward the direction of the feminine screams, and I see Ester thrashing and screaming her head off while two guards drag her across the manicured lawns. Abbie stands up, and Gannon turns to look up the hill in the castle's direction.

"Ha, serves her right," Abbie chuffs, and I look at her from where I sit, wondering what happened to Ester that she is being escorted out.

"What did she do?" I ask curiously. Abbie turns and looks down at me and gasps before her head turns to Ester, still thrashing as they lead her toward the front of the castle, toward the enormous iron gates.

"I worry that it may upset you, but nothing happened. The King woke up before she could do anything," Abbie tells me as she looks down at her hands, picking at her nails.

"Before she did what?" I ask, suddenly feeling sick. Especially knowing she had been with Kyson in the past, and clearly has a thing for him still. Despite what everyone said about him looking for a replacement maid before I arrived, the thought still makes my stomach turn. I must admit it had crossed my mind who he would replace me with in his quarters. The thought sickens me.

"The King woke early this morning in his office to Ester fondling him," Abbie says, and I feel like I will be sick at her words. Bile burns my throat as my heart aches. A whimper leaves my lips before I can stop it as I think of her touching him. Panic bubbles within me, and I feel like I am choking. My ability to breathe is suddenly cut off as my bond screams out for him.

"Hey, hey. Nothing happened, I promise. I heard the guard talking this morning. When he woke, he was livid and tossed her out. He then banished her from the castle, so I guess they finally found her. He did nothing with her, Ivy. I promise you, he never touched her," she says, clutching my face in her hands.

"That's it. Breathe, Ivy. He didn't betray you," Abbie whispers as I try to stop my panic attack. She wipes my tears. I feel so stupid, so weak. How can a bond have such an effect especially after he threw me out? I had hoped it would lessen, yet it's only growing stronger.

"So, he didn't sleep with her?" I ask, letting out a breath finally.

"No, apparently, she ran naked from his office crying like her bum was on fire," Abbie snickers.

Yet, I can't find the humor in her words. The thought of her being near him so intimately sends a sharp pain through my chest. However, it is odd because I also feel bad for her, knowing exactly what it's like to be tossed away like trash by him. I guess Ester and I have that in common.

Then again, I never found pleasure in another's pain, even if it is justified. I guess it's because I've known so much pain myself, I wouldn't wish it on anybody else. Abbie is about to say something else when a whistle catches our attention. Abbie and I look up toward the hill, and we see Clarice wave to us. Abbie gets up, and I know it is time for her to go, but that doesn't stop the tears knowing I am now alone, just me and the horses.

"I gotta go, but I will try to visit you later," Abbie says, briefly hugging me before rushing off back down the wharf. I follow, watching as she runs past Gannon and up the hill to Clarice. Damian, I notice, is coming down the small path leading toward the stables. As I reach the stable doors, I wait for him.

"Sorry about this morning, Beta," I tell him, baring my neck to him.

"You don't do that for me, Ivy. You're my superior, not the other way around," Damian tells me, and I shake my head.

"A superior who is in the stables because her King can't bear the sight of her," I tell him, and Gannon wanders over. Damian looks away and clicks his tongue before he clenches his jaw.

"He will get over it, Ivy; he just needs time," Damian says with a swift nod.

I doubt it.

TEN

ABBIE

After my heartbreaking visit with Ivy, I leave to grab the few groceries Clarice has ordered from the grocer. It's a beautiful day as I go over the mental list of chores I still need to complete before the guest Alpha arrives. As I walk toward the main gates, I notice the King talking to a man whose back is to me. But as the breeze shifts, every muscle in my body tenses, and I find myself unable to move. It feels like my body goes into some sort of shock.

"Abbie, are you okay?" Liam's voice reaches my ears, yet I still can't bring myself to move. My heart leaps in my chest when his hands gripping my arms jolt me out of the odd state I am in. Liam turns me so I face him.

Yet my eyes automatically go to the stranger standing with the King. His suit is a light gray, his jacket open, and he has his hands in his pants pockets. My eyes roam over his body. The white shirt he wears fits his body in a way that I can see the outline of his abs pressing tight beneath it.

When his eyes meet mine, he appears curious while every part of me screams, mate. "Abbie?" Liam's voice says, and I notice the man's eyes go to Liam's hands gripping my arms. His lips move in a way that tells me he doesn't like Liam touching me. I shake my head, coming out of my daze and looking at Liam, who stares worriedly at me. He glances over his shoulder at the man the King is with.

"Sorry, I forgot what I was doing," I tell Liam before quickly rushing out the gates while every part of me screams I should be running toward that mysterious man... towards... I gulp... *my mate*... not away from him. Yet he makes no move to stop me, and once I am walking down the road, I shake my head, thinking I must have imagined the feeling I had heard about for so long. I make my way into town, yet that nagging feeling in the pit of my stomach never dwindles. If anything, it only gets worse. I had always heard when you laid eyes on your mate, you just knew. And in that crazy moment, it felt like I just knew. As the time passes, it feels harder and harder to conjure up the initial feeling. All I know is something is off.

The entire walk is a daze. Even after I retrieve the goods I'm sent for, I step out of the shop, having no memory of even entering. I'm on autopilot, my mind consumed with the man back at the castle. So consumed, I don't even notice he has followed me to the small town until I walk right into him.

"You didn't stick around to introduce yourself, a little rude, don't you think, little mate?" A deep voice comes before hands slide up my bare arms, leaving tingles from his touch.

I take a startled step back, and he puts up his hands in what I assume is supposed to be an apologetic gesture. "Your name is Abbie, isn't it?" he asks.

I say nothing. Despite him clearly being my mate, he's still a stranger, though every fiber of my being calls for me to go to him, submit to him.

He glances around, and I follow suit. No one is around, which only makes me more nervous in his presence. "Liam told me your name. No need to be scared. I won't hurt you, love," he tells me. But my brain doesn't seem to be able to function, and he sighs loudly. "I'm Alpha Kade, but you can call me Kade."

"Nice to meet you," I tell him, trying to step around him, knowing no Alpha would want a rogue for a mate. His aura isn't as strong as Gannon's or anyone else I've met here, so I know he is a werewolf, yet there's power behind it that tells me I'm right in thinking that. He sidesteps, blocking my path again.

"Trying to escape me, are you? I don't mind a good chase, though I would rather not cause a scene here," he tells me, making me look up at him. He catches my chin between his fingers, forcing me to meet his gaze. His eyes flicker, and I watch his tongue dart out between his lips as he looks at me.

"You realize who I am to you?" he asks; his tone is curious, as if probing to see how much I know.

"You're my mate," I whisper, bracing for his rejection so I can go about my day. He chuckles softly, leaning down, so close his lips are almost brushing mine.

"Hm, if you know, then why are you trying to run from me?" he asks.

I blink at him, and my brows furrow at his words. "I'm not; I am…" I stop myself, realizing that's exactly what I am trying to do. He raises an eyebrow at me, his thumb brushing over my bottom lip.

"Good, I am a busy man and don't have time for silly games of hide and seek. So shall we?" he asks, letting me go and motioning toward his car. I glance down at my bags in my hands, knowing Clarice needs them for dinner tonight.

"I'll return you to the castle after lunch. The King has already okayed it," he tells me.

"You told the King who I am to you?" I ask. He nods his head, reaching for the bags I grip, so tightly my knuckles are straining against my skin.

"Of course. Now come on, there's a café down the road," he tells me, and a giddy feeling rises in my stomach. My mate wants me? He wants to keep me? He's not rejecting me! I thought for sure when he said nothing, that meant he was going to reject me.

Chewing my lip nervously, I glance at his car. It's sleek and modern. He opens the door and motions for me to climb in. My mother would have scolded me for getting in a car with a stranger, but mom always said mates were our biggest blessing. They would love us unconditionally and never leave us. When I was younger, I craved to have a relationship like my mother and father had. Though, over the years, I never thought it would be a possibility for me. No one would want a broken rogue for a mate.

Mom's words flit through my head, a vague memory I hold. "If you find your mate, and I hope you do one day, it will be the most magical experience of your life. You'll know instantly they are yours, and you are theirs. It's a love that compares to nothing else," she tells me, and as I look at him, I wonder if I will have that with this man. Mrs. Daley always told us we would never have a mate, that we were unlovable and vile. Hearing that enough over the years, I started to believe her. Yet as Kade waits patiently for me to climb into his car, I wonder if Mrs. Daley had it all wrong.

"I mean you no harm. Don't you feel the pull?" he asks, and I nod.

"You're not thinking of rejecting me, are you, Abbie? You wouldn't shun the Moon Goddess in such a way, would you?" Kade asks.

"No, of course not. I just didn't expect you to want me back," I answer honestly.

"Of course I want you. You're my mate. Now, who doesn't want their mate?" he asks, and my cheeks heat at his words.

"So shall we?" he asks again, motioning toward his car. A giddy feeling bubbles up within me, and I nod, climbing into the car. He leans over me, plugging in my seatbelt before pausing as he steps away. His hand cups my cheek, his thumb brushing below my eye gently.

"You are a pretty one," he murmurs, and tingles rush across my face, his scent inviting. I can't help myself as I inhale deeply, his scent strong, like peppermint and white chocolate. Kade chuckles softly.

"Good to see the feeling reciprocated," he whispers, his eyes sparkling as they go to my lips. He then clears his throat, letting me go and shaking his head as he shuts my door.

CHAPTER
ELEVEN

ABBIE

As we drive, Kade turns on some music, and his relaxed demeanor starts to soothe my nerves. I can't help but steal glances at him, taking in his strong features and the way his muscles subtly shift under his shirt as he drives. We arrive at the café, and Kade guides me inside, his arm casually draped over my shoulders, leading me to a table.

We sit across from each other, and Kade orders us both coffee and sandwiches. He maintains eye contact with me, creating an intense atmosphere that makes the air between us feel heavy. It feels like he's studying me.

"Tell me about yourself," Kade says, breaking the silence.

"I'm just a rogue," I reply softly, feeling a bit out of my depth.

"Come on now, Abbie. There must be more to you than that," he presses, his gaze piercing. I shift uncomfortably in my chair, not used to talking about myself. Sensing my reluctance, Kade decides to talk about himself instead, which relieves me.

"You know, my pack is lovely," Kade begins, a hint of pride in his voice. "They are going to be so excited when I bring you home. You'll love the pack house, it's beautiful."

"You want me to leave with you?" I ask, surprised.

"Of course, you're my mate. We are supposed to be together. You wouldn't turn your back on what the Moon Goddess wants, would you?"

I shake my head, but my thoughts instantly turn to Ivy. I have never been without her. Although he is my mate, he'll look after me, and I won't have to be a maid, but what will become of Ivy?

"Once I have you home, and we complete the mating ceremony, and I mark you, then I'll introduce you to the pack," Kade adds.

"Mating ceremony?" I ask nervously.

"Of course, why is that an issue?" he inquires, his eyes narrowing slightly.

I say nothing, the idea making me feel a mix of emotions and none of them are good.

"So once you're back, you should pack what things you need because once I am done helping the King, we'll be leaving."

"I don't know if I can go, that is up to the King," I tell him.

"Nonsense, don't worry, I will handle the King. Besides, it's the law; he can't stop you. Mate bonds are protected," Kade assures me, his tone confident, almost dismissive of my concerns.

Yet, the thought of leaving Ivy behind weighs heavily on me. I've never been without her, and the idea of leaving her feels like abandoning a part of myself.

It's just about dark by the time I return to the castle. Kade drops me at the front gate and I can't wipe the smile off my face. My mate wants me and he seems nice. He tells me all about his pack and the packhouse, about duties I am expected to perform as his Luna. It's nice, though I am still a little wary. I wait for the other shoe to drop, keeping an eye out for the rejection, but it never comes.

Walking through the gates, I nearly jump out of my skin when Liam moves off the wall beside the iron gates.

"Gannon has been looking for you," he states, and I swallow

nervously. While with Kade, I completely forgot about Gannon for those few hours. Guilt swamps me and my heart beats faster.

"You need to tell him, Abbie," Liam tells me. I say nothing because I don't know what to say. I never thought I would be put in a position where I have to choose.

"Are you going to reject Kade or turn Gannon away?" he asks, stepping closer, and for the first time since meeting Liam, I take a step back from him. He doesn't look happy with me, and his entire demeanor is off. He looks like the callous killer I have heard rumors of.

"He's my mate, Liam," I answer softly.

"Yes, but you're a werewolf, you can reject your mates," he says. My brows furrow in confusion at his words.

"You want me to reject my mate?" I ask him, knowing doing that would be shunning the Moon Goddess for the gift she gave me.

"Kade is not a good man, Abbie." He doesn't elaborate further. Instead, he turns on his heel and walks off before calling over his shoulder.

"You need to tell Gannon, if you don't I will," Liam states, not bothering to stop.

"Wait," I call out to him while chasing after him. He slows, but doesn't stop as he walks through the double doors.

"You can't tell him. I barely know the man. You're acting like I am about to run off with him," I snap, annoyed at the accusation in his tone. Liam turns on me instantly, and I back up at the murderous look he gives me. My back hits the stone wall, and I gasp at his closeness.

"That is exactly what you will do. You will run off with your piece of shit mate and forget him. Just like she did. Then I will be left to pick up the pieces," Liam snarls.

"He's my mate," I whisper, suddenly feeling tiny next to this man with the way he has me trapped and cornered. Everything he's saying goes against everything I've ever learned about mates. We are supposed to be with our mates, not reject them. He reaches a hand up and I flinch, but he only twirls a lock of my hair around his finger.

"Gannon loves you. Kade doesn't. That man isn't capable of love. I guess you'll find that out the hard way," he whispers before letting go and stepping back.

"What's that supposed to mean, Liam!" I growl. He glares at my tone. I didn't mean for it to come out the way it did, but it's too late to take it back.

I like Liam... but I don't exactly trust his character analysis of other people given his own rather sociopathic tendencies. Maybe he's just saying all of this to mess with me.

"Do the right thing, Abbie. You need to tell him. If you don't and I have to, I will skin your mate alive and make you watch. If you want to be with your mate, fine. But don't lead Gannon along. You hurt him like she did? Not even Gannon will be able to save you from me," he says, his tone of voice turning darker along with his eyes. Tears prick the corners of my eyes at his words.

What is he talking about? Who is 'she'? I don't want to hurt Gannon, I think, feeling overwhelmed by my own thoughts.

"I don't want to hurt Gannon," I tell him.

"Then you'll tell him, or reject your mate. If you want to be with that twat, Gannon will understand. But if he finds out because he caught you or I had to tell him, it will destroy him. But know this, Abbie. Just like you and Ivy are forever bound together, so are Gannon and me. Nothing will come between us," he says while stepping toward me again.

His canines slip out, and his claws extend from his fingertips as he grabs my face. His thumb brushes over my cheek, and I swallow, feeling more like prey than I ever have in my life.

"You hurt him, and he may forgive you," he tells me while his hand moves to my throat, his fingers wrap around my throat, his claws grazing the back of my neck and making my skin prickle with goosebumps as he leans in so close his stubble brushes my cheek.

"But I won't. And I am not the sort of man you want to make an enemy of," he whispers next to my ear.

A tear rolls down my cheek, and I nod before feeling his tongue move across my cheek, licking up the tear that brimmed and spilled over.

"So just keep that in mind. Like you and Ivy come together, so do Gannon and I. He is a good man, but I'll let you in on a little secret. I'M NOT," he growls before pecking my cheek and walking off, leaving me feeling sick with fear.

I stand there petrified, watching him leave when the door across from where I stand opens up. The King walks out of his office and stops, stunned to see me standing there crying.

"Abbie?" the King asks, and I look at him. His eyes go to the end of the hall where Liam is before he turns toward the stairs and disappears. The King sighs and pushes his door open wider, nodding toward it.

"Are you okay?" he asks, and I nod.

"I need to get back to my room," I tell him, walking off.

"Abbie, is this over Kade being your mate?" The King calls out, and I stop suddenly angered that he would dare mention mates when he has locked his own mate away and rejected her over who her mother was.

"Even if it is, you would be the last person I would ask advice from, especially when your mate is rotting in a stable like a damn farm animal," I snarl before walking off. I hear his growl behind me, and I half expect him to order me out of the castle too, but as I reach the stairs and look back at him, he stands by the window looking out at the stables. Good, I hope the bastard feels guilty.

CHAPTER
TWELVE

I VY
Later that night.

I'm awoken by Gannon's voice outside. Sitting up, I shiver while rubbing my arms trying to warm them. "Kyson, I won't let you-" Gannon's words cut off abruptly, and I hear a grunt and a splash. My heart rate quickens at the sound, before it nearly leaps out of my chest when I hear the creak of the door.

Hastily moving, I sneak into the closest stall, trying to hide, his footsteps echo loudly, and the horses become unsettled. His aura ripples out violently, and I bite my lip to refrain from screaming out to Gannon.

Hiding amongst the hay, I wonder if Gannon is alright when I hear the crunch of footsteps coming nearer. I hold my breath, burrowing deeper into the hay. Peering out, I can't help the whimper that escapes me when I notice Kyson, only it isn't his normal form but that of his Lycan side. The moment the noise leaves my lips, I clamp a hand over my mouth at my mistake.

He turns swiftly in my direction, and I hold my breath. A few tense seconds pass by, and I hear him sniff the air while my heart beats rapidly, drawing his attention further. His growl is thunderous, as he starts ripping through the hay, claws slashing violently as he searches for me. Within seconds, he finds me hiding, and I peer up at him, seeing his chest rising and falling heavily while his eyes blaze with fury. I clench my eyes shut when I see his hand coming toward me, only to hear him grunt. The thud of him hitting something makes my eyes jolt open to see Gannon has tackled him. He is dripping wet, which confirms he is the one that was tossed into the lake.

"Ivy, go, but don't run!" Gannon urges, but it is too late by the time I hear the last because I wasted no time getting to my feet and running for the doors when I hear more fighting. Then, a loud crash. Peering over my shoulder, I see Gannon's body crumpled on the ground against the stall opposite to the one I was hiding in.

Distracted by Gannon momentarily, I turn to keep running, only for my body to career forward when somebody collides with me. My scream is deafening, and the horses go wild in their stalls.

I brace myself for impact, wishing I hadn't when I hit the dirt in a stiff heap. The air rushes from my lungs and I groan as I get to my hands and knees, to find blood dripping on the floor. I wipe my chin. Having fallen face first, I'd split it open. My busted fingers throb even more as they take my weight when I tense, hearing Gannon's voice behind me.

"Ivy, don't move."

My heart leaps frantically in my chest when I feel the heat of him press against my back as he shoves me back to the ground. His nose presses to the side of my neck, and he lets out a menacing growl while I freeze beneath him.

"Kyson, you don't want to hurt her," Gannon speaks softly but it earns him a feral snarl before I am suddenly grabbed and ripped away. I shriek as I roll onto my back, his huge form towering over me possessively as he glares at Gannon before returning his attention to me.

His claws rake my skin, tearing my clothes, and I can smell the copious amounts of liquor he has been drinking. "Kyson," Gannon speaks, though I hear the underlying fear lacing it, which only scares me more.

Suddenly, the stable doors open and his head whips in the direction of the noise. So does mine to see Damian enter and freeze. Kyson growls, baring his teeth, which are only inches from my face. Damian raises his hands, kneeling, his eyes trained on his King and me trapped beneath him.

"Ivy, are you okay?" Damian asks when Kyson's paw presses into my shoulder, his claws slicing my flesh.

"No!" I whimper. "He's going to kill me," I sob.

"He is not in control, but I don't think that is his intention," Damian speaks calmly, while I feel anything but calm. Kyson, though unfazed by Damian's presence, returns his attention to back me trembling beneath him. He lifts his hand, and I feel my blood pooling in the crook of my neck and chest. He sniffs my blood, instinctively I grip his fur, petrified he'll bite me or eat me. He growls, shaking his head, yet my hands don't let go.

"Kyson please, you're scaring me," I whimper.

"He's scenting you Ivy. Kyson may not have control, but he'll recognize his mate," Damian tries to reassure me. Kyson sniffs me, then licks the scratches he gave me, healing them. I cringe, as he continues licking me, while also tearing apart my clothes with his claws. He becomes almost frantic each time, he slices me quickly healing me with his tongue.

"Kyson!" Damian calls. His head twists in Damian's direction, but he drags me closer, pulling me further under him.

"I'm not taking her, but stop. You're scaring her."

Kyson huffs but peers down at me, nearly coming nose to nose with me. I freeze with him so close to my face when I feel his tongue roll across my chin, healing the gash before frantically licking and nipping my neck. I grab his face, my hand tugging on his ear, and he growls at me.

"Stop it," I cry out only for him to snarl, which sends a shiver down my spine when he suddenly grabs me with one arm like I weigh nothing. Gannon jumps to his feet.

"Easy Gannon," Damian warns him, and I turn my head to find Damian also standing.

Kyson, not worried by them, drags me off to one of the stalls. I am about to start thrashing to get out of his grip, when he suddenly lays down, pulling me on top of him. I hear Damian exhale loudly. While I am frozen in my fear. I carefully try to climb off him, only for him to snap his teeth at me and pull me back.

Damian enters the stall and at first. I think he is going to help me escape, but instead he keeps his distance and sits on the floor across from us when Kyson growls in warning not to come closer. Kyson rolls, his huge furry body pressing me into the stall wall, obscuring my view. "I'm not going anywhere, Ivy, sleep. His beast is just restless, and he obliterated himself drinking."

I try to move, only every time I do I am dragged back, and he presses closer. I fist the fur on his chest, my body stiff. "He'll sleep, just leave him be, he won't hurt you."

"What happens when he wakes up," Damian chuckles softly.

"Oh, he'll be furious, but I won't let him hurt you, we'd die stopping him if we needed to," Damian says, making me remember Gannon mentioning the pact.

"I promise, I'm not going anywhere, sleep. He tries anything. I'll stop him," Damian says, then I hear him yawn. I remain still, his furry face pressed into the hollow of my neck, eventually fighting sleep becomes impossible, and I drift off to sleep cocooned in his scent and warmth.

)⊙(

The next morning, I wake to the feeling of Kyson moving I'm unsure when he shifted back, but now his knee is pressed between my legs, his arm wrapped around my torso, his face next to my shoulder. I try to sit up, and carefully move his arm off me, only for him to lurch upright. His eyes are wide as he scans his surroundings while I shuffle backward to get away from him. My movement, however, doesn't go unnoticed by him, and he pins me with a glare.

He takes in his surroundings, and peers down at the filth he had us lying in, earning a growl from him. The noise instantly wakes up Damian, who snaps to attention. Kyson glares at me as he gets up, his rejection of me loud and clear. My bond screams out for him, and I flinch when he takes a step toward me, only for Damian to speak behind him.

"Touch her Kyson, we'll have problems," Damian warns him. Kyson peers at him over his shoulder and I watch him, petrified about what he'll do next. His jaw clenches and his hands fist at his side when he abruptly turns and walks out of the stall toward the stable door. I let out the breath I am holding, and Damian scrubs a hand down his face.

"Are you okay?" Damian asks, and I hastily nod, only to notice Gannon, Dustin, and Liam all out in the main area of the stables. My lips part in shock when I feel fabric touch me and I jump, peering up at Damian, but his gaze is averted, and he is shirtless.

"My Queen, you have no top," he tells me, and I notice all the guards looking toward the stable door. I take it, covering myself while my face flames with heat.

"As I said, we won't let him hurt you."

"You didn't stop him last night," I mumble, feeling angry and scared all over again.

"But did he hurt you?" Damian asks as I pull his shirt on. I swallow looking down, but besides my busted fingers, I am unscathed. "He scented you, nothing abnormal for Lycans. We are rougher, but his intention wasn't to hurt you. Unfortunately, Gannon panicked, which escalated things. But I don't believe his intention was to hurt you."

"Then what was his intention?" I ask, baffled, remembering him healing the deep gashes he left in my skin.

"His bond craves yours, Lycan aren't meant to be apart once they've found their mate. I know you don't understand since you aren't one, but the bond pulls a lot harder for us. He wanted you close, the moment he got and everyone calmed down, he went to sleep," Damian tells me.

I peer out at Dustin, Damian and Gannon. "Then why are they here?" I ask him.

"Just in case, we weren't sure what he would wake up like. In his Lycan form, he is more beast than man, running on instinct. But as a man, he runs on emotion, which can be far more lethal than his animalistic traits when it comes to you," he warns me.

"So what am I supposed to do when his animalistic side comes for me again?" I blurt, worried that his beast would be creeping around every night.

"Usually, Kyson has control except when drunk, but if he does come," Damian crouches in front of me. "Don't run, my Queen. You never run from a Lycan, you do, and he will chase. And that is one race he will always win," Damian warns.

I swallow, glancing at Gannon, but I nod. Damian smiles sadly.

"Hopefully, the King will come to his senses soon, for now, I need to shower, and you need your breakfast," he tells me. Oh, how I wish to shower myself but after my last attempt, I've given up on the idea. Though, maybe I could try to bathe in the lake. But what if I drown? I'm no good at swimming. Yet, Kyson's scent covers every inch of me, one part of me hates it because it makes me long for him, another part of me wants to savor it, not knowing when I would see him next.

CHAPTER
THIRTEEN

I VY

When dawn breaks, I go without a visit from Abbie, leaving a void that's hard to ignore. Had Kyson forbid her from coming to visit me? I try to shake off the feeling of abandonment, telling myself she must be busy, but the ache in my chest doesn't ease even as the day comes to an end. Today I've barely seen anyone. Damian told me Kyson went on a rampage after waking next to me and has kept everyone busy ordering them around. In an attempt to distract myself, I decided to help Peter with his outside chores, and now we are picking oranges.

Damian had mentioned it was alright, as long as I did not venture into the castle. And after last night, I don't want to risk any run-ins with the King, so that isn't something he has to worry about.

As I move from orange to orange, my hands mechanically go about their task, but my mind is somewhere else. I think of the castle, the King and his people, of our complicated lives interwoven in a sticky web of mistrust and secrets. The simple task is a small comfort, a momentary escape from the chaos until I suddenly see him out of the corner of my eye.

Kyson emerges from the treeline, clad in just shorts, a clear sign that he has just returned from his run. His presence sends a jolt of anxiety through me. He's always an imposing man, but today, with his casual attire and intense demeanor, he's particularly daunting. He stops when he notices me, eyes taking me in as mine do the same to him. For a few seconds, he simply stands there studying me as if trying to make up his mind about something. There's something in his eyes that speaks of pain and longing, and I can't help but wonder if the bond torments him the same way it does me. All I want to do is throw myself in his arms and beg for forgiveness but I remain where I am, too scared to move while I watch him back.

His hair is messy, cheeks flushed and chest heaving under the sunlight while beads of sweat run down the valleys of his abs. He is tall, with broad shoulders and strong arms. His legs are taut, his stomach toned and sculpted. He's in peak physical form, no signs of weakness or weariness. While standing near him, I feel even more inferior, weak. The only sound out here is his ragged breath as he stands watching me, trying to decide what to do with me, to say to me.

"Orange my King," Peter, ever so kind, offers Kyson an orange, cutting through the awkward tension but the King's reaction is anything but gracious. His voice is sharp, laced with command.

"Why is she here?" he demands. Peter looks back at me in confusion when I hear the door behind us open that leads to the kitchens and laundry. Kyson turns his attention and I see Damian step out the door.

"I thought I told you she wasn't to come to the castle," he snaps at Damian, his tone icy.

"She isn't in the castle. She is picking oranges, Kyson," Damian tries to explain, his voice tinged with a plea for understanding.

Not wanting to cause more trouble, I quietly retreat to the stables, the King's voice still ringing in my ears as he and Damian argue. Peter follows, worry written all over his face.

"Are you okay, Ivy?" he asks, his voice filled with concern.

"I don't want to get you in trouble, Peter. Please, just go," I whisper, urging him away. He hesitates, torn between concern and also not wanting to earn the King's wrath, but eventually leaves me alone, and I continue walking back to my new home, the stables.

In the stables, I try to make a bed out of old sheets and Kyson's clothes, which Gannon had sneakily provided. But emotions get the better of me, and I start tearing the clothes apart as frustration and sadness grips me. Each rip feels like a release, but it brings no peace, only a sense of deepening despair. I want to scream, want to cry, want anything other than this empty grief that fills me. I feel like I am rotting from the inside out, that my life is decaying before my eyes. At least back at the orphanage, I knew how each day would be with Mrs. Daley. Now I can't prepare for the next five minutes. His mood swings are unpredictable.

I could prepare for back breaking chores and frequent lashes. I endured it, and lived and breathed and choked on that life. Yet coming here gave us hope, we could finally breathe, we were finally free. But why does this hurt more? Why does the bond sting feel so much more intensely brutal? Here, it's more than just my body suffering. It's my heart... my soul. The glimpses of a different kind of life, a safe life... only to have it ripped away as quickly as it came.

When I finally calm down, I peer down at my makeshift den by the furnace only for another wave of devastation to hit me. I've ruined Kyson's clothes. Desperately, I snatch them up, sniffing for his scent, but it's gone. My tantrum has robbed me of that small comfort, and it breaks my heart painfully as I ignore the shooting pain of my hand while searching for his scent, yet all I get is a nose full of earth and dirt. The lack of even that minor comfort makes the hollow feeling inside my chest worsen as my bond cries out for him.

Curling up in a ball, with the shredded remnants, I lay there, feeling more alone than ever. The echoes of the King's anger and the loss of his scent haunt me, replaying in my head. Now my own mind taunts me, telling me how stupid I was to let my anger get the better of me, now I am not only without my mate but without anything to keep me warm. I close my eyes, seeking escape, even if it's just for a moment. But escape doesn't come, and I'm left with the stark reality of my situation, a reality that's becoming increasingly difficult to bear.

CHAPTER
FOURTEEN

KYSON

As I storm away from the confrontation with Damian over Ivy, my anger is a storm brewing inside me. Damian is right on my heels, frustration evident in his voice as he adds his opinion to the mix, fueling my anger more.

"Everything alright?" Clarice's voice cuts through the tension as she steps out of the back doors of the laundry.

"He had her near the castle," I snap, my words laced with venom.

Clarice sighs heavily, her disappointment palpable.

Why the heck is everyone taking her side? She isn't even the Queen! I haven't marked her. Have they forgotten Claire already?

"She is picking oranges, Kyson," Clarice tries to reason, but my glare turns to fix on Ivy. However, when I turn to confront her, I find she's already gone. Damian curses under his breath and moves to chase after her, but my growl halts him in his tracks.

"No, Gannon can watch her. We need to go over the Rogue murders and the information Kade gave us," I command, my voice leaving no room for argument.

Damian freezes, his frustration with me reaching a boiling point.

68

"Was it necessary to be such a prick? She's having a hard enough time as it is, and you just keep hurting her. You're digging yourself a grave, Kyson. You're risking everything!" he yells.

"No, her mother ruined everything," I counter coldly.

"Exactly, her mother, not her. But still, you punish her for it, punish yourself," Damian retorts.

"I am not punishing myself," I snarl, but the words ring hollow even to my ears because I've felt nothing but agony without her. Yet she does not deserve my love.

"Really? Then how do you explain getting so fucking drunk that you lost control last night?" Damian challenges.

I growl, ignoring him and storming inside the castle, trying to escape Damian's accusations. The kitchen staff scatter as I enter, sensing my foul mood, and I keep moving toward the foyer.

"Are you seriously going to continue ignoring the bond? This is your only chance at having a mate, but you can't see past your hate," Damian continues.

"Damian, enough. I have a headache," I snap, heading towards my office.

Out of the corner of my eye, I catch a glimpse of Ivy walking across the lawns. Through the windows, Peter chases after her before stopping her. I watch her for a second as she talks to Peter. She looks longingly at the castle, making a pang of guilt wash over me. Peter wanders off, leaving her alone, her figure deflated in defeat, while Peter looks at her with worry. She has everyone convinced she is not a monster but I know otherwise.

"Can you at least fucking try to talk to her? She frets without you," Damian's voice rings in my ears and he grabs my arm. I snarl, but he doesn't back off when Gannon opens the foyer doors and steps inside.

"You can still fix things, it's not too late, Kyson," Damian pleads but I shake my head.

Ignoring him, I brush past Gannon, who steps into my path with

69

a glare. "What's happened now? What did you do?" he instantly accuses me.

I'm at the end of my tether. Do they have any idea how it feels knowing you're housing a monster's daughter? They all witnessed what Marissa did, yet they expected me to accept her daughter with open arms.

"Everyone, patrol now!" I scream, my patience worn out. My command erupts violently and Gannon gasps clutching the wall as he fights to remain where he is.

Damian resists, straining against my command. "Remove the command," he grits out. I hate commanding them, they know it, and guilt hits me for it, but I won't back down. They need to let me get my head straight and come to terms with this; she is not the only one grieving the bond.

"No, I'm sick and tired of hearing about her, sick of you telling me how to handle my mate when YOU DON'T UNDERSTAND," I snarl back, watching as Gannon, unable to resist any longer, rushes out the door.

"You'd leave her defenseless," Damian accuses.

"She has Dustin," I snap before storming off.

"Dustin, you ordered him to go into town for you with Liam earlier. It's nearly dark, Kyson!" Damian shouts at me, but I ignore him, and keep walking, only to hear his body smash against the door, unable to resist my command any longer.

In my office, I reach for my bottle of liquor, immediately chugging half of it in an attempt to drown out the bond that's gnawing at me. Time slips away as I sit there, consumed by thoughts of Ivy, of Claire, and the state I found her in. It all rushes back, the guilt of leaving that day, her last words replay in my mind on a loop that morning, I didn't want to go. Why did she make me leave? She would probably still be here if I'd stayed.

Some time later, Clarice enters, her disappointment evident. "If you're here to scold me, don't," I warn her.

"Just collecting your tray," she responds, her tone tired. But I can tell she is holding her tongue. She wants to speak, but also knows her place. Little does she know, it's not her words I fear. It's breaking her heart. Clarice knows me better than one here, she helped raise me, raise Claire, more than my parents ever did.

I glance at the clock, realizing hours have passed. Clarice sighs and picks up the tray. "You too. Why do I bother cooking for you if you don't bother eating it," she mutters with a shake of her head.

"Did you remember to send food down for—" I stop mid-sentence, the guilt unbearable.

"For your Queen?" Clarice finishes for me, her eyes holding a mixture of pity and reproach. "I left it for her, but she never touched it. Abbie tried to get her to eat, but she refused, said she wasn't hungry," she informs me.

"She refused?" I growl, anger flaring again. "She should be grateful I let her live, yet she refuses what we provide." I snarl, seeing that her refusal has upset Clarice too. I get up from my chair.

But Clarice blocks the door, her eyes hard. "I used to think you were a good man, but now I am not so sure anymore. You hurt her..." her words trail off unfinished but I hear the threat loud and clear.

"You'll what, Ma? Quit?" I ask her, and her bottom lip quivers, and she glances away. I instantly feel bad for the words and wish I could take them back.

"Do you not remember? Have you forgotten already?" I ask her, and her gaze hardens as it turns to me.

"No one has forgotten, though I wish I could... I wish I could, Kyson, I've lived through hell and back but nothing broke me more than losing her. I won't live through losing you too. This kingdom won't survive losing their Queen. We've lost too many," she snaps.

"She is not Queen!" I yell.

"But your kingdom won't accept anyone other than her. She is your true mate, our true Queen. You need to realize that because if you lose her, you lose all of us!" she says before walking away.

I stare at her. They barely know her! I punch the wall in frustration, feeling more furious than ever. Snatching my bottle, I drink every drop, yet it still doesn't help, doesn't numb the bond.

Stumbling down to the stables, a fresh liquor bottle in hand, I find Ivy curled in a ball, surrounded by shredded clothes, and the scent of her tears fills the air. It's freezing inside, and my guilt intensifies as the draft rushes over me. Leaving her, I step outside to gather wood, hearing a noise in the forest, but I dismiss it as one of the guards when they don't come closer.

Returning with the wood, I find Ivy awake, struggling to light a fire with one hand. "Finally, Damian, can you please light—"

She stops mid-sentence when she notices me. "Sorry, sir," she murmurs, fear evident in her voice as she quickly stands.

I notice the tremble in her words; she is scared of me. No, that is not an accurate word. She is petrified of me. I take a step toward her, and she takes one back and the way her heart rate picks up doesn't go unnoticed by me; it bothers me for some reason. Perhaps because I spent so long trying to get her out of her shell, only to see her reverting back to the way she was when she first came here, maybe that bothers me.

I study her, seeing her straighten her spine, and stare past me. Despite the pain it causes her, she clutches her hands behind her back, just like Mrs. Daley taught her. I know because I feel it. Pain shoots up my hand, and I drop the wood.

Ivy gasps and moves to pick it up. "It's fine, my King; I can wait for Gannon," she tells me, then freezes.

"I mean," she pauses. "Do you need me to send someone up with wood?" she asks yet won't meet my gaze. Now she is questioning whether I got the wood for her or for myself.

"Leave it," I tell her, not trusting myself with more than those words. She rises, and I snatch the piece of wood out of her hand. She bows her head, moving back to her makeshift den of torn blankets, when I notice a few of my shirts. I shake my head and she tries to cover them, realizing what I am staring at.

Ivy's face turns pink with her embarrassment while I load the wood in the furnace. I can feel her eyes watching me, smell her fear. I start the fire, and once I am satisfied, it will remain going, I close the little hatch and get to my feet, walking out but not before glancing back to see her rush towards the warmth.

As I walk back to the castle, the weight of my actions, my guilt, and my loneliness press down on me, heavier with each step. My own bitterness and anger are turning everyone against me, and I can't seem to stop the spiral. The night air does nothing to ease the turmoil inside me. When I hear a noise, I pause for a second, staring out at the treeline across the small lake. When I notice nothing, I keep walking.

CHAPTER
FIFTEEN

IVY

I watch Kyson leave, and once I am sure he has left, I rush toward the fire, trying to warm myself, my bones ache from the cold, and my teeth chatter uncontrollably when an unexpected noise outside startles me. My first thought is that it might be Kyson, and I immediately worry that he's angry with me. The fire crackles in front of me, providing little comfort against the chill that has nothing to do with the cold night air. As I glance around, the hair on the back of my neck stands on end. There is a strange scent in the air, familiar, but I can't place it. The stables are deathly quiet, too quiet, and the horses all stand with their eyes trained on the stable doors. I strain my ears to catch any sound that might tell me more. Rising to my feet, I go to see if someone is outside... perhaps one of the guards.

I see a large, dark shape come into view in the stables. At first, I wonder if it's Kyson in his Lycan form. Only, just then, the horses start to go wild. My heart stops for a moment before racing uncontrollably. It's a bear. And a large one by the looks of it. I can tell by its hunched shape and slow prowl.

I stay rooted, frozen in place, watching the bear sniff the ground, raise its head, and turn its attention to me. I've never seen a bear before, but I do recall you weren't supposed to run from them. It's massive, with dark fur and eyes that reflect a wild hunger. My feet feel rooted to the ground and I stagger as I take a step back. It growls and I slowly take another step back.

As the bear stalks toward me, a deep, paralyzing fear grips me. *I'm dead,* I think to myself, not seeing a way out of this. As I scramble backward, a bit faster this time, my hand shoots out, pulling a burning stick from the fire without thinking, burning my hands painfully. The bear lunges when I hiss and drop it. My scream is blood-curdling as I quickly move out of its way, adrenaline pumping, I don't feel the burning stick as I grab it. I wave it frantically, hoping to scare the bear away, but it only seems to anger it more. I scream for help, my voice shrill and desperate in the quiet night.

The bear lunges at me, and at that moment, I prepare for death. But then, out of nowhere, another huge, black shape tackles the bear. At first, I think it's another bear before realizing that it's a Lycan. It's Kyson, his form massive and intimidating as he collides with the savage bear, it turns on him quickly, and he's thrown back, crashing into a stall with a loud thud. My heart is in my throat, helpless, as I watch the bear turn to finish him off. Acting on instinct, I rip a piece of wood from the stall and hit the bear with all my strength.

Pain explodes across my face as the bear turns and slices me with its claws down my face. Blood blinds me, hot and sticky, trickling down my skin as I stagger back clutching my face. I'm sure this is the end, as I swipe my face frantically, trying to clear my vision, but then I hear the sounds of a fierce struggle. Kyson, in his Lycan form, is attacking the bear, driving it back with powerful blows. He punches the bear, makes it sniff and paw at its nose before Kyson plunges his own claws into its side. With a final injury to the face from Kyson, the bear retreats, fleeing into the night.

Shouts echo outside from the castle. The noise has alerted the guards, who rush into the stables. They burst inside but instantly back up when they're faced with the King in this form. I don't recognize a single one of them and Kyson, still feral in his Lycan form, moves to attack them. Heart hammering in my chest, I move, grabbing his fur knowing he won't forgive himself if he attacks his men. He freezes when I grab his fur. He whirls around, snarling at me, and I drop to my knees in submission, my hands shaking as I clutch at the fur on his thick thighs. His eyes blaze with a wild light, and I brace myself, certain he's going to attack.

But then, to my surprise, Kyson's Lycan demeanor changes, recognizing me. He lowers his head, his rough tongue licking my arm, healing the gash the bear left. His attention moves to my burnt fingers, and he gently licks them, soothing the pain when his licking becomes frantic on my face.

The guards hesitate, watching us warily. Kyson's Lycan side seems to sense their presence and growls, his protective instincts kicking in. He drags me around like a prized possession, pulling me into one of the stalls. The guards back away, unsure of how to approach the situation. It's clear that his Lycan is not hurting me, but rather protecting me in his own way, even if it is from his own guard.

"I'm fine, he won't hurt me," I murmur to them, hoping it's true, even though his Lycan is unpredictable. I peer up at him, and he growls, tucking me closer.I shriek when his long claws nick me. The guards hesitate, looking at me worriedly.

"Get Damian," I stutter. They rush off immediately.

I'm still trembling, the shock of the encounter with the bear and Kyson's unexpected defense of me overwhelming. Kyson curls around me, his massive body a protective barrier between me and the rest of the world as his weight crushes me into the hay. I move trying to get out from under him, but he snarls snapping sharp teeth at me. I freeze momentarily, my eyes meeting his when I show him he's crushing me. He sniffs me but my huge beast of mate seems to understand because he moves off me. When I try to climb out entirely though, he growls again making my heart race. I nudge his huge shoulder, trying to get him to understand. He doesn't budge, so I tap his chest. Still nothing.

Leaning forward, I press my ear to his chest, listening to the hard steady thump of his heart. That seems to work because he rolls on his back, dragging me onto his chest before turning slightly so I can't see past him. It's like he's using himself like a wall separating me from everyone else, or maybe trying to stop me escaping. I press my hands against his chest, trying to warm them, and feel him sniffing my hair.

The warmth of his fur and the steady rhythm of his breathing slowly calms me down.

As I lay there, tucked safely under Kyson's protective Lycan form, I realize the complexity of our relationship. He may be harsh and distant at times, but his instincts are still to protect me. Or his Lycan instincts are. He can deny the bond, but the bond will remind him, just as it did tonight when he came back for me.

The guards maintain their distance, but I know it's one of the royal guards but not Damian or any scent I immediately recognize, but they're respecting Kyson's clear message to stay away and keep their distance. I'm grateful for their understanding, knowing that any attempt to intervene might provoke him further.

I lean against Kyson, my mind slowly processing everything that has happened. The fear, the pain, the relief – it all mingles together in a confusing bundle of emotions. But through it all, there's a newfound respect and understanding for Kyson.

The night wears on, the fire in the stall flickering softly, casting a warm glow around us. I close my eyes, allowing myself to relax in his embrace. The events of the night have drained me, and despite the chaos, I feel safe here with him. Even if I can only feel safe with him while he's in this form.

CHAPTER
SIXTEEN

I VY

The morning light filters through the cracks of the stable, casting a golden hue over the hay and dust particles dancing in the air. I wake up alone, the space beside me cold, telling me that Kyson is gone and must have left a while ago. However, someone has draped one of his blankets from his room over me, making me wonder if he sent someone to get it because it's covered in his scent. My heart sinks a little deeper, the loneliness once again settling in like an unwelcome guest. I sit up, rubbing the sleep from my eyes, the events of last night replaying in my mind like a nightmare I can't escape.

The bear, the fear, Kyson's unexpected rescue—it all feels surreal, like a twisted fairy tale where the prince is also the monster. I shiver, pulling my blanket closer around me. The stables, now once again, feel like a prison.

As I gather my thoughts, the sound of footsteps approach.

The stable door creaks open, and Damian's silhouette appears against the morning light. He looks concerned, his brows furrowed as he surveys my disheveled state. The sight of him, a familiar face in this whirlwind of chaos, brings a small sense of relief.

Damian's voice breaks the silence, carrying a hint of hope that I cling to desperately.

"Morning, my Queen," he says excitedly. Confused by his cheery tone, I get up, my body hurting from the rough ground and the emotional turmoil that won't let up.

"Morning, Damian," I manage to say, my voice hoarse from the tears and screams of the night.

He steps closer, his expression softening. "You've had a rough night," he observes, extending his hand to help me up.

I nod, accepting his help. As I stand, the stiffness in my muscles reminds me of the ordeal I've just been through.

"We need to get you cleaned up and into a more comfortable place," he suggests, and I glance at him, wearing a silly smile I hadn't seen before.

"I'm allowed to shower?" I ask as he guides me out of the stable. The fresh air hits me, a welcome change from the stale, heavy atmosphere inside.

As we walk, I can't help but glance back at the stables, the scene of so much fear and confusion. It's hard to leave it behind, even harder to face the uncertainty that awaits me in the castle.

Damian leads me along the path, his grip firm but gentle. I'm grateful for his support, for his understanding. He doesn't press me for details, doesn't bombard me with questions like one would expect, but I know Kyson and the guard would have filled him in.

"Yes, I have some good news," Damian says, "Come on!" he tells me.

Confused, my brows furrow as he waves his hand in front of me to grab my arm. I look at it before placing my good hand in his. He places it on his arm and tucks his arm to his side. I raise an eyebrow at him as he starts up the path leading back to the castle. For a second, hope flares to life, only to die down when he speaks again.

"The King said you can stay in his old quarters; you will be more comfortable up there," he says, and I stop. Beta Damian also stopped and looked down at me.

"He said I could come back?" I ask hopefully. Beta Damian glances at Gannon for a second before turning his gaze back to me.

"He didn't, did he?" I ask, sorrow hitting me once again.

"I convinced him, but he is aware you will stay in his old room," Damian tells me.

"His old room?" I whisper, holding back tears.

"Yes, the room he currently uses used to be his sister's," Damian explains.

"Before my mother killed her," I sigh, still unable to believe she killed someone. It all feels surreal. Nevertheless, Damian escorts me back to the castle, and as we approach the castle doors that lead into the foyer, the door opens, and Kyson steps out.

He stops in his tracks before eyeing my hand on Damian's arm. His eyes flicker and he growls. I yank my hand away before his eyes go to mine for a second before going to Damian.

"Find me when you're done," the King says, not bothering to acknowledge my existence before he turns and stalks off toward where the cars were waiting out front of the castle.

I stare after him while pain ripples through my chest at his dismissal of me. Gannon growls before following him, and Damian looks down at me.

"Come on, I will show you where he put you," Damian says, tugging me inside.

"You mean where you decided to put me? He doesn't look so happy I will be here," I tell him.

As I enter, I notice the room is bigger than Kyson's, though I could tell it has remained untouched by the thick layers of dust on the furniture and appliances. One of the servants is in here trying to clean it up, uncovering all the furniture that was covered by sheets. It feels weird watching her try to clean the place, and I move to help her when Damian stops me, pointing to the bathroom.

"Bathroom is through there. I will help her. Go take a shower and get cleaned up. I placed some of Kyson's clothes in the closet for you. It might help with the discomfort. Gannon said you struggled last night, my Queen."

The female servant watches me curiously at his words. I frown that she is expected to clean this room, all because I would be staying in it. It's too big of a task for one person.

"I will help. Go get cleaned up," Damian says, nudging me toward the bathroom. With a sigh, I give up.

I smell terrible after spending all night in the stables. The girl had already restocked the bathroom, everything shiny and clean. A fresh towel hung on the side of the huge spa bath that sat in the center. Across the far wall stood an open shower, no screen, just two shower heads protruding from the wall and a drain that ran along the entire back of the bathroom.

All the counter space was made of black marble and the floors slate. All the finishings are gold and it has double basins. It makes me wonder if Kyson stayed in the other room just to feel close to his sister because this room is much more luxurious and as big as his entire quarters. I shower quickly, washing all remnants of the stables off. Finally feeling clean, I emerge out in my towel, wondering where the closet is that Damian spoke of.

I go to ask when I notice the room is empty, yet all the furniture is uncovered, and the curtains are drawn. No dust in sight makes me realize just how much quicker Lycans are than common werewolves.

Wandering through the room, I open a door, finding an untouched office with the furniture still covered. I quickly close the door before opening another and finding a library. However, the shelves are bare, and the room is dark. Not that I could read anyway, so there's no point in a stocked library. Yet it makes me think of Kyson and his love for reading.

Moving across the room, I roll my eyes, having missed the door next to the bathroom, which would be the most obvious place for a closet. I walk over to it and grip the handle, pulling it open.

His scent hits me like a punch in the chest. A few of his clothes are hung, but I recognize a few pieces I knew were from his room. Stepping in, his scent becomes even more overwhelming, and my heart aches as I clutch it. It brings me to my knees.

Not caring for my injured hand, I start ripping the clothes off the hangers. I need his scent, need him as I curl up in a ball among his clothes. Some primal, instinctual part takes over all rational thought and sends me wild with uncontrollable grief.

My entire body is anxious as I claw at the ground. I feel unhinged, uncontrollable, and I curse him as much as I longed for him. Surely no one could survive this sort of heartache.

My instincts are all over the place. Time stands still, and I have no idea how long I've been in here when the door opens.

A violent growl escapes my throat, and my claws sink into the soft gray plush carpet, slicing through it like a hot knife through butter. A woman, whoever was at the door, jumps back, startled, pulling away from me just in time to see her face. Recognition returns to me, and I scramble after her to apologize, but she is already gone.

The door shuts behind her with a soft click. My skin feels like it is crawling as I claw at it, suddenly feeling cold, and I have the urge to go back to my den. The smell of food hits my nostrils, and I peer over at the table between the armchairs and fireplace to notice the bowl of hot soup. I wrinkle my nose because the strong odor is tainting the scent of my mate. Turning, I walk back to the closet and shut the door before burrowing back inside my den.

As I nestle deeper into Kyson's clothes, their familiar scent wraps around me like a cocoon. It's a bittersweet comfort, a reminder of what I long for and what seems so out of reach. My thoughts drift to Kyson, to the complexity of our bond, and to the pain that seems to be its constant companion.

The loneliness is overwhelming, suffocating. I close my eyes, trying to escape into memories, into a time when things were simpler, when my heart wasn't torn in two. But the memories are elusive, slipping through my fingers like sand.

CHAPTER
SEVENTEEN

K YSON
Two Days Later

The carpet is wearing down from my constant pacing. My fingers throb and ache, causing me to growl. My entire being vibrates with the urge to track her down, knowing she is just on the other side of the castle. It has been two days since I last laid eyes on her, and the bond hammers into every aspect of my senses. I shouldn't have agreed to let her back in the castle, yet since the bear attack, I can't leave her out there either.

This bond is driving me crazy, taking over every aspect of me. My Lycan side, which I can barely contain, seeks her out whenever my guard is down. Now, I'm scared to sleep, scared to stay awake too. I can't win. I want it gone. I busy myself with work, but it's nearly impossible when my fucking hand won't stop throbbing.

How is my hand throbbing? My Lycan healed her. Maybe the bear hurt her hand? Annoyed, I reach for the bottle, my vice, when I feel like I'm losing control. We should be investigating the recent deaths, but the bridge remains closed.

So, relief floods me when Gannon enters the room to report it is now open. I need to get out of this place and away from Damian. He has been incessantly annoying me to go see her.

"The bridge has reopened, my King," Gannon tells me.

I nod, pouring some whiskey into my glass before downing it. "Get the cars ready; we are leaving," I tell him without looking over at him as I pour another drink.

"Yes, my King, but Ivy," he starts.

"Do not speak her name," I bellow, tossing my glass across the room. It explodes, smashing against the brickwork around the fireplace. The glass shatters everywhere. Gannon, who is used to my anger, doesn't flinch. However, I feel as though I am on the verge of exploding. He would run then; they all did.

"As I was saying, she has not left the closet in two days. No one can get into her room or near her, not even Abbie. She hasn't eaten, and her fretting is getting worse," Gannon says, ignoring me.

"Not my problem. I let her back into the castle. Tell Damian to deal with her," I snap, annoyed at their worry for her. She is a traitor's daughter.

"My King... your Queen..."

"She is not my Queen or your Queen; she never will be," I snarl. Anger is the only thing keeping me alive.

Gannon growls before turning and walking out. My shoulders sag as he leaves, and I clench my hand, my fingers aching before opening the mindlink.

'Dustin, have the car ready. You drive with me today,' I tell him.

'My king, Beta Damian usually...'

'I said you drive with me, send a maid in to clean up the glass in my room,' I tell him, cutting him off.

'Yes, my King,' he says, and I cut off the link. After retrieving my wallet and phone, I grab my jacket before leaving the room and heading downstairs. I toss my jacket to Dustin, who catches it, placing it over his arm. When I walk downstairs, I hear Clarice and Abbie excitedly talking about something, and Abbie is glowing vibrantly and nearly bouncing on the spot.

The groceries in her arms nearly topple out of the basket she carries. Clarice tries to get her to contain her excitement over whatever it is that has her bouncing with joy.

They cut off abruptly, noticing me, and Abbie bows respectably, bearing her neck to me. Gannon stands off near the doors, glaring angrily at the wall.

I step past them, heading out. The sun is setting, and I'm eager to get to town before nightfall. Despite all the pain, I'm still driven to put a stop to those killing rogue children and their families. Gannon follows me silently; his brewing anger behind me only makes the throbbing in my hand worse, bringing the pulse in my hand back to the forefront of my mind and fueling my anger more.

Clarice catches up to me with a duffle bag, obviously having escaped the gushing Abbie.

"For fuck's sake, can someone send a doctor to look at her fucking hand?" I snap before twisting and punching the stone wall.

Pain flares up my arm, and Clarice drops the bag in her hands. My anger diffuses, and my burning hatred dissolves as my Lycan side settles. It's becoming too much. Gannon's mood also changes, and Clarice stands quivering beside me. Eventually, I sigh, dropping my aura, unsure of what came over me.

"No one can get close to her. We've tried, my King," Clarice murmurs. Her voice trembles, and I glance at the woman. Her face is pale from the fright I've just given her.

My knuckles bleed, and I ball my hand into a fist as though I'm ready to fight. The dull throbbing is driving me insane. The fact she's not allowing anyone in is pissing me off. Does she not know I can fucking feel it? Is she doing this to annoy me?

Days I've been complaining and asking them to tend to her. With a snarl, I turn and stalk off toward my old chambers when Gannon's hand falls on my shoulder, and I stop, turn my head, and glare at him.

"Mind your place, Gannon," I warn him.

"Your intentions first, my King," he says, clenching his jaw. The man is tempting my rage to come forth again. They're all pushing me to my limits.

They know they're no match but would die trying, and for her, their rogue fucking Queen I haven't even marked. Complete idiocy on my part, making them swear to that pact it would override me every damn time, but they would never be a match for the beast that lives in me.

No one is a match for the Lycan King. They know it too, and I know they would die for her, no matter who brought them their demise.

I keep walking, Gannon's hand falling from my shoulder as I stalk toward the castle entrance.

"My King," Gannon calls.

"Kyson," he bellows, but I ignore him, stalking up the steps before turning in the opposite direction of my quarters to go to my old room.

Gannon jogs to keep up with my long strides as I hunt her down before approaching the double doors leading into the room. I shove them open, and Gannon tries to grab me. I turn and growl, my aura slamming into him and stunning him.

"Out!" I order. The command grips him instantly. They may have the pact to uphold, but they can't fight a direct command. I slam the doors as he stands stunned, unable to cross the threshold.

Turning around to face the room, I notice it's completely dark. The curtains are closed, and I reach over and flick on the light. I'm completely shocked at the state of the room. The mattress is torn to shreds; the linens are shredded. Plates sit by the door, still full, like they merely slid the trays through the gap. The stench is horrendous from the rotting food, and I gag before picking up the trays and opening the door. I thrust them toward Gannon, who takes them looking disgusted.

"Get rid of it," I snap, shutting the door.

Wandering through the room, I check the bathroom, but there's no sign of her. Her scent is everywhere, stuffing from the mattress scattered all over the floor when I hear the remnants of a low muffled growl.

Turning, I face the closet. The door is closed, yet her scent smells most potent in this corner. Crouching down, I grip the door handle, opening the door to find two blue sapphire eyes illuminated in the darkness. Her canines protrude as she lifts her head from amongst the stuffing and shredded clothes. My clothes and the linens from the room cover the floor where she built her little den.

I feel strange, like a trespasser in her den, a threat to her area. I don't think she recognizes me. Her feral instincts and guilt try to strangle me for what I've let become of her. She moves from beneath the linens, her hand falling on the carpet in front of me. Clawed nails slice through the carpet as she calculates her attack.

Ivy may not have shifted or been able to, but she-wolves are just as dangerous when they feel threatened.

Wild gleaming eyes peer back at me before a feral snarl is cut off as she sniffs the air. She honestly looks more animal than the Ivy I'm used to. I did this to her, made her this way. The guilt flooding through me eats at me.

I have destroyed her. Yet I push it aside, trying to remember why I came up here. I crawl a little into her space, and she growls, my body's own reaction to settle her reacting without my say as I purr, calling her out of her den.

Briefly, I wonder if it will work because it's clear to me that she's been left to fret about the bond I've denied her. But still, her whimper tells me the bond isn't completely lost.

Eyes narrowing, Ivy launches forward before halting at my command before she can touch me. She falls forward onto the carpet, belly down, submissive. I look away; it's essentially what the calling is for, making them submissive, yet it pains me seeing her this way, using it against her this way, so I let it drop.

Immediately, she lunges at me, a wild energy fueling her attack. I stumble backward, caught off guard, as she starts to tear at my clothes, seeking my scent, my skin. I let her maul me, a storm of emotions raging within me, knowing I'm responsible for this savage she has become.

She rips at my shirt, her tongue lapping at my chest, her actions raw and primal. Yet, amid her frenzy, I notice she's favoring one hand, keeping it close to her chest. She is rabid in her need for my scent. While she mauls me, I pry her hand away from her chest. There are no obvious wounds, but I realize her fingers aren't aligned correctly — my Lycan had healed her, but improperly.

Guilt washes over me, knowing I need to re-break her fingers to heal them correctly. So I flood her with my calling, trying to sedate her enough to examine her hand better. Despite the calling acting as a sedative, she squirms as I grasp her fingers. Even under the influence of my calling, she still feels pain, evident when she starts fighting against it, attempting to pull her hand away.

"I have to rebreak them, Ivy. I know it will hurt, but I can't heal them when they're misaligned," I tell her, dropping the calling so she understands what I'm saying. I instantly regret dropping it. She responds with a savage bite, turning wild as she tries to force me to let her hand go.

I let the thrum of my calling resonate through my chest, trying to pacify her. "I have to do this. You won't like it, but I have no choice." I contemplate calling Gannon to pin her down. But as my thrumming spills out, she presses her ear to my chest, purring in response. My hand finds its way into her hair, massaging her scalp gently.

I hold her head tight to my chest, flooding her as best I can to lessen the pain. It's one thing sedating her for minor injuries she wouldn't notice, but breaking her fingers... she'll definitely notice that. I break the first finger. She squirms, but I maintain a firm grip on her head, forcing her to remain submissive under my calling. I feel the pain in my own hand, resonating with hers, and quickly reposition the second and third fingers before sucking on them, my teeth slicing her skin, forcing my saliva into her wounds.

When I finish, I release her, sliding out from under her, only for her claws to sink into my leg. Her breath hitches, and her other hand reaches for me again, desperate for contact and seeking the bond.

She growls, the sound ticking in her throat as she hooks her claws deeper. I growl, blood seeping down my leg. Yanking her hand away I order her, smashing her with the calling and my command. "Stop," she whimpers.

My heart jolts, witnessing her total submission to the bond, enslaved to its will in any form she can have it. I kneel in front of her as her breath catches, and her other hand snakes out, desperate to grip my knee. I try to ignore the sensation of her hand on my leg, her nails carving through fabric and skin. I avert my gaze; she's completely naked, her skin marred by claw marks she inflicted upon herself.

"I need to leave," I utter emotionlessly, though inside, I'm torn, yearning to envelop her in my arms and soothe her. I pull off my shirt and drape it over her, trying to offer some comfort.

"You need to eat; you can't stay hidden here. I think you require some time outside.. I'll return in two days," I inform her matter-of-factly before leaving.

CHAPTER
EIGHTEEN

I VY

As the days slip by, his scent lingers a little less. Each day passes, my senses sharpen, my mind clears, and I slowly rediscover remnants of who I am. After so much solitude, I have gradually returned and found my identity, no longer ruled by unfamiliar instincts.

Agony is the only word to describe it. One thing becomes clear: I cannot shift. It saddens me, and I wonder if it's because of the bond like Gannon mentioned all those days ago, or if I'm just a failure in yet another aspect of life.

I have vague memories of the King coming into the room. I remember him healing my hand, but that was the last time I saw him. The King said he'd be gone for two days; however, it's been much longer. I don't know how long it's been since I left this room, left my den, but I feel a considerable amount of time has passed.

As the days drag on, they become more manageable, a little less painful. Once Kyson's scent is gone, and only my scent remains in the room, I realize that my den no longer fulfills its original purpose, and the bond is now only a distant memory, or so I hope.

Eventually, I can see my surroundings again. Clarity returns, and the fog lifts. It's like someone flips a switch, and everything either goes numb or dies off. I'm not sure which one, but I don't care. I can finally breathe, finally feel more like myself than I have in days.

As one of the servants slides a tray across the floor just inside the door, I'm drawn to the sound of the door creaking open. I get up and move toward her, and she shrieks, the noise startling me and making me jump back and away from her. She quickly slams the door shut behind her. The smell of eggs wafts to my nose, and my stomach rumbles hungrily. How long has it been since I've eaten?

Looking down, I realize I have no clothes on, making my eyes widen in shock. How long have I been naked? Shaking my head, I rush to the cupboard to find some clothes. Everything is shredded.

I look at the torn sheets and curl my lip in disgust as I scoop them up and sniff them. My scent is potent on them, and I definitely need to find something clean to wear.

Claw marks have shredded through every scrap of cloth in this room, which makes me look at my fingertips. How did I do that? When I can't even shift? It puzzles me - like I had been in some sort of trance and someone else had taken over.

Shaking my head, I grab some of the longer pieces and make a sarong out of them. I look like a peasant. I chuckle at the thought as I stand in front of the mirror in the bathroom.

Mrs. Daley would have whipped me good for my seamstress skills, or lack thereof. Oh well, it did the trick. Wandering out of the bathroom, I retrieve the tray from the floor by the door.

I move toward the fireplace and sit on the floor by the coffee table. My hands tremble as I pick up the fork. I practically inhale my food, barely tasting any of it.

I am ravenous. When I finish, I wander around the room, wondering if I'm allowed to leave it. An hour passes and no one enters, so I walk to the bedroom doors leading in with my empty tray in hand.

No one is standing outside my door, no guards or anything, so I figure I must be allowed to leave the room. I look down at my lovely bedsheet attire and shake my head.

Yep, I'm doing this; I'm going to walk down to the kitchen and pray no one sees me in my sheet sarong or notices the fact I have no clothes on underneath it or peek at my ass, which I know isn't fully covered because I can feel the draft from the open bedroom window caress against me. This is mortifying, but seriously, it can't be any worse than the King rejecting our bond, so I shrug and step out. If I can survive that agony, then I can survive a little embarrassment.

As I move through the corridors trying to remember the way, one thing becomes obvious. No one is on this side of the castle. The place is ghostly and quiet until I come to the stairs.

Straight across are the King's quarters, yet here too is also silent, and no guards stand or line the corridors. It is eerily quiet, maybe because it is so early in the morning. The sun is only just rising. However, I think it's a little strange. Descending down the stairs, it is the same.

Where is everybody? I can't figure it out. I find the kitchen is also empty as I make my way to the laundry room and retrieve a servant's uniform. I'm not daring enough to enter the King's quarters in search of clothes.

I'm afraid my nose will pick up his mouth-watering scent and I'll be plunged back into the darkness the bond held me in for days.

The sound of a horn in the distance makes me move to the laundry window as I button up my uniform to see everyone down by the river running back to the castle.

The entire palace must be down there, I think to myself. Grabbing some flats from the shelf, I slip them on my feet and step out the back door to where the long clotheslines are.

This side of the castle is surrounded by fruit trees and gardens. Sheets flap along with the breeze as I make my way down the back to the hill, where I can see everyone standing still as statues, staring out at the horizon. I keep close to the trees, wanting to know what's going on, but also to go unseen.

All uniformed guards stand in rows, and people from the town outside the castle gates take up most of the hill. Unable to see, I walk out of my hiding place and stop beside one of the guards. I peek my head around, trying to see what's going on.

The guard looks down at me, and I peer back at him in confusion when I see his eyes glaze over. Moments later, Gannon is beside me. He leads me down the hill, bringing me to where Abbie stands at the front with Clarice and the castle servants.

Only then do I realize why everyone is gathered here. It's a cemetery. Hundreds and hundreds of black marble headstones line the flat before the river.

CHAPTER
NINETEEN

I VY

My stomach drops, and I look at Abbie, who seems shocked to see me, but she stays quiet. She reaches over and grips my fingers with hers. The King stands at the front, where I see 13 fresh graves dug. He stares off vacantly toward the path leading to the surrounding forest.

I can only see his side, but he must sense my stare because he turns his head and looks at me. His eyes meet mine, and my heart sputters in my chest. He then turns his gaze away, as if I am merely another servant or member of the public.

Time seems to stop, and I suck in a breath when I see the open graves. I peer around before seeing a succession of coffins being carried to the grave sites where the King stands.

I have no idea what happened, but one thing is clear to me: most of the coffins belong to children or small adults. Four of them, I can tell, are adult-sized coffins, but the other nine are child-sized coffins.

The guards carrying them stop by a grave and set them down before music starts playing from a violinist who I hadn't noticed was at the side by the water. It's complete silence while we wait for the coffins to be lowered into each grave.

Nobody speaks or even whispers. We merely watch. Something happened; that much is apparent. I wonder briefly if this is where the King had gone. If so, when did he return to organize all this?

When it finishes and the coffins are laid to rest, a horn blares again. After a few minutes, everyone starts climbing the hill and leaving. The place is packed.

However, I notice the King remains. Abbie grabs my arm and tugs me up the hill, back toward the castle. I feel she's almost vibrating beside me, squeezing my hand like she can't believe I'm holding it.

We go back in through the laundry, following Clarice. The moment I step inside, I am crushed between the two of them as they smother me in their warmth.

"You're back?" Abbie gushes while squeezing me tight. Clarice cups my face in her hands, her eyes teary, and she lets out a breath. I'm about to ask what happened when the King suddenly enters the room. His scent hits me like a brick to the face, and I'm stunned in my tracks.

"Get back to work," the King snaps at us before stalking past us without so much as a backward glance. I swallow and stare after him as he passes through the kitchens.

Gannon and Damian follow him as he leaves without acknowledging my existence. I bite the inside of my lip. The pain helps the pang of hurt that courses through my chest as the metallic taste of my blood washes over my tongue.

"He will come around," Clarice tells me, gripping my shoulder, but I'm sick of hearing it. Sick of losing days to a bond he broke. I'm not going to wait around and hide in my room for him.

Nope, I decide to keep busy, and everything can go back to how it was. Just me and Abbie against the world, the way it used to be. So, with that, I grab some cleaning supplies, ignoring Clarice's protests that I'm not a servant, and follow Abbie to help her do her chores, which she's excited about.

Finally, I'm doing something other than wallowing and hiding away from everyone. Abbie tells me the King returned yesterday morning and spent the day hand digging the graves himself, refusing help when the guards tried to step in and take over. He apparently spent the night destroying his room before Damian dragged him off to train with the guards.

The day passes by quickly as we busy ourselves, and it feels good to move around, using muscles I barely used in days. However, Abbie becomes antsy and jittery towards the end of the day.

"Are you okay?" I ask her, as she's practically bouncing on her feet.

Suddenly, I hear Gannon growling behind us. He's been following us around for most of the day; I don't know if he chose to or if Gannon was ordered to follow us by the king. I'm not sure, and I never ask. If the king is going to pretend I don't exist, that's fine, but I'm not waiting around for him to change his mind any longer.

Clarice sighs and looks over at her, where we stand on the other side of the kitchen counter. She then rolls her eyes before speaking. "Go on then," she says with a dismissive wave. Abbie squeals before grabbing me, pecking my cheek, and rushing off out of the kitchen.

"Wait, where are you going?" I call after her, but she's already gone and out of earshot. I turn to Clarice, who clucks her tongue and shakes her head.

"You should head up to your room, Ivy. I'll send someone up with your dinner," Clarice tells me, and my brows furrow. What's going on? I turn to look at Gannon, who's glaring at the wall above our heads. Clarice clears her throat, which seems to snap him out of the homicidal stare-off he's having.

"Right, I'll escort her up," Gannon says, but I wave him off. Only he insists on following. When I reach the top of the staircase, I notice Damian coming out of the King's room with a tray.

He starts walking toward us, but I quickly rush off to find my room before locking myself in with a sigh. Abbie and I fixed the room up and cleaned it earlier today, but I'm met with silence as I sit on the sofa in front of the fireplace. This room is too big to just sit in by yourself.

The silence surrounding me is deafening, and after a few hours of absolute silence, I go in search of Abbie's small room, which I know is in Beta Damian's quarters.

However, when I reach the lower level and find her room, her bed is empty. Abbie's small room is much like the one I was originally in when I was still the king's servant. Her scent perfumes the room and brings me comfort, so curling up on her bed, I wait for her to return.

CHAPTER
TWENTY

ABBIE

I'm waiting with Clarice for the burial to start. We're holding a luncheon in the ballroom for the staff, but I won't be attending. I've agreed to meet Kade this afternoon, but still, I help set it up after my altercation with Gannon. I notice Gannon coming down with the King. It saddens me when he looks my way, only to look away. Guilt courses through me, and I turn my attention straight ahead, holding back the emotion that threatens to choke me. In an ideal world, Gannon would have been my mate, but I have a mate and can't throw him away either. I've never had anything, and Kade is mine, and I will fight for that, even if I don't know what I'm fighting for exactly.

The ceremony is just beginning as everyone waits on the hill. It's only moments later when I notice movement at my side and glance in that direction to find Ivy.

My shock must be apparent because she smiles sadly before looking ahead, and I don't miss how her eyes instantly seek out the King. I grip her fingers, giving them a squeeze. She's missed so much, and I have so much to tell her, but for now, it'll have to wait.

The King is standing at the front where I see 13 fresh graves dug. He's staring off vacantly toward the path leading to the surrounding forest. I feel Ivy's arm brush up against mine, and I can tell she's trying to figure out what's going on.

Time seems to stop, and the only noise is the soft breeze and the birds in the trees. I swallow when I see the open graves that have been freshly dug. Glancing around, we see movement in the far corner before a succession of coffins is carried to the grave sites where the King is standing.

Most of the coffins belong to children, making me think of Tyson. What if he's one of the children? What if Mrs. Daley killed him? It makes my heart clench in my chest. Most of them aren't large enough to be adults. Four of them, I can tell, are adult-sized coffins, but the other nine belong to children.

The guards carrying them stop by a grave, and they set them down before music starts playing from the violinist who stands by the river. It's complete silence while we all wait for the coffins to be lowered into each grave. Nobody speaks or even whispers. We merely watch.

When it finishes and the coffins are laid to rest, a horn blares again. After a few minutes, everyone starts climbing the hill and leaving to go back to work. The place is packed with people, but I only pay attention to the most important person to me here, Ivy. I grab Ivy's arm and tug her up the hill, back toward the castle. Excitement bubbles within me as I try to contain my excitement about having her back in a semi-normal state.

This place was lonely when I was the only werewolf in the castle besides her. Not that she's shifted yet, but now she's returned to me; I feel like I can finally breathe again. Finally, I can let go of the pressure building on my shoulders because with her it's a little bit lighter, and I'll endure it for her, knowing she's by my side. We go back in through the laundry, following behind Clarice. The moment Ivy steps inside, I wrap my arms around her and so does Clarice.

"You're back?" I murmur while squeezing her tighter. Clarice cups her face in her hands, her eyes teary, and she lets out a breath that could not be mistaken for anything other than relief. Ivy grips her hands and opens her mouth to say something when the King suddenly enters the room. She stops, staring over her shoulder at him, and I notice Gannon step in behind him.

"Get back to work!" the King snaps at us before stalking past us without so much as a backward glance. I press my lips in a line when I see the heartbreak on her face. Is the mate bond not the same for Lycans? How could he treat her so badly?

I swallow and look away as Gannon and Damian follow after him. Gannon doesn't even look in my direction, just clenches his jaw as if he couldn't bear to be near me. I bite the inside of my lip before returning my attention back to Ivy.

"He will come around," Clarice tells her, gripping her shoulders. Ivy shakes her head and looks at me. I smile at her sadly, and I hate how she put on her old maid's uniform. She's supposed to be happy! Happy because the King is her mate, but here she is, forced back into a position I wished I had never needed to see her in again. She ignores Clarice's protests that she isn't a servant and shouldn't help me when Ivy insists.

"I want to help Abbie. I am not his mate anymore. He has made that perfectly clear," Ivy tells her.

"You'll always be my Queen," Clarice whispers, and I see Ivy swallow. Seeing her sadness just makes the decision to leave with Kade all the more torturous. I can't leave her with the King while I run off with my mate. Ivy follows me to help me do my chores, which I am excited about. It's the most time we've really spent together since being here.

I tell her about how the King returned yesterday morning and spent the day hand digging the graves himself and half the night, refusing any help when the guards tried to step in and take over. I also tell her about the castle gossip. However, I'm too scared to tell her I found my mate and may be leaving her. Yet as the day goes on and the time to meet Kade draws closer, I'm becoming more excited.

That giddy, excited feeling bubbles in me at knowing I'm seeing my mate soon. Only for it to dampen when the guilt returns. It's like waves of pure happiness, then guilt over Ivy and Gannon, then fear of the unknown and excitement that I've found my mate, blissfully painful, a torturous combination.

Yet when the time comes, I can't help the spring I have in my step as we walk into the kitchen. Clarice sighs and looks over at me, where we stand on the other side of the kitchen counter. She then rolls her eyes before speaking. "Go on then," she says with a dismissive wave. A little excited squeal escapes me before I grab Ivy, quickly pecking her cheek, before rushing off out of the kitchen.

"Wait, where are you going?" Ivy calls after me. However, I don't stop. All day I've been trying to figure out a solution to my problems, one being that I can't leave Ivy, the other Tyson. I have to ask if there's any chance Kade would help me get him from Mrs. Daley. The other thing I have to ask is if he would allow Ivy to come with me, because if she can't come, I'm not leaving her behind by herself.

Kade is waiting for me out front by the gates. He smiles when I slip out the doors, and I return the smile and walk over to him. He holds my door open, and I don't hesitate to climb in, loving his scent that I know saturates his car. Kade takes me to a different place today. Instead of a cafe or restaurant, he takes me for a picnic by the bridge.

"Are you excited about leaving in a few days?" he asks as we set out the blanket and sit on it. I frown and look at the river running under the bridge.

"I have to leave, Abbie. I can't stay here. I have a pack to run back home," he tells me when I say nothing. He passes me a sandwich and pulls some grapes out of a container. He pops one in his mouth, watching me.

"What's wrong?' he asks, watching me. "Is it that Gannon you always talk about?" he demands, and I'm shocked to hear the anger in his tone.

I say nothing, scared to anger him further.

"Sorry. I hate how close you are. And I hate the way he stares at you," Kade says.

"I've hardly seen him," I tell him.

"He was watching you when you ran out to the car," he tells me while taking a bite of his sandwich. I swallow, tearing apart my sandwich and popping a piece into my mouth.

"Do you know Ivy? My friend?" I ask him, and he glances at me.

"The King's mate?" he asks, and I nod.

"Yeah, I've heard of her. Why?"

"The King hasn't been nice to her recently. I wanted to know if she could come with us," I ask, and Kade scoffs.

"And how would that be possible?" he laughs, and my face falls. I sigh, leaning up against the tree.

"I can't steal the King's mate, he would kill me, Abbie."

"And I won't go without her," I tell him, and his eyebrows raise.

"You would choose your friend over me?" he asks.

"She's more than just my friend. We grew up together," I tell him, but he shakes his head.

"You're asking the impossible of me."

"We could sneak her out. The King doesn't even need to know. He will think she ran away," I try to reason.

"I can't believe you are serious about this. I knew you were simple, but damn it, Abbie, the King is a Lycan. Do you have any idea what they are capable of?" he says, a sharp edge in his tone.

He's right. I'm being foolish. It's a stupid idea. I look away, embarrassed, and blink back tears.

"I didn't mean to call you simple. Sometimes I forget it's not your fault," Kade says, reaching over and gripping my hand.

"I can't read, but that doesn't mean I am simple," I respond to Kade, feeling the sting of his words more than he probably realizes. He's the last person I expect to use such names against me.

"As I say, I don't mean it the way it comes out. I'll think about what you say about your friend. Maybe we can figure something out. Now, what's this other thing you mention in the car you want to ask me?" Kade squeezes my fingers, trying to smooth over his earlier comment.

I explain to him about Tyson, watching as he listens intently, nodding. "I know Alpha Brock. I can request the boy for you, if you want. See what he says," he offers.

"Really?" I ask, excitement bubbling up. He's willing to help me get Tyson back?

"Only if you behave. And show me that you can look after him when we get back home," he conditions. The way he says 'behave' strikes me as odd, as though I am a child too. I'm not quite sure what he means by it.

But he's willing to help me with Tyson. I could keep him and raise him, give him the safe refuge that I have found. Now, all I need to do is convince Kade to let me sneak Ivy out. I can't wait to tell her that we might have a way to be free from this place.

CHAPTER
TWENTY-ONE

KYSON

The door opening has me looking over my shoulder from where I sit in my seat by the fire. Damian walks in and glares at the glass in my hand. He knows better than to say anything. "Ivy finally came out of the room," he tells me as if I don't already know. Saying nothing more, he sits across from me.

"I noticed," I say simply before bringing my glass to my lips and draining the last remnants. Damian sighs and stands back up when I hold the glass out to him. He moves toward the bar area and pours another glass before handing it back to me.

"Do you plan on just drowning out the bond?" he asks. I hum mindlessly, and he snarls at me. His aura slips out in his anger, although it has no effect on me.

"You have already destroyed her bond toward you. She had little to no reaction when she saw you," Damian spits as if I'm not aware of that.

"If only I were so lucky to have it break," I tell him, earning another growl.

"You're a fucking idiot. There are no second chance mates like the werewolves; Lycans don't get those, nor can you reject her, either. The bond won't sever for you, Kyson; it will always be there, so why do you choose to ignore it?"

"Because I can," I tell him, sipping my drink and enjoying the taste as it coats my tongue.

"If that were true, why is it that every time I see you, you have a drink in your hand?" he asks, glaring at my glass of whiskey. He shakes his head and clutches his hair in frustration while pacing in front of the fireplace.

"My relationship with Ivy is none of your business, so leave it," I tell him, not caring for his input.

"She is my Queen," he bellows, his face turning red in anger and his claws slipping out. He fists his hands and takes a deep breath, closing his eyes before dropping back into the seat across from me.

"She is your mate and Queen. She should be ruling alongside you, not rotting away in a room by herself."

"And what good is her being Queen when she can't even shift? I can't even change her now, so there is no point in getting attached to her when she will be dead in fifty years, anyway. Then what, Damian, you seem to think you know everything?" I ask him.

"She can fucking shift; you just severed the bond, forcing her wolf-side dormant. You know as well as I do, if you spent time with her, you could lure it back out," he fumes while I scoff.

"We don't know that. Ivy was a rogue for so long; that is probably why she can't shift."

"Then mark her!" he bellows at me. I shake my head at his words.

"You are making a mistake, Kyson. She may not accept you back if you leave this too long. You could ruin any future you thought you would have with her," Damian says.

"She isn't going anywhere; I am not stupid. Do you think I would let her leave the castle or me and have her weaken me?"

"You're selfish. You can't expect Ivy to just wait around for the day you will change your mind, Kyson. Don't be fucking cruel; you can't live without her, you will grow weak, and this whole kingdom will grow weak. Remember, her not being able to shift puts her at risk of not only her werewolf-side remaining dormant but the bond completely severing for her; she will feel nothing toward you, then what? A few years down the track, and you pull your head out of your ass, you think she will just take you back?" he asks.

"If that happened, which it won't, she wouldn't have a choice. I will force her or use the damn calling on her."

"You disgust me," he spits at me, and I shrug, uncaring for his words.

"I am King. I can do as I please with my mate."

"Then do the right thing. You're better than this," Damian snarls.

"And if I'm not?" I ask him as he goes to walk out. I look over the back of the lounge to see him stop by the door.

"Then you're not my King," he says before yanking the door open and walking out of my room. I glare at the burning fire, angered that it had to be this way.

She didn't even react when I saw her earlier. I expected some emotion, anything from her, but all I got was a blank stare. I can hardly feel her anymore, although the bond and pull to her have only grown stronger, crushing my chest and heart more with each passing day. With that, I get up and pour another drink, trying to drown the ache the bond causes.

When the alcohol can no longer satiate the urge, I do what I do every night and go to sit by her door. It's the only thing that drives the pain away. I walk toward her room before peering inside.

Only when I do, I see the lights are still on. I check the closet, but she isn't in there or any of the rooms next to the main one. My brows furrow when I notice her guard is also not around. I told him to remain unnoticed while up here, but that didn't mean hiding from me.

'Dustin, where are you?' I ask through the mindlink.

'In Beta Damian's quarters, my King. Ivy has gone into Abbie's room.

She hasn't come out for a while,' he answers, and I sigh. At least she is with Abbie.

'*I take it Abbie has returned from visiting her mate in town?'* I ask him.

'*No, my King. I peered into the room before she* had *fallen asleep in Abbie's bed; Gannon also left to go find Abbie.'*

I chew my lip. Gannon had taken the news pretty badly. He really had fallen hard for the girl, which is surprising.

Gannon isn't one for feelings and hardly leaves his station, but I have noticed he follows Abbie everywhere when not busy. I always catch him wherever she is, though she is oblivious to him shadowing her.

Abbie seems over the moon to have found her mate, though I worry about what will happen when the Alpha leaves to go back to his pack. We don't really associate with other packs, but he always offers a lending hand and has been the biggest help when coming to the hunters and rogue issues.

No doubt he wants to remain in my good graces, but an ally is an ally, and we don't have many amongst the werewolf packs. Sure, they obey orders, but only a couple go out of their way and seek me out, offering to help in any way they can.

Gannon has expressed concern for her already. He, too, is worried about her leaving with Kade, but if she asks, I can't deny her. Mate bonds aren't to be denied if they both want the same thing, so I would tell her yes if she asked.

Alpha Kade is a well-known man whore. I know he is already married, though he never marked the woman. They have three kids together, and he has countless women on the side. I know Gannon tried to tell Abbie that, but she refuses to believe him.

The mate bond has a good grip on her, and Abbie refuses to see him any other way than the bond would allow. God knows what he has told her. She will see for herself if she decides to leave with him. Yet I also wonder how Ivy would take that news. He is scheduled to go in a couple of days, if not sooner.

Not realizing I left the mindlink open, I jump when I hear Dustin's voice flit through my head. *'Is that all my King?'* he asks.

'Yes, and you can leave your station. Damian will probably be down there soon, and I am on my way anyway,' I tell him.

'I don't mind staying,' he says. Of course, he doesn't. He would lay his life down for her over the pact my main five guards made.

'You can go; I am only a few minutes away,' I tell him, cutting the link.

CHAPTER
TWENTY-TWO

IVY

Abbie hasn't returned, and I wake up cold and shivering. Yet I know the room isn't cold, and I am bundled beneath the blankets. So, I wonder why I am awake at such a ghastly hour and this freezing. Tossing the blankets back, I get up.

It is still dark outside, and I can't think of any reason why Abbie isn't back. Deciding to see if she fell asleep in the servant's rooms downstairs, I stretch and yawn; rubbing my arms, trying to warm them, and grip the door handle. Only when I twist it, I feel the weight against it, and it flies toward me.

I jump back to see the King suddenly sprawled on the floor. His eyes fly open, and he growls, lurching forward before freezing as he turns, spotting me.

I take a step back, wondering why he was leaning against the door or why he is down here in the first place. Was he here looking for Abbie, and if he was, what for?

My stomach sinks with the possibilities, and before I can stop it, a whimper slips past my lips. The King stands abruptly and scrubs his hand down his face before looking out into the hall and back at me.

A wave of fear crashes over me, and a desperate whimper escapes my lips, betraying my terror. The King's face hardens as he stands abruptly, the muscles in his jaw twitching with barely contained anger.

"Where is Damian?" he growls, his eyes darting around the hall before settling back on me. Trembling, I point to a door across from Abbie's room. Without another word, he storms towards it.

"Were you sleeping?" I blurt out, trying to break the tense silence. He pauses for a moment, his hand hovering over the door-knob before answering.

"That is none of your concern. Stay on your side of the castle," he barks before wrenching open Damian's door. My heart pounds in my chest as I realize I've angered him again.

"I-I was just looking for Abbie," I stammer, backing away and retreating back to my room.

"Ivy."

I freeze, too scared to turn and face him. He strides over to me and drapes his jacket over my shoulders, tugging it closed with rough hands. His piercing gaze bores into mine and I can't look away.

"Go back to your room," he orders gruffly before stepping back. Confused and shaken by his sudden change in behavior, I quickly leave the room and retreat to my own. Unable to shake off the feeling of unease from our encounter, I search for Abbie, but she is nowhere to be found in the servants' quarters.

There is no sign of her in the bathrooms either. I even asked some guards, but they shake their heads, so I go back to my enormous, empty room. Pushing the door open, I shiver at how cold it is. The fire has gone out, so I flick a light on before wandering around and looking for matches and some kindling.

My hands shake as I try to light the match before using it to light the scrunched-up pieces of paper, which burn out before the wood can catch. With a sigh, I go to see if I can find a guard and ask them to light it for me because I am having no luck getting it to catch onto the wood.

Stepping out of the room, I navigate my way back through the halls and walk toward the stairs. Only when I turn onto them, I see the King walking toward me.

"Why aren't you in your room? Were you trying to leave?" he snarls, and his eyes flicker black. I gasp at the sight and take a step back from him while shaking my head, wondering why he is mad all of a sudden. I did nothing, yet once again earned his anger.

"Then why are you out of your room, Ivy?" he asks, stalking up the last of the steps toward me.

"The fire went out. It's cold. I was hoping to find Dustin or a guard," I admit. He sighs before looking toward his quarters.

"I'll send someone. Go back to your room," he says, stalking off down the hall toward his room. I watch him leave, only he stops at his bedroom door and looks back at me. He growls and I scurry off back toward my room before slipping inside. Nobody comes while I wait. I climb into bed, dragging the extra linens over me. I do not know how long I have been asleep when I hear a noise and sit up. Light flickers in the room, and I look toward the fire that has been ignited, only to see someone crouched in front of it loading logs into it.

Getting up, I drag my duvet with me, only to stop by the couch when I notice it is the King in front of the fireplace. His back tenses. He looks over his shoulder at me, and then turns to glare at the fireplace and its flickering flames. I wait for him to leave, but he doesn't, so I crawl onto the couch.

This side of the room is significantly warmer. I observe the King from where I sit. He says nothing, just loads the wood in, and then gets up and walks over to the armchair and sits in it, resting his head back and closing his eyes. Only now can I see the deep bruising under his eyes, like he hasn't slept in days. He looks dead on his feet. He growls again, and his eyes open, looking at me.

"Go to sleep," he says, closing his eyes again.

"You aren't going back to your room?" I ask.

"I can't sleep," he says simply.

I want to ask him why, yet his eyes open again to peer over at me.

"The bond keeps me awake," he says, clearly unhappy about it. I bite the inside of my lip and nod before laying back down, snuggling under my blanket, enjoying the warmth and his soothing scent.

It isn't until he starts snoring lightly that my eyes open to look over at him. Getting up, I sniff my blanket, which is drenched in my scent.

The bond tugs at me to comfort him, but I also don't want to wake him and have him get cranky at me. So instead, I drape my blanket over him before laying in front of the fire only for his snoring to change to purring, and I glance up to find him hugging the blanket, burying his face in it.

The following day I wake in my bed, my duvet chucked over me, and I peer around the room. There is no sign of the King, and if it wasn't for his scent tainting the blanket, I would have thought I imagined it.

All day, I look for Abbie before finally giving up. Gannon is also missing, and I am beginning to worry, but when I am sitting in my room bored out of my mind, the door bursts open. Abbie rushes into the room excitedly and runs over to me, where I sit in front of the fireplace.

Relief floods me. "Where have you been? I have been looking for you," I ask before grabbing her. She is beaming with happiness and hugs me back before holding me at arm's length.

"I didn't want to upset you, but I have some news. I found my mate," she gushes, almost bouncing on the spot. Her face is flushed, her hair frazzled with excited energy.

"Oh, that's wonderful, Abbie. What's he like?" I ask her.

She blushes and then starts gushing excitedly, telling me all about her new mate. I am happy for her until she turns a little nervous, which in turn makes me nervous, and she looks down at her hands.

"He's great, but he asked me to leave with him. I just need to get permission from the King."

"You're leaving?" I feel my heart sink through my chest. This can't be happening.

She nods sadly. "Yes, in a few days, but I had a plan. Come with me?" she asks, clutching my hands. I only look at the floor, knowing what the answer will be.

"I will convince him. He will help me get you out. We can come up with a meeting spot," Abbie says.

"Abbie, he won't go against the King," I tell her.

She shakes her head. "I will convince him. You'll see. He will let me bring you." I chew my lip nervously, hoping she is right. I didn't want to be here without Abbie.

CHAPTER
TWENTY-THREE

A BBIE

"If he says yes, will you come?" I ask her.

"But he won't. No one would dare go against the Lycan King. Kyson would kill him if he took me, you have to see that?" she says.

"He won't know you're with us. I'll figure it out, you'll see. I will get you out," I tell her, and she sighs.

"I don't want to get you in trouble," she says, but I shake my head.

"I'll convince him, you'll see," I tell her quickly, getting up and pecking her cheek.

After dinner, I head to my room, and when I step inside, I find Gannon sitting on the end of my bed. I stop at the door and peer over at him, wondering if he is here to argue more over Kade.

"Please Gannon, I don't want to argue with you," I whisper.

"I'm not here to argue, just come here," he says, patting the spot beside him on the bed. I glance at the spot before being nudged into the room from behind, and I jump, looking over my shoulder to see it is Liam.

"She can use my old phone," he says, tossing it to Gannon.

"I factory reset it," Liam says, and I look at Gannon, wondering what they are talking about and why both of them are suddenly in my room.

I move closer to Gannon, slightly nervous next to Liam. When I am close enough to him, he reaches out and grabs my hand before moving further back on the bed and pulling me to sit between his legs.

Liam shuts the door and Gannon wraps his arm around my waist, resting his chin on my shoulder. I try to get up, but his hold is too strong.

"Watch," he says, holding the phone out in front of me.

"Gannon?" I murmur, knowing Kade wouldn't like me sitting on the man's lap, though it is hard not to lean into his warm embrace, his scent soothing and familiar.

"Abbie, stop. I am not stopping you from going, but this? You need to learn, or I will risk the King's wrath and order you to reject him," Gannon says.

"What?"

"In case you need me, please. Just this once, listen to what I am saying. I understand you made up your mind. But I need to show you how to use this," I sigh, but decide to go along with it.

He shows me some features on the phone, opening and closing messages and the phone book.

"Gannon I can't send texts, I can't read," I tell him.

"This button here, you just speak into it and it will convert your speech to text, then hit send. Liam also set it up so it will read messages back to you," he tells me while showing me how to work the device.

"You want me to text you?" I ask him, and he nods his head against my shoulder.

"Mine and Liam's number are in here, so is the King's. If you want to come home, ring me or Liam. We will answer, no matter how late it is. Anything, Abbie, you ring us and we will come get you," Gannon tells me.

"Gannon, Kade isn't ..."

"I know you don't want to believe anything bad about him, but just take the phone, Abbie," he says, placing it in my hands. I take it and he switches the screen off.

"Now unlock it," he says, and I do.

"Show me how to use it, like I just showed you. I am not leaving until I know you can work this phone," he says, and I focus back on the screen.

It takes a few tries and Gannon corrects me, but I eventually get the hang of it. When he is satisfied that I have it figured out, he sighs before leaning down and passing me a bag he had by his feet. "I got you a few things and Clarice went into town and bought you a few different sets of clothes."

"Gannon, you shouldn't ..."

"I can't come with you, so stop. Let me do this and just accept it," he says, tapping my leg for me to get up. I let him up, and he stares at me for a few seconds before wrapping his arms around me and pressing his lips to my forehead.

"Keep practicing with the phone, Liam put credit on it for you, already," he tells me, and I nod my head. He then leaves me, walking out of the room, and I sit back down on the bed.

The next morning I am woken early by someone knocking on my door. Before I can even get up, it opens and Liam strolls in. I sit up, worried. He holds his hand out in a placating gesture.

"Gannon is on patrol. I am just checking if you can use the phone properly, Gannon asked me to double check again. He said Kade is picking you up this afternoon," I nod my head and he unplugs the phone from the charger sitting next to me and hands it to me.

"Now show me how to use it. You take this phone with you no matter where you go. Make sure you answer it if he rings, because if you don't, I know he will go to hunt you down. The king can be brutal when punishing us and you don't want Gannon punished, Abbie," he tells me.

I nod and show him. "I will take you to see Kade this morning," Liam tells me, and I gulp, looking up at him with worry.

"I won't hurt him, but I will be waiting with you while he picks you up," I sigh, knowing not to argue with him. Liam would do as he pleases.

He waits outside my door as I get changed before escorting me downstairs. We wait out the front, and when the car pulls up, Kade gets out, and I can tell he is a little frightened of Liam as he ushers me into the car.

"Liam," Kade acknowledges. Liam tilts his head to the side, watching Kade but remains silent. Kade quickly gets in the car and pulls away.

"That man is strange. I don't like you hanging around him," Kade says as we drive into town.

"Where are we going?" I ask him, ignoring his statement.

"To the cafe, we leave today," he tells me.

"And Ivy?" I ask him.

"I am still thinking about it. I have yet to decide," he says as we pull up out the front. We head inside and sit at the back tables, and Kade hands me a menu, but I set it down on the table.

"Right, I forgot you can't read," he exhales before clicking his tongue. "That is going to be an issue. I hope you're a fast learner. You will have to earn your keep. I can't have a useless Luna," he says, staring at the menu. I shrink in my seat a little, not wanting him to know how much him saying that affects me.

The waitress comes over, and Kade orders for us. I remain quiet, picking at my food. "Why are you quiet? You aren't second-guessing about coming I hope. I can't remain here, I have a pack back home to run," he tells me, and I shake my head.

"I am just worried about Ivy."

He presses his lips in a line, seemingly annoyed.

"She is the King's mate, she will be fine. Time to cut ties with her," he says, and I look over at him in shock and disbelief. Setting my fork down, I get up.

"Abbie?" he says as I grab my phone off the counter, about to text Liam or Gannon to come get me.

"Abbie, where are you going?" he asks, but if that is how he feels about Ivy, then my mind is made up. I am not going.

I walk outside and unlock the phone when it is plucked from my fingers. I glance over at Kade, who had come up behind me.

"You don't just walk out during a conversation," Kade scolds me, looking livid.

"I am not going. If Ivy can't come, I am staying here," I tell him.

CHAPTER
TWENTY-FOUR

IVY

    I haven't seen Abbie since she told me her mate wants her to leave with him. She spends all her time with him, which doesn't bother me. Besides, I am happy for her. If it couldn't be both of us, I'm glad one of us found a loving mate. But, I know she is anxious about the King not letting her leave.

However, the King is acting strangely too. Every night, I wake to find the King in my room asleep, only for him to be gone when I wake up in the morning.

At first, I thought I was going crazy. The King is here at random hours during the night; I always wake to his scent. Then, by morning, it's like he was never here at all. His coming and going is making it harder. If he doesn't want me, he needs to just leave me be. It's selfish of him to keep putting me through this agony.

His coming and going is driving me insane.

He never says anything, and just stares if I catch him and accidentally wakes him, or he ignores me completely. My heart tugs painfully for those two nights. I don't know what he wants, but it's clear he doesn't want me. But as his scent settles in the room each night, it feels like being rejected all over again. I start praying Abbie can convince her mate to let me join because I can't live like this.

The breeze is cool as the day slows down, and all the servants prepare for dinner and end-of-day tasks. Tugging the white sheets from the clothesline with Abbie, we fold them, bringing the corners together and placing them in the basket. Our interactions have been flat out most of the day, and she has been quiet for most of it. I know she is itching to tell me something because she tries a few times, but then she falls quiet because someone is always around.

A guard, another servant, so amongst the blowing winds and the flapping sheets, she moves closer to me before reaching over and dropping something into the front pocket of my apron.

I glance down before putting my hand in the pocket and feeling around for what it is. My fingertips brush something cool and metal, and I twist my wrist in the oversized pocket and look at what it is. It's a watch.

"When the big hand is on the twelve and the little one on the seven, I am leaving," she whispers, and I look at her, feeling scared. She chews her lip before glancing around nervously. Then she reaches into her shirt and produces a small key from her bra. She drops it in my pocket.

"I stole the key from Gannon; it's for the laundry door," she whispers, nodding to the one we just came out of. Behind the kitchens, it runs alongside the far gardens where the fruit trees meet the forest.

"Run along the river and head west. Keep going, and you will find a bridge. Meet us at the bridge. He said he would help me get you out. Be there at 7 pm sharp," she whispers, and I nod, pulling another sheet down from the clothesline. My lips quirk in the corners.

"You convinced him," I smile, feeling my heart leap inside my chest.

"Yes, but he said if you're late, we can't wait. He said he doesn't want to be caught waiting outside the town limits," she tells me, and I nod. Looking at the sky, the clouds are moving in dark and heavy, and it's going to be one hell of a storm when it hits. I just hope I won't get caught in it.

"And you're sure he won't tell on me?"

"He promised me," she whispers before reaching over and gripping my arm. "We will be free, just not the freedom we used to long for, but actual freedom, freedom to live," she whispers, with tears in her eyes. "Always and forever."

"More than my life," I say in return.

"More than my life, always more," she repeats. We finish dragging the clothes in off the line and walk back through the laundry doors when Abbie shrieks. I turn to look back at her as she rubs a spot on her back and growls. Laughter reaches my ears, and Abbie turns to see a rotten apple splattered against her back.

"Peter, you little shit," Abbie hisses, dropping her basket and chasing after him, picking up rotten apples that had fallen beneath the trees. Peter, the stable boy, always finds a way to cause mischief and get away with it. I watch his mop of curly hair bounce up and down as he runs off, dodging Abbie's advances.

Abbie shrieks when he pelts another her way. She lobs one back, and I laugh, watching her try to hit him with the apples while her shrill cries and his laughter fill the silence.

Abbie retrieves another apple and tosses it where he goes to dart behind the castle wall just as Dustin walks around. The mushy apple smacks him in the face, and he freezes on the spot, stunned for a second before wiping the mush off.

Abbie snickers, trying to muffle her laughter at hitting the guard. Peter hides behind him before popping his head out and sticking his tongue out at Abbie. Dustin wipes the mushy apple off his clothes, growling. I laugh at the sight of bits of apples sticking to his crisp, clean uniform, and a chunk stuck in his stubble.

Dustin's eyes go to Abbie, and she points at me; my eyes widen, and I shake my head, but he looks ridiculous with apple mush stuck to his face, and I chuckle. He raises an eyebrow at me.

"You think this is funny, my Queen?" he asks, a hint of a smile on his lips. I snicker before stopping when he walks over to the apple tree, making Abbie squeal and rush toward me before using me as a shield. Dustin picks up a gross-looking apple that's nearly crumbling in his hand.

Dustin tosses the apple in the air a couple of times, letting it mush up more before he laughs and throws it. I shriek and duck, falling on top of Abbie, only to hear him gasp, and Peter burst out laughing, holding his tummy and pointing behind us. Abbie and I look behind us to see Clarice covered in the rotted mush.

We both tense, waiting for the scolding as she steps closer, examining her soiled apron.

She looks back up, and her eyes go to us on the ground. Abbie and I both point to Dustin standing by the apple tree with Peter. We look in their direction to find Dustin pointing the blame at Peter.

Clarice glares, and we all freeze in place as the old woman stalks toward us before ripping her apron off. "Apple war it is then," she huffs, a look of wild excitement on her face. Then she runs over and scoops up some apples. Abbie and I giggle before jumping up and joining the fray.

CHAPTER
TWENTY-FIVE

K YSON

Damian stands by my office window, his gaze lost in whatever he's watching outside. His chuckle catches my ear, and I glance up, curious but trying not to show it because I know that will give them an excuse to try to pull me away from work.

I keep my focus on the maps spread across my desk, tracing the patterns of the recent attacks along the river. The river isn't deep enough for boats, just canoes, maybe. Each body found is a taunt, marked with a hunter's or rebel's patch, a gruesome display designed to provoke. No scents, no clues, nothing - it's like chasing ghosts.

Yet they were always laid out and on display like they wanted them found and were merely taunting us.

The location they were always found was never near enough to any packs to pinpoint one, and they were nowhere near any human settlements, so it was a mystery, as always. One that had been doing my head in for years.

Yet the main perpetrator of the werewolf rebellion that was

helping the hunters was proven dead. Marissa, Ivy's mother, has been dead for years, so who was leading them now??

It made no sense to me. It was also the reason after my sister's death, no werewolves could set foot in my castle grounds except Alpha Kade, and of course, Abbie and Ivy, who were the first werewolf servants we had in over a decade. Werewolves couldn't be trusted, and everyone was scrutinized before ever entering through my castle gates.

But the laughter from Gannon and Damian is a distraction I can't ignore for long. "They wanna run now. That old woman has a good arm on her." Gannon's amusement pulls me from the frustrating puzzle I've been trying to solve for decades.

I look up from examining the dots on the map. I am looking for some sort of pattern to see Gannon and Damian watching out the window. Both of them held silly grins of amusement on their faces.

"Oh, that had to have hurt," Damian snickers.

"What are you both looking at?" I ask, and Gannon turns slightly to look over his shoulder at me.

"Apple war," he laughs.

My eyebrows raise, and he turns back to the window before snorting at whatever he is watching. Intrigued, I finally give in, leaving my desk and walking around it, standing and joining them at the window. Below, in the gardens, a chaotic scene unfolds. Clarice, Abbie, Ivy, Dustin, and the stable boy, Peter, are engaged in an impromptu apple war. The sight is absurd yet somehow endearing. Peter, the mischievous kid who once pelted Damian with horseshit, now ducks and weaves, dodging the girls lobbing apples at him.

I remember the day the cheeky little shit threw horseshit at Damian, and man, did he go off. Damian had thrown him into the small lake by the stables that day. The kid was always up to no good, but he was a breath of fresh air around the typical somber mood.

I watch, unable to suppress a smile, as Ivy attempts a throw, her apple flying wide off the mark. Dustin, quick to retaliate, hits her squarely on the head with his own projectile. The look of mock horror on his face when she rubs the spot is priceless. She charges at him in a moment of daring foolishness, only to slip and tumble, both of them landing in a heap.

Their antics, so carefree and light-hearted, are a stark contrast to the weight of the world outside these castle walls. Yet, I can't shake a twinge of envy as she lands on top of him after Dustin slips on an apple in his haste to escape her a second time.

The nervous glances I receive from Gannon and Damian as they continue to wrestle each other are not missed like they expected me to blow up over them mucking around, but I know Dustin is no threat to me or her.

Peter rushes to help Dustin as Ivy manages to get him to the ground, only for Peter to be smashed with an apple by Clarice, who triumphantly fist pumps afterward. .

I see Ivy laugh, climbing off Dustin before leaning down and smearing her hand over his face before she ducks off. Suddenly, thunder cracks across the sky, echoing my inner turmoil. The sky darkens as I watch Ivy, jealousy coursing through me. The laughter and shouts below fade as the group looks skyward, sensing the impending downpour.

Then, Abbie slumps her shoulders, and Peter follows suit. Ivy wipes her clothes off as she makes her way back to the laundry door, stopping beside Dustin and offering him a hand up.

He takes it, and she pulls him to his feet before he bows to her. Ivy shakes her head and waves goodbye to Peter. Abbie skips back over to her, wrapping an arm around her waist and pressing her head against Ivy's shoulder as they walk inside together, arm in arm.

"They seem to be having a good time," I murmur with a nod before walking back to my bar and grabbing a glass. I pour some whiskey in it and scull it then pour another glass. Yet after the third glass, I realize no matter how much I drink, it won't subdue the jealousy coursing through me at seeing her muck around with the guard.

"I wonder if Abbie has told Ivy she is leaving this afternoon,"

Gannon says, and I look over at him from where he is sitting in the armchair at my desk.

"Well, she will know tomorrow when she wakes up, and Abbie isn't here anymore," I tell him with a shrug.

"You should have said no," Gannon growls.

"He is her mate, and she asked to go with him. I won't deny her wishes if that is what she wants," I tell him. We warned Abbie and she wouldn't listen, believing whatever lies Alpha Kade fed her. Sometimes you just have to let people make mistakes. Plus, I couldn't risk tension with Alpha Kade now. I needed him and his pack's support to get to the bottom of this rogue business.

"He doesn't deserve her," Gannon growls, glaring at my desk, and I sigh.

"She will see reason," Damian tells him, gripping his shoulder.

"By then, it will probably be too late," Gannon snarls.

"If not, and she wants to come back, you gave her your number. She also has the King's and mine so she can get a hold of Ivy if she wants to come back."

"We will go get her," I finish for him, and Gannon sighs but nods his head.

"What if he hurts her?" Gannon asks, looking tortured at the thought.

"She's his mate; he can't hurt her without hurting himself," Damian assures him, but that wasn't true; she-wolves are always at a disadvantage when it comes to men, especially Alpha men, though we didn't admit that in front of Gannon though he would be fully aware.

"There are other ways to destroy someone; you don't have to physically hurt them to break them," Gannon says, and my brows furrow at his words.

TWENTY-SIX

KYSON

His words make me think of Ivy when I found her in her closet, and the den she had made. I swallow, suddenly feeling guilty, before shaking the feeling off.

Around 6:30 pm, after everyone has dinner, I make my way downstairs. Alpha Kade is coming to retrieve Abbie, and I need to thank him for his recent help. I wait out front on the stone driveway when his BMW pulls in.

Abbie waits, sitting on the step. She has a small bag with her that Clarice had made up for her, so she has a few things to take.

She smacks into his chest the moment he gets out of the car, and he wraps his arms around her, burying his face in her hair before pecking her lips softly. I turn my gaze away, giving them some privacy. Also, it disturbs me to see how doting he is with her, especially with knowing his home situation. It was all a façade, we just couldn't convince her.

It was the only thing I didn't like about the man. He was alright other than that, as far as I know. Though nobody truly knows what goes on behind closed doors.

"Get in the car, my love; we need to head home," he whispers, cupping her face in his hands. Abbie comes over and bowed to me, and Damian gives her a brief hug before she looked around.

"Where did Gannon go?" she asks, looking a little disappointed. Alpha Kade grips her shoulder.

"You said goodbye to your friend?" he asks her, and she looks up at him, nodding. He inclines his head toward the car, and she slowly walks back to it before climbing into the passenger seat and clipping her belt.

"Let me know if you need anything, my King. Now to go home to my wife and introduce this new one to her. I'm sure she will kick up a fuss but not to worry," he clicks his tongue and shakes his head with a laugh. "Lucky, I am Alpha right?" he sighs. I say nothing on the matter; it sickens me how he treated women as mere objects to please him. I only hope he's discussed this with Abbie.

"Thank you for your help; I will be in touch," I tell him, glancing at Abbie, who was peering out the closed window up at the castle. Alpha Kade looks over his shoulder at her before looking back at me.

"Now, please don't be upset, my King, but in order to get her to come with me, I may have made a deal with her," he says, and I tilt my head to the side, observing him.

He has a slim face and beady eyes, a smirk playing on his lips like he thinks it's funny he had to cut a deal with his own mate to get her to agree to go with him. Only Abbie and Ivy are very similar The only time I had seen her ask for anything was when she asked to go with her mate. Other than that, she never asked for anything unless it was for Ivy. *Ivy!*

"I told her I would, but I have no intention of stopping. I thought I should let you know your mate, Ivy?" he says. I nod, wanting to know what it is he agreed to for Abbie.

"She is supposed to meet us at the bridge leading out of town, I was supposed to smuggle her out, I agreed, of course, but I had no intentions of taking your Queen, but I thought I should let you know, we can't have runaway Queen now," Alpha Kade murmurs while looking back at the car like he was worried Abbie may overhear.

I growl and glare at him before clenching my jaw. I hate the way Alpha Kade smirks, as if I can't control my own mate. Damian's hand falls on my shoulder, warning me not to lose it with Abbie present. Not to alert Abbie that we know of Ivy's plans.

"I suggest you leave Alpha Kade. You never should have made that deal; you have potentially put my future Queen at risk," Damian snarls while I fight the urge to shift and kill the bastard, bloody foolish werewolf.

"Where is she?" I ask the Alpha. He flinches away and quickly answers.

"She is probably along the river somewhere, my King. She was meeting us there at 7 pm" he answers, and I nod. Alpha Kade quickly rushes back to the car, Abbie glances at us nervously and waves and we play along, waving back to her, trying to keep my fury in check.

I watch them leave and go out the gates. The moment they do, I turn on my heel to go find her and drag her back. Damian grips my arm, making me come to a stop, and my entire body trembles with the need to track her down.

"Calm down," he says, but I shrug him off.

'Fucking find her,' I bellow through the link. The forest air is thick with tension as I barrel through the underbrush, my paws thudding against the damp earth. Each stride is fueled by a tumultuous mix of anger and concern. How could she think of running away? The very thought tightens my chest, a mixture of hurt and bewilderment coursing through me. As I run for the river and shift mid run, Damian explains what had happened, and howls filled the night sky.

'Kyson!' Damian bellows through the link.

'How fucking dare she try to run from me,' I say, seething.

'You need to calm down,' he says before I see him shift, racing to catch up to me.

'I will calm down once she's back locked in her room. Who was

supposed to be watching her?' I snarl and I hear Dustin whimper through the mindlink. I growl at him before shutting the link.

'We will find her, but please be rational about this, my King. You don't want to scare her.'

'She will be lucky if I don't chain her to my fucking bed. Enough with your chatter, Damian. Fucking find my mate,' I snap, and he nods beside me.

Damian keeps pace, a silent, solid presence to my left. His occasional glances speak volumes - concern, caution, but he knows better than to voice them now. My mind is a storm of emotions, thoughts swirling chaotically. The betrayal stings sharply, but beneath that, there's an undercurrent of fear - fear for her safety, fear of losing her.

We're nearing the river, the sound of its rushing waters growing louder with each step. I pause for a moment, lifting my nose to the wind. Her scent is stronger here, intermingled with the damp earth and the crisp river air. It's unmistakably Ivy - a mix of her shampoo and something uniquely her, something soothing that usually calms me. But now, it only fuels my determination.

As we approach the riverbank, my eyes scan the area, every sense heightened. The sky is a canvas of darkening blues and grays, the impending storm mirroring the turmoil inside me. Lightning flashes in the distance, followed by the low rumble of thunder. The atmosphere is electric, every nerve in my body on edge as I search for her.

She would regret running from me.

CHAPTER

TWENTY-SEVEN

I VY

A couple hours earlier.

Abbie and I hurry to change into fresh clothes and we both take quick showers in the staff bathrooms before she has to leave to speak with the King about the arrangements for her departure. As she prepares to leave, she squeezes me tightly, her touch conveying a mixture of affection and unease at what we are about to attempt. "Don't be late," she whispers, her warm breath brushing against my cheek as she plants a tender kiss.

Since her departure, I have been restless, pacing back and forth in my room. Even when the servant brings up my dinner, I find myself too consumed by nerves to take a single bite. With trembling hands, I rummage through the cupboard, exchanging my light attire for warmer clothing. I also grab a pair of flat shoes, anticipating the possibility of having to run.

Moving towards the door, I cautiously crack it open, ensuring no one is watching, before retrieving the small key from my pocket. I am astonished that Abbie managed to obtain it from Gannon, shaking my head at the risks she has taken. The unease in my stomach grows, causing me to abandon my dinner and make my way down to the kitchen.

As I enter the bustling kitchen, the evening staff pays me no mind, their attention focused on their end-of-day tasks, thankfully this hour is one of the busiest. I swiftly pour myself a glass of water, desperately seeking relief in its coolness. However, to my dismay, the liquid only seems to intensify my nervousness, sending waves of anxiety coursing through me. Realizing I need to relieve myself, I hurriedly make my way to the servant bathroom, wasting precious time before returning to the kitchen.

Thankfully, the kitchen staff has left to enjoy their own meals, leaving me free to slip out through the back door into the laundry room.

Ignoring the towering shelves and giant washers and dryers that surround me, I make a beeline for the back door. With the key in hand, I insert it into the lock and turn it with a mixture of fear and hope.

A sigh of relief escapes me as the door swings open, revealing a world beyond the confines of the castle. Soon I will be free, I just need to get to that bridge.

Stepping outside, I feel the wind pick up slightly, rustling the leaves on the trees surrounding the place, and the sky darkening from the approaching storm, so far the sky remains free from heavy clouds. But I can smell the rain in the air, making everything feel heavier. I slip out, careful to close the door quietly behind me, and seek shelter under the protective canopy of the fruit trees as I try to make my way to the river at the back of the kingdom grounds.

Using them as cover, I race along the row of trees, pausing occasionally to ensure that no guards are watching before continuing my mad dash. I maneuver over the hill and through the graveyard, my heart pounding in my chest, until I reach the river that slivers along the back of the castle grounds. Peering back at the castle, I don't see guards moving from their posts or sense any issues, and I let out a breath of relief.

Heading west, I start jogging, keeping my body low to avoid detection. With each step, I feel a sense of liberation building within me. I can't believe I am breaking free from the suffocating confines of the castle and from the oppressive bond that has tormented me for far too long now.

The thought of a future filled with endless possibilities brings a smile to my face, even as my tired legs protest. Finally, I am going to be free, free of the castle, my mate, and free of the bond.

No more of the King silently sitting in my room and making the bond wreak havoc, no more of his scent tormenting me. Excitement bubbles in me as I think of my future possibilities. It will be just me and Abbie again, and, of course, her mate. But I can survive anything as long as I have her by my side.

By the time I reach the halfway point, darkness has enveloped the sky completely. Glancing down at the watch Abbie had given me tightly clasped in my hand, I check the time once more. She instructed me to run straight and follow the river, yet there is no sign of a bridge or any roads up ahead.

The storm overheard is moving in, and it seems like I'm attempting the impossible. Is Abbie sure of the directions? Or is it simply further than I thought?

Coming to a halt, I bend over, resting my hands on my knees as I struggle to catch my breath. Nearly half an hour of relentless running has taken its toll on my weary body. The chill of the night air sends shivers down my spine, and as the moon's feeble light is swallowed by the encroaching clouds, a sense of anxiety settles over me. I don't like the dark, and the shadows creeping nearer from the trees have my anxiety levels rise.

My teeth throb from breathing against the cool wind and the strain of exertion, and my legs scream in protest, but I push myself to continue knowing this is my only chance at escaping. Determined to find the spot Abbie has described, I strain my eyes, searching for any sign of it in the darkness. Fear gnaws at me as I stand alone in the inky blackness, unable to shift and relying solely on my human senses. The scent of rain hangs heavy in the air, adding to my growing unease as it starts drowning out other scents.

Every noise, every snap of a twig, sends my head spinning in all directions. Slowing my pace slightly, I squint into the distance, straining to make out any sign of the bridge Abbie's mate had mentioned.

It is at that very moment that distant howls reach my ears, carried on the wind from the direction of the castle which sends my heart into a frenzied flutter. *He knows.*

My heart skips a beat at the sound of the howls, as the guards communicate with each other, they sound from every direction and I know I am running out of time. The hairs on the back of my neck standing on end. The howls resonate with a haunting familiarity. A chill runs through my veins as I realize that those howls belong to the wolves that guard the castle grounds.

Fear grips me with an iron fist, my mind racing to find a way out of this predicament but the only one I can see is finding that bridge.

TWENTY-EIGHT

I VY

Forcing my legs to move, I start running. My heart thumps erratically, and I take off before hearing one howl so loud and angry it can only be the King. Panic seizes me, and I glance ahead, knowing that being by the water, I am far too exposed. With that knowledge, I take off for the tree line, deciding to stay as near to the edge of the forest as possible, so I don't get lost. I also won't be spotted out in the open of the clear space running alongside the river.

Adrenaline courses through me as I take off, praying I make it to the bridge. Tears burn my eyes as the wind whips my face, making it sting. The sounds of running through the forest send fear coursing through me. What took me half an hour to run through, they cover in a matter of minutes. I can hear them in the woods gaining on me. I glance behind me only to look ahead and I skid across the ground, coming to a halt. My feet skid across the loose rocks and leaves making me fall on my side when a huge black Lycan with impenetrable eyes flashes between the trees in front of me.

"No," I gasp, knowing he's found me. Knowing I can't escape his Lycan.

He prowls through the trees toward me. His growl sounds menacing, furious, as I scramble backward, trying to get to my feet. However, the leaves and damp earth make the ground slippery as I hear the crunch of twigs beneath him.

"You were warned," he growls angrily, and I shake my head.

Kyron's fur is so dark, it has a blue hue to it under the moonlight filtering through the trees. He stalks closer to me, growling, his teeth sharp and gleaming, chilling my bones as he stalks closer. His chest rises and falls heavily with his burning anger, and his aura is suffocating. His claws slash down a nearby tree when he stops, tilting his head.

"Don't," he warns, anticipating what I am about to do. But my mind doesn't listen.

My scream hurts my own ears when he suddenly runs at me, as my feet finally get leverage on the ground. I sprint off, only to get about five steps when his weight hits my back, shoving me forward into the dirt. The air in my lungs completely leaves me in a huff as I hit the ground. His weight never lands on top of me, yet I feel the rumble of his growl against my back, his clawed hands on either side of my face.

Fear momentarily paralyzes me, and I can feel the fur on his legs brush against mine as he traps me beneath him, caging me in.

The crunch of twigs makes me look up to see Damian step out of the trees in just a pair of shorts. Worry etches into his facial features as he looks at me pinned beneath the King. I want to yell out to him for help but my voice is suddenly mute with the fear wrapping around me.

"Leave us," the King commands him.

"No, please," I beg my voice a whisper in the breeze that goes unheard. My eyes meet Damian's fleetingly before he disappears within the trees, leaving me with Kyson. His chest rumbles with his growl against my back, and he buries his nose in my neck, making me whimper.

Tears stream down my cheeks as I try to claw my way out from under him, only for him to press his chest firmly against my back, forcing me to the ground. His teeth nip my shoulder, making me cry out when I try to move.

"You would dare attempt to leave me, to leave your King," he snarls next to my ear, his gravelly voice sending a shiver up my spine. My entire body shakes beneath him, his aura slamming down on me, dominating me and forcing another whimper to leave my lips.

"You're mine, mine Ivy, and you will remain with me. I will chain you to my damn bed if needed," he growls. "You won't be escaping me again, you were warned never to run from me, and now you'll learn the consequences of your actions."

My fingertips burn and throb, anger mingling with my fear and claws slip from my fingertips, enraged by his words, although petrified at the same time. They dig into the earth, and he snarls again, nipping my shoulder and making me flinch as he breaks my skin and blood trails down my shoulder blades.

I was so close, so close to freedom.

"Submit," he growls in warning, and I feel my eyes flicker before my own growl slips out of me uncontrollably. My vision changes, illuminating the darkness and making my surroundings brighter. His hand falls on my shoulder, claws sinking in as his weight lifts. Before I know it, he flips me on my back with a swift yank before dropping his weight against my abdomen and legs. Trapping me once again. His aura smashes against me, and he roars in my face.

"I said submit," he growls, yet as his words wash over me and instead of a whimper, rage emerges out in the form of my thunderous growl.

"No!" I scream back at him, thrashing beneath him trying to escape.

His fists come down on either side of my face on the dirt. "I am your fucking King. You will submit to me," he snarls, then pressing his chest against mine.

"The same King who doesn't want me for a mate," I snarl back, and my eyes flicker, my vision making his features clearer as my eyes adapt to the darkness, turning a luminescent blue, which makes his glare harden as his eyes examine my face. He uses his nose, turning my face, his fur brushing against me before he snarls.

"You're mine," he seethes, shaking with rage above me and the bond flares, making me angry.

"I'm not anymore," I growl at him, and he roars in my face before punching the ground beside my face. I squeeze my eyes shut and inhale deeply but refuse to submit like his aura tries to make me. The feeling of it caressing over me makes nausea build. Yet I shove it back, shocking myself at my own ability to not give in when I feel his tongue swipe across his bite marks on my shoulder and arm.

"You will submit, one way or another," he purrs, and I hear his bones snap and rearrange before his warm skin presses against me. I feel the calling, making my skin tingle as he forces the bond to the surface, and I gasp that he would use it on me to get me to submit to him.

I scream as he awakens the stupid calling. Willing to do anything to get away, I thrash beneath him, wanting him to stop, not wanting to submit to him when I feel the weight of it start to relax me. With a last-ditch effort to stop him, I start hitting him and thrashing for him to get off me.

The King snarls, shoving the calling on me again as I scramble, kicking my feet and pushing away and out from under him. He snarls, flashing his canines at me, and my hand moves with speed I never thought possible and connects with his face. Only after they do that, I realize my fingers... no... my *claws* are out, razor-sharp as they slash down his face.

Blood spills and sprays across my face, and I gasp at what I've done while his head whips to the side. The deep threatening growl that leaves him makes my blood run cold as he slowly turns his face back to look at me. Deep claw marks streak down his cheek, across his lips, and over one of his eyelids. *How did I do that?* My bravado wears off immediately as he snarls before pouncing on me and crushing me beneath him. His blood drips on me, covering me like a leaky faucet.

My claws retract instantly and I whimper, waiting for him to tear into me when he purrs, the calling washing over me, and I sob as I feel my body go lax beneath him, giving in to his demands. He buries his face in my neck and my hands feebly try to push his face away.

"Shh, my Queen," he whispers, nipping my fingertips and burying his face in my neck.

"You're mine now," he purrs before I feel his teeth pierce my skin. He sinks them deeply into my neck, through the layers of skin and tissue and I gasp as sparks rush from head to toe, every inch of me tingling and my body feels foreign to me. Even my toes curl as immense pleasure washes through every part of my body. I feel him take something from me, like he stole a piece of my soul as it embeds and transfers to him. My eyelids flutter, heavy as the fight drains out of me and I feel his teeth slide out of my neck, his tongue rolls over my mark.

His calling grows louder, taking everything, forcing me to relax while exhaustion, like never before, slivers through me.

"Sleep my Queen, your King has got you," he purrs. My head falls back as he scoops me up in his arms, his chest vibrating against me as he continues to purr, clutching me close while I become entirely limp in his arms. He starts walking, nuzzling my neck as I try to fight the exhaustion. Unable, I blink once more and everything goes black.

CHAPTER
TWENTY-NINE

A BBIE
An hour earlier

The time finally comes for me to leave, and I am waiting out front of the castle, sitting on the steps. A small bag sits between my feet that Clarice has made up for me, so I have a few things to take with me until Kade organizes for more clothes. Yet as the car pulls in, I jump to my feet and rush over to him. The bond tugs me to my mate, and I am ecstatic that Ivy can come with us. That I will eventually get Tyson back. Today is a good day, everything's coming together, though I will miss this place. Miss Gannon and Clarice, but Kade promises I can visit whenever I want.

I smack into his chest the moment he gets out of the car, and he wraps his arms around me, burying his face in my hair before pecking my lips softly.

"Get in the car, my love. We need to head home," Kade whispers, cupping my face in his hands. Looking around, I try to find Gannon but can't see him. So instead I turn to the King and give a quick bow to him. Surprisingly, Damian gives me a brief hug before I look around again. He was just here seconds ago. Where did he go?

"Where did Gannon go?" I ask, a little disappointed. Alpha Kade grips my shoulder, turning me toward the car.

"You said goodbye to your friend?" he asks me, and I look up at him, nodding. He inclines his head toward the car, and I slowly walk back to it before climbing into the passenger seat and clipping in my belt. Kade shuts my door and I watch as he talks to the King, my hands sweat and I wipe them on my pants.

After a few minutes, he climbs into the car, starting it. I wave to the King and those waiting. The King stiffly waves back and I peer up at Kade. "The King looks angry," I tell him.

"Probably busy," is all Kade offers. We drive to the bridge where we are supposed to meet Ivy, yet as time slips on, and the closer it nears to 7 pm, the more nervous I get. I pace along the walkway, looking to the path below. Once 7 pm comes and goes, I hear howls fill the sky, and Kade gasps.

Nervously I look at Kade. "I don't think she is coming, love, she must have changed her mind."

I shake my head, knowing she wouldn't have.

"No. She'll be here," I tell him, pacing again.

"Abbie!"

"No, she will be here," I tell him, and he growls behind me. I peer over my shoulder at Kade, and he presses his lips in a line.

"The King knows of her plans. The gardener told him when he heard you speaking," Kade tells me. But the gardener wasn't there to listen.

"Abbie, don't make me do this, I don't want to hurt you, but we need to leave. Kyson will come for me when he finds out I was in on it."

"How do you know about the gardener?" I question.

"One of the guards sent me a message just now," he says, coming over playing with his phone. He shows me the screen.

"You know I can't read, do the voice to text thingy," I tell him.

"My phone doesn't have that feature," he tells me.

"No, we need to wait. She will come. I know she will," I tell him.

"Abbie, get in the car," he repeats, and I shake my head.

"Just go," I tell him, waving him off and turning toward the steep incline to go look for her when I feel his aura slip out and wash over me.

"Stop this nonsense and get in the fucking car! You are testing my patience. Now!" he bellows the order, and I whimper as I try to fight his command, yet my feet carry me to the car with frighteningly quick steps.

Kade growls, slamming my door before I barely get my legs in. I sit there, shaking at his commanding. He climbs into the car and starts it before he sighs heavily.

"The King is mad at me. You don't want me hurt, do you? What would the Moon Goddess think if you got your mate killed, all because you foolishly wanted to wait?" he asks.

"What if she tripped or something? What if she's hurt?" I ask, worried.

He puts the car in drive, and it starts moving. I reach for the door handle, but Kade's hand drops on my thigh, his nails digging in.

"Do you not love me? Did you not hear what I said about the King looking for me?" he growls before once again his aura slips out. "Sit there and be quiet! Think about the consequences if the King finds me. Imagine all the ways he could hurt me," he orders, and I blink.

My mind is overpowered and does everything he asks. For hours, I imagine possible torture scenarios, my bond aching and cringing when finally he squeezes my fingers.

"I dropped my command. I'm sorry, love. I shouldn't have commanded you," he tells me, and I peer out the window, feeling sick. If only he knew how tortured my mind already was and then he does that. Forces me to envision his death while my bond tugs painfully in my chest. The guilt forms an endless pit in my stomach.

"I'm sorry," I whisper.

"That's okay. You are forgiven. I bet you're hungry. There is a truck stop ahead." At the mention of food, my belly rumbles. He pulls in and there is a small diner. Stepping inside, we take our seats and Kade orders for us. He orders our food, yet when it comes out, I stare at the measly plate.

"You need to watch your figure. Can't have a fat Luna," he says as I stare down at the bowl of lettuce. "Lucky, I am here to look out for you. I'll make a Luna of you," he says. I look at his eggs and bacon, but not wanting to sound ungrateful, I tuck in. My belly rumbles after we finish eating and climb in the car. I am still very hungry, and I pinch my shirt that is far too loose, wondering if I am overweight. Surely, someone would have told me? Maybe not, but I don't think I am. I've never had enough to eat and I've always thought I looked sickeningly skinny, with the way my hip bones jut out and my ribs show.

The drive takes hours, and I reach into the backseat to retrieve my bag, pulling my phone out. I have multiple text messages from Gannon. Yet some part of me tells me not to listen to them in the car. Kade makes it very clear about his dislike for Gannon and Liam, and I don't feel like arguing with him over any message he sent.

So I tuck the phone back in the bag when my fingers touch a wrapper. Excitement bubbles in me and I pull the bag of candy clouds out. I open it and pop three in my mouth while reaching for the dial on the radio. Only Kade slaps my hand.

He had never done that before. He always let me choose the station when in his car. "I'm listening to that! What has gotten into you? You're acting out of sorts!" he snaps, glancing at me.

Am I acting out of sorts? Is it me? Why do I suddenly feel so uncomfortable in his presence? It's like all of the warmth and safety has melted away. Guilt smashes me for even thinking I was uncomfortable. The Moon Goddess would strike me down for my terrible thoughts about my mate. A gift she bestowed me.

"What have you got?" Kade asks when I pop another candy in my mouth. I show him the bag, offering him some.

"Strawberry clouds, do you want one? They are..."

He rips the bag out of my hand.

"I knew you were acting up! For fuck's sake, you shouldn't eat candy. The sugar goes to your head." He winds the window down, tossing the bag before I can try to grab it. "You're so talkative and loud whenever you eat that shit he gives you!" he snaps and I shrink in my chair.

"Seriously, Abbie, think of your health. And my sanity. It drives me up the wall when you're blubbering and bouncing on your feet!" he scolds.

He never complained before, and Gannon never said I talk too much. That sinking feeling returns, and I turn my gaze out the window.

Wiping a stray tear with my fingers. "You're not seriously crying over candy?" he huffs, and I feel myself slip into a mask I had learned at a young age. A mask Mrs. Daley earned from us. One of emptiness. Tears won't help you, no, they would get us beat back at the orphanage. Kade mutters something under his breath.

I turn my thoughts inward, blocking out the world and everyone in it. Going to a place no one can touch me. Going to a place I only visit in my dreams. Grandma's house. Where my childhood was good before it all got taken away from me when we had to go on the run.

CHAPTER
THIRTY

K *YSON*

Damian panics the moment he sees me step into the foyer with her in my arms. Her blood runs down my arms, although it has slowed considerably. Ivy infuriated me; I wasn't supposed to mark her, but when she refused to submit, I lost control.

She hasn't shifted yet, but she did partially shift when she slashed me, so she must be close to shifting, and now I could have put everything at risk.

Damian's eyes fly wide open when he notices the blood trailing down my arms, and he tries to rip her away from me. I pull her closer, and his arms drop as his eyes take her in looking for any injury.

"I marked her; she is fine," I spit through gritted teeth, annoyed at how he goes straight for her as if I have fatally hurt her. He exhales, and his shoulders sag with his obvious relief.

"Not ideal, but we can work with that. Just means changing her will be harder and require a few attempts," Damian sighs. Ivy looks like a ragdoll in my arms. Looking at her, it almost looks like she is dead with how floppy her body is in my arms. Moving her around, I pull her closer, so her head rests on my shoulder instead of craning back awkwardly.

"Help me get her upstairs," I command, and he walks ahead, opening the doors for me before finally opening the bedroom door. I stop, peering around my room before walking back out.

"What is it?" Damian asks, and I look down the hall toward the other wing.

"I can't stay in there with her; I don't trust myself," I tell him.

"Kyson, you can't just mark her and lock her away in her room and leave her there," Damian says, and I look down at her in my arms.

"Just have them move my stuff tomorrow to hers, just not... It's Claire's old room; I can't," I tell him before walking off toward her room.

"But you will stay with her. You will move back to your old quarters?" Damian asks.

"I said I would. I know I can't leave her now; I fucking marked her."

"And you do not seem the least bit happy about that," Damian states.

"Damian, stop. Just leave it be."

He chuckles and shakes his head.

"Whatever you say, my King," he adds as I step through the threshold, tugging Ivy closer. Damian moves toward the fire, throwing another log in it before walking into the bathroom, and I hear the bath running. I glance at him as he emerges, and he shrugs.

"What, do you plan on putting her to bed filthy and covered in blood and dirt?" he asks.

"I know what you're doing," I growl at him.

"And what is that, my King?" Damian smirks, and I narrow my eyes at him, his lips tugging into a smirk. He knows exactly what he is doing, trying to force me to break down the walls of the bond. He knows the more time spent with her would awaken the bond, awaken her shift.

146

"Don't play dumb," I snap at him before looking down at her. She looks filthy, mud matted in her hair, and her porcelain skin is now stained red. Blood also drenches my chest, neck, and face from her claw marks, and I sigh.

"I will have some clothes sent over for you," Damian says before turning and walking out of the room.

Biting the inside of my lip, I sigh. I move toward the bathroom before sitting on the edge of the giant bathtub with Ivy on my lap. Quickly stripping her bare, I look away from her naked body. My urges tempt me to taste her flesh and smother her in my scent.

The bond may be weak for her, but it has never been stronger for me, especially as I feel her essence weave through mine. Reaching over, I shut the taps off before stepping into the bath and settling her on my lap, keeping her head above water. Her back rests against my chest. Reaching for a cloth, I begin to wash her.

Not once does she stir as I clean her, her mark still weeping with blood as it tries to heal. It isn't until Damian clears his throat from the bathroom doorway, his back turned slightly, that I realize I am licking her. I shake my head, not remembering when I gave myself over to instinct. Her neck and face are completely clean, and I glare at the ceiling. A growl slips from me at Damian's following words.

"Does she taste good, my King?" he taunts.

"Are you trying to irritate me on purpose? I didn't fucking realize I was doing it until you made a noise," I snap back.

"Instinct shouldn't be ignored," Damian says simply. That's easy for him to say. He hasn't found his mate, and his mate probably isn't a traitor. "Clothes are on the bed, towels by the sink," he says, walking out.

I glance at the sink basin and shake my head before reluctantly climbing out and bringing Ivy with me. What a mission it is trying to dry her and me when she has no movement.

Giving up on trying to dress her after pulling one of my shirts over her head, I lay her on the bed, tugging the blankets up over her before pulling on the shorts Damian brought in for me. Moving back to the bathroom, I examine my face. Her claw marks are deep, especially across my cheek and temple. I prod it, and it starts bleeding, so I grab a hand towel, pressing it against it as I walk back out of the bathroom. Grabbing her hand, I examine her fingers.

I wonder how she managed to claw me up so badly. Werewolf claws could do some damage, but it's like I was slashed with a knife. The only damage that causes this sort of destruction to a Lycan is usually caused by another Lycan's claws.

Placing her hand down, I move toward my old bar, searching for liquor. Finding none, I call for Dustin to retrieve it for me, along with a set of handcuffs, before settling on the couch by the fire. I turn my chair so I can see her while I wait for him.

)◐(

A few hours later, whiskey in hand, I watch her. The dimly lit room casts shadows on her face as she sleeps across the room from me, her eyes closed. Her hair cascades over her shoulders in waves, the moonlight catching hints of blue. Ivy's hair is that black, it gives off strange hues under the lighting.

The air is filled with the rich aroma of whiskey, its spicy notes mingling with the smoky scent of the fire. Underneath it all, her sweet honey nectar scent invades every inch of the room, sending my senses wild. Her scent is intoxicating to me.

As I take a sip of the whiskey, the smooth liquid burns down my throat, leaving a warm trail in its wake. Its flavors dance on my tongue, hints of caramel and oak, but it does nothing to stop the ache in me to go to her, to bundle her up in my arms and devour her essence. I feel out of control and it's all because of her. She will send me insane with love or hate. They seem to blur into one these days. I can't stand to be near her, yet it pains me to be away.

For some reason, I can't shake the image of her eyes glowing with an unearthly light, or the surprising strength she displayed as she struggled against me. It was clear that she was angry, and it took nearly all my strength to subdue her.

What really bothers me is how she resisted my command in her anger. The calling overwhelmed her, but my command, she fought. It puzzles me. In those moments, Ivy had a strength that seemed beyond what a werewolf should possess. She fought my command, but couldn't withstand the calling. I keep telling myself it's because she's my mate, yet something nags at me as I ponder.There must be more to it.

The sun is just beginning to peek over the horizon when I finally climb into bed next to her. She stirs and rolls into me. I growl at her touch, her small hands pressing into my side, seeking me out, but then I notice she's still unconscious, just reacting to the bond. Reaching over to the bedside table, I grab the handcuffs I placed there earlier and clamp one around her wrist, securing it to the headboard.

I can't risk her waking before me and trying to run again. Now that my mark is etched into her skin, there's no place she can hide from me. She'll learn that her place is with me, and whatever I choose to do with her rests solely with me. She has no choice in the matter. So until she learns that, I'll make the choices for both of us. Settling back beside her, I rest my head on the pillow and close my eyes.

Sleep takes me almost instantly with her by my side. I haven't slept completely since I forced her out of the castle, but now, with her snuggled into me and her scent enveloping me, I plunge into oblivion.

THIRTY-ONE

ABBIE

My sense of time slips away, and it is only when Kade shakes my shoulder that I snap back to reality, startled by his touch. "We have arrived, my love," he murmurs, and I blink, disoriented.

Already? I cast my gaze about, taking in the late hour and the unfamiliar surroundings. This is not the grand packhouse that Kade described to me; there are no sprawling gardens, no elegant fountains, no tall hedges. Instead, my eyes land on a dilapidated cabin, nestled in isolation, surrounded by an imposing forest. I thought he is supposed to be Alpha of some great pack.

Confusion fills me as I inquire, "Where are we?" The desolation of this place is palpable.

"It's a safe house," Kade explains, his voice tinged with concern. "We have been experiencing troubles with neighboring packs. We cannot risk alerting them to your presence. It would put you in grave danger." I furrow my brows, about to voice my worries when he steps out of the car without another word. The wind bites at his figure as he circles around to open my door. I step out, rubbing my arms for warmth before retrieving my bag.

"How long will we be staying here?" I inquire, my eyes tracing the tiny porch with its uneven slope and the door that bears the signs of weathered neglect—a gaping crack and a missing chunk from the bottom corner.

"You will remain here until we can resolve the conflict with the other pack," he replies, fumbling with his keys.

"But...you won't be staying with me?" I question, glancing apprehensively into the shadows cast by the looming trees.

"No," he responds gently, his eyes filled with regret. "I must return home to maintain appearances. If I do not, they may grow suspicious and come searching for me. It would not be safe for you." The weight of his words settles upon me as a deep pit grows in my stomach.

"But is this place truly safe?" I ask, seeking reassurances. It sure doesn't look safe. He nods, his expression solemn.

"For the time being, it is," he assures me. "I will stay for a while longer to ensure your comfort. My men have stocked everything you may need. Come, let me show you inside." Urging me to follow him, he unlocks the stubborn door with a few firm kicks, its swollen frame revealing the damage inflicted by water. As I step inside, the disarray of the cabin assaults my senses, litter strewn about like remnants of forgotten lives, reminiscent of abandoned buildings I encountered near the orphanage.

Within the confines of this forsaken dwelling, a double bed – or perhaps a worn futon – occupies the space, its mattress heavily stained. Kade flicks on the lights, their feeble glow flickering as he moves toward the minuscule kitchen, so cramped that I could easily stretch my leg from the bed to touch the counter. He returns with a box of matches, placing them in my hands.

"I must depart now, but I shall return tomorrow," he informs me. "Firewood can be found at the back; you may need to chop some for yourself. Fresh bed linens are over there, and there is food in the pantry and fridge."

"Wait," I plead desperately. "Can you help me start the fire? I've always been dreadful at it. Either Gannon, Liam, Dustin, or sometimes Damian would always take care of it back in my little room at home."

"Don't be silly," Kade dismisses kindly. "It is dreadfully late, and I must hurry home to shower for work. You will manage just fine for one night. I will return around lunchtime tomorrow."

"Please, let me come with you. You can sneak me into the pack house. No one will see me; it's late night, no one will be up at this hour," I tell him, not wanting to stay here by myself.

"Abbie, love. I need to go. I haven't got time for theatrics. Behave, and I'll be back tomorrow," he says, pecking my forehead before turning to leave me here.

With those words, he kisses my forehead before turning to leave me here. I survey my surroundings, settling onto the creaking mattress that digs into my backside. The chill in the air seeps into my bones, causing them to ache.

I glance around, sitting on the creaky old mattress, the springs digging into my backside. It's freezing here, so cold my breath makes clouds in the air.

I will myself to get up and start the fire. After mere moments of sitting, the cold seeps deep into my bones, making them ache from the inside out. Too cold to even start a fire, I reach for the sheets and blankets huddling beneath them, and pull my phone from my bag. Switching on the screen, I sigh wearily, realizing it is far too late to call Gannon and disturb his slumber. Instead, I replay his messages, his voice filled with longing and a telling me to call him.

As I lie there in the frigid cabin, I can't help but wish for the comfort of Gannon's presence and the warming fires of the castle. The weight of solitude settles upon me, amplified by the biting cold that lingers in the air.

CHAPTER
THIRTY-TWO

I VY

My muscles throb with an ache as I force my heavy eyelids to flutter open, my gaze landing on the plain expanse of the ceiling. A dull throb pulses through my head, leaving me feeling groggy and disoriented as I shift on the bed. But as I attempt to rub my eyes, a shock of icy metal snags my wrist, freezing me in place.

With a tilt of my head, I discover that one of my hands is shackled to the headboard, the cold handcuff biting into my flesh. A gasp escapes my lips as I jerk my trapped wrist, desperate to break free, only to find that the restraint refuses to yield. Panic slithers its way through my veins as the memories of yesterday surge back with a vengeance, flooding every corner of my mind.

A tightness constricts my chest, making it difficult to draw a full breath as my free hand instinctively travels to my neck. The tingling sensation of his touch lingers on my skin, accompanied by a stinging reminder of how he marked me.

The haunting echoes of his threats to bind me to the bed reverberate in my thoughts as I scan the room for his presence, but he remains elusive, nowhere to be found. Judging by the soft glow filtering through the window, it appears to be midday. My struggles against the restraints intensify, the unforgiving metal digging deeper into my wrist, leaving behind angry bruises as I desperately try to free myself.

Warm tears carve their path down my cheeks, proof of the inescapable truth that he has ensnared me, trapping me within the confines of this bed, leaving his mark upon me.

I sob at how easy it was for him to hurt me and chain me up like this. My head swivels, angling towards the entrance as his intoxicating scent wafts towards me. The King strides into the room, his gaze momentarily flickering over me in my futile attempt to break free.

"There would be no need for such measures, but I cannot trust you," he asserts, making his way towards the bar area. Clutching a book in one hand, he observes my struggle while pouring himself a drink, placing the book on the coffee table before settling into an armchair.

"You tried to flee," he remarks casually, as though that alone justifies his harsh treatment. Yet all I can think of are the countless times Mrs. Daley confined and imprisoned us, triggering my claustrophobia to soar to unbearable heights. Despite the room's ample size, being trapped on this bed with a hand rendered useless makes the space feel small, as if its very walls conspire to suffocate me.

"You're afraid," he states matter-of-factly, taking a sip from his glass and studying me intently over its rim.

"Release me, Kyson," I stammer, my voice trembling.

"Never, Ivy. What part of 'you are mine' did you fail to comprehend? Did you believe that being destined to a King would grant you the freedom to depart without consequences?" he challenges, eliciting a defiant glare from me. I glare at him. My sudden anger doesn't stop the tears from sliding down my face or the feeling of unease at being trapped. His presence only makes me more nervous. I turn my gaze to the closet before lying back down on my side.

The sound of his glass gently clinking against the coffee table and his footsteps growing nearer indicate his approach. "You cannot simply walk away; the bond forbids it, at least for me," he declares, his voice drawing closer as he edges towards the edge of the bed.

"Then reject me and be done with it," I tell him.

"Lycan's cannot sever their connection to their mates. Even if I desired it, I would be incapable of doing so, and truth be told, I have no desire to sever that bond," he confesses, though his words seem more like an attempt to convince himself rather than me. It doesn't offer me any hope.

"I will release you from these handcuffs once I sense that I can trust you again. As long as the anger coursing through our bond persists, you shall remain restrained. Do you understand?" The words catch in my throat when I feel his fingertips firmly grip my chin, tilting my face upwards to meet his gaze.

The faint scarring from my claw marks on his face had healed, leaving behind a subtle trace of our encounter. Strangely, these marks only seem to enhance his god-like good looks, adding character rather than detracting from them. His features remained as striking as ever, despite the evidence of our conflict.

With a cool detachment in his voice, he spoke, his thumb brushing lightly against my lips. "All you had to do was submit," he said. I instinctively jerk my head away from his touch, a small act of defiance that seems to disappoint him. A sigh escapes his lips as he continues, "But since you didn't, I can't guarantee that you won't try to run again."

His words hung heavy in the air, a reminder of my captivity and the powerlessness that came with it. As he turns away, retreating to his whiskey, I find myself lost in a sea of memories. The silence of the room amplifies the haunting echoes of my past, particularly those from the orphanage where I was bound and restrained, trapped both physically and mentally.

In these moments of silence, my mind becomes another prison, leading me down paths I desperately wished to forget. I yearn for the presence of Abbie, whose whispers had once kept me grounded during such torment, usually because she would be locked in that cramped space with me. But now, all I have is the suffocating silence enforced by the king, a silence that threatens to consume me.

My muscles ache from the lack of movement, reminding me of the stagnant existence I am now leading. Somehow, this feels worse than the orphanage. Suddenly, the urgency to relieve myself washes over me. Almost as if reading my thoughts, he appears by my side, undoing the handcuffs with an air of impatience. "Go," he commands, nodding towards the bathroom.

"You forget I can feel you, Ivy. Now hurry up."

"Then, if that were true, you wouldn't have me handcuffed to the damn bed."

He seems perplexed at my reaction. He tilts his head to the side, observing me, but I pay him no mind. I stumble over my own feet as I climb off the bed before rushing to the bathroom.

Emerging from the bathroom, my gaze is immediately drawn to the handcuffs in his hand as he stands waiting by the door. My heart rate quickens, anxiety coursing through my veins, as he observes me with a tilted head. His fingers graze his chin in contemplation.

"Come here," he murmurs, and I take a step back, shaking my head, my eyes darting to the handcuffs. He takes a calculated step toward me.

"I thought you were scared of me," he muses, raising the handcuffs as if they are a symbol of fear. My heart lurches in my chest, pounding relentlessly. He studies me for a moment before shifting his gaze to the handcuffs.

"But these are what scare you?" he questions, frustration etching lines on his face. He sighs and runs a hand down his tired features, biting his lip as he ponders. Meanwhile, I stand frozen in place, shifting my weight nervously from one foot to the other, bracing myself for the inevitable moment when he will force the cuffs back onto my wrists.

"Do I need these?" he asks me, he watches me intently and I swallow the lump forming in my throat.

"If you try to escape again," he warns, his voice laced with a dangerous edge as he steps closer. "I will lock you in the cells beneath the castle, or perhaps I'll resort to using these again," he states.

"Am I understood?" he asks, and I bite down on my lip.

"Ivy!" he growls when I don't answer him. Tears burn my eyes, and I nod in reluctant understanding, aware of the consequences that await any further attempts at defiance. He curses under his breath, shaking his head then tosses the handcuffs onto the bed.

"One chance, Ivy," he states firmly. "Don't ruin it. I don't take pleasure in punishing you." His words hang in the air like an unspoken promise, though lately it seems that punishment has become an all too frequent occurrence.

"Then don't give me a reason to," I whisper defiantly. He glances over at me, a low growl escaping his throat. He storms toward me, reaching forward and gripping my wrist tightly. In one swift motion, he yanks me toward him, pinning me beneath his weight on the bed. The suddenness of his movements leaves me breathless, caught off guard and vulnerable.

"You can be a stubborn little thing," he growls, a trace of frustration evident in his voice. The calling surges through my veins, his proximity drawing out an instinctual response within me that I am beginning to despise. His hands lock around my wrists, pulling them above my head and holding them captive with a strength that leaves me powerless underneath him. His chest presses against mine, the vibration reverberating through my entire body, the clash between desire and anger intensifying as he uses the calling.

His nose trails along my cheek, inhaling my scent before pausing near my ear. "You can fight me all you want, Ivy," he purrs, his warm breath sending shivers down my spine. "But I possess something you don't." His tongue grazes the seam of my lips, eliciting a moan from deep within me. My body betrays me, succumbing to his touch even as tears threaten to spill from my eyes.

"I don't want to force you," he whispers against my lips, his voice laced with a hint of desperation. "I've told you this before. I don't want to become that kind of monster."

He thrust his hips against my barely clothed body, the pressure causing another moan to escape my lips, mingling with the whirlwind of conflicting emotions inside me. I know that if he desires it, he can use the calling to make me submit completely, to surrender myself entirely to him.

"See, Ivy," he growls, an edge of control in his voice. "I have power over you. Don't make me abuse it. I don't want that, and I know you don't either." With those words, he abruptly withdraws, the overwhelming sensation vanishing as quickly as it had appeared leaving me feeling suddenly cold.

"Tread carefully, Ivy. You don't want me to snap," he growls before rolling off me.

The moment he does, my entire body shudders like it's going through withdrawals. It takes everything in me not to throw myself at him and rub myself on him, needing his skin, wanting to bite him. He smirks knowing the war he has caused inside me before his face falls when I don't give in to the urges, my anger at him overshadowing them, and I grit my teeth.

"You're fighting it," he snarls, his voice dripping with frustration and impatience and he grips my face with his fingers. His eyes bore into mine, searching for any sign of surrender.

"You would rather be in pain?" he asks, his tone laced with a mix of concern and anger. His brows furrow as he waits for my response.

"I used to love it when you did that. Now, you just make me hate it because you're taking my choice," I tell him, my words tinged with bitterness. He lets me go. The weight of broken promises hangs heavily in the air between us. "You promised I would have a choice. But you never meant it did you?"

He looks away from me, his gaze fixed on some distant point in the room. I catch a glimpse of his throat bobbing as he swallows, a flicker of guilt crossing his features before he masks it.

"You've given me no choice. You want to make choices. Then

don't make me take them," he pleads, his voice tinged with desperation. "Stop fighting the bond and you don't run from me again."

A bitter laugh escapes my lips, laced with a tinge of disbelief. "You're a hypocrite," I spit out, the words dripping with venom. "You say don't fight it or deny the bond, but you broke mine. You had no issues breaking me. I won't allow you to do it a second time."

My anger boils over, my voice rising in volume until it fills the room, leaving me breathless. He seems taken aback by my outburst, his eyes widening momentarily before he regains his composure. Without saying another word, he gets up from his seat and storms toward the door, his steps heavy with frustration.

"You try to leave this room before I say, and you will find yourself in the cold confines of the cells," he snaps, his voice sharp and cutting.

With one final glare in my direction, he walks out and slams the door behind him, the sound reverberating through the room like a gunshot. I jump at the sudden noise, the bond between us flaring to life, tugging at my very core, urging me to chase after him.

It takes me days, endless nights of torment, for the bond to ease its grip and allow me to breathe again. But it takes him only seconds to force it back, to tighten its chains around my heart. One bite, one act of dominance, and he is destroying me all over again.

Only now, in the aftermath of our heated exchange, do I recognize the signs, the insidious influence he has over me. The twisted way the bond works against me, stripping away my autonomy. It isn't fair, and with Abbie gone, I fear I may not survive the relentless push and pull of this bond, the agony of losing it once more if he so chooses.

Yet, despite the overwhelming despair that threatens to consume me. One thing has become startlingly obvious: he is fighting the bond just as fiercely as I am. He may have the calling, and the power that comes with it, but I am not entirely powerless. I have this bond, this connection that binds us together. And if he wants to break me, to shatter every piece of my being, then I will make sure he breaks too.

I'll show him how intertwined pain and desire truly are. There can be no winner unless we are both scarred. Every touch brings a sting of pain, yet pain itself is an old acquaintance, a constant shadow in my life. What are a few more scars to a soul already so deeply lacerated? My skin might heal, but the soul remembers.

He awakened feelings in me, a dangerous stirring of life where once there was only numbness, he gave hope, only to take it away. Now, I find myself craving the cold embrace of that void again. And soon, so will he.

THIRTY-THREE

I VY

The next few days went the same. The King forces me to go with him wherever he goes, making me follow around like a lost puppy and it's starting to get on my nerves. I stare longingly out toward the forest through his office window at Clarice and Peter.

Peter has a bucket and a scrubbing brush in his hand. Clarice is talking to him, and it looks like she is about to hang out the washing. I press my forehead against the cool glass. Fresh air would be good, anything to get away from the king or the guards, even if only for a few moments.

"I will take you outside later," the King says, as if he can read my mind. He is staring down at his laptop screen, not paying any attention to me whatsoever. For the most part, we ignore each other. However, I can see he is becoming bothered by it. It is almost as if he is picking fights with me when we do talk, just to give him a reason to grab me or touch me.

He never hurts me, but I don't believe that is his intention, anyway. The bond draws him closer to me, and Damian has admitted that is why the King drinks the way he does; to fight off the urges for him to give in to the bond, something I have refused to do myself. I have also been refusing to sleep in the bed with him even though I can hear him pacing because of it. It gives me some weird sick satisfaction that it disturbs him. Like I am winning at something while being held prisoner. Though it pains me refusing him, I am becoming desensitized to the pain. It's not like I know anything else, but I see how frustrated it makes him.

He can't complain about it because he said I can't leave the room, and technically I hadn't or tried to, so he has no reason to force me into bed with him or use the calling on me though I can see the temptation too clearly on his face.

"Can I ring Abbie?" I ask, and he briefly looks over the laptop screen at where I am sitting.

"You tried her earlier, and she never picked up. You may try tonight, and if she doesn't answer, I will call her mate, so you can speak with her, that is if you behave and eat tonight," he adds. I turn my gaze away and glare out the window. I have had no appetite since being back. Just the smell of food makes me want to throw up.

"Can I go help, Clarice?" I ask.

"No, I am busy," he growls, and I chew my lip. It is boring sitting here and that's all I ever seem to do, sit around, and wait for him to drag me somewhere else.

"Damian can take me," I say, and he sighs, sitting back in his chair, staring at me.

"Damian and Gannon are working; I can't pull them away from their duties just because you're bored, Ivy," he says. A growl slips from me, and he folds his arms across his chest, arching an eyebrow at me while pressing his full lips in a line.

My eyes stare at them, and I have to pull my gaze away, making me lick mine. I notice he does this when he is debating with himself and not liking his own trail of thoughts.

I stand up, seeing his eyes watch me make my way over to him before I stop next to his desk. He swivels in his chair to face me straight on like he thinks I am about to make a run for the door.

Then, I notice his computer screen. Seeing my gaze, he glances back at what is a beautiful woman on the screen and hurt rushes through me. There are lots of them, all tiny pictures of women displayed in different stages of undress and posed for the camera.

"It's not what you think," he murmurs, and I look at him. He reaches for me, but I jerk my hand away. He has been sitting here this entire time looking at other women while I sit across from him unable to do anything but stare out a window because of the pain he's causing me.

"Ivy, come here," he snarls, leaning forward and wrapping his fingers around my wrist. He pulls me on his lap, locking his arm around my waist when I try to get up.

"Let me go," I thrash trying to escape his grip. Kyson growls and nips my shoulder with his teeth, his grip tightening.

"I'll show you, stop," he growls.

"I don't want to see your side pieces," I snap at him. At that, his arm tightens around my waist. His growl turns menacing as he presses his teeth against the back of my neck.

"You are overreacting, settle down," he warns. "I don't have side pieces, only you. Now stop it," he growls, moving the mouse around and clicking on one. I growl at him. I can't help it until the image clicks open, and then the screen opens up to her mutilated body. My stomach lurches, and I look away, my heart thumping in my ears loudly and my eyes widen in horror.

"Are you still jealous of a dead woman?" Kyson asks as I turn my gaze away, unable to handle looking at the screen.

"Get rid of it," I whisper as tears burn and sting my eyes at the thought of what she endured to look like that.

"I clicked out of another file. I didn't think about the picture on it, or I would have shut the screen completely down."

"Why are they all half-naked? Did they not have better pictures?" I say, wiping a stray tear. I can't get the image out of my head. It seared forever in my memory. The way she is torn apart and the look of anguish in her dead eyes.

JESSICA HALL

"Unfortunately, no, their owners didn't take normal pictures of the girls, they wouldn't sell if they did," the King says.

"Wouldn't sell?" I ask, confused.

"Yes, these women are rogue sex slaves, Ivy. We have been trying to find out where they are kept, and we also believe the children's bodies that have been washing up belong to some of these women. We know the hunters are behind it, yet we don't know why so many are suddenly popping up or why the children are older each time."

"Older?" I ask and he nods.

"Yes, most are children, but they seem to be targeting young adults or late teens. Barely above 18. I'm now wondering if the children are just collateral damage now because every time new bodies show up they are mostly women." He answers.

164

CHAPTER
THIRTY-FOUR

I VY

"The children you buried the other week?"

He nods before dropping his chin on my shoulder. "Correct, the rest were women not much older than you," he adds.

"Who would do such a thing?" I murmur, staring back at the women.

"Some very sick individuals, unfortunately, the hunters have help from one of the packs. We have found a few of the rebel insignia patches too along with the bodies," he says, reaching over to the drawer beside him and pulling out a sandwich bag full of fabric patches. He drops it on the desk, and I pick it up. The moment I turn it over, I gasp and clutch my ears as screams suddenly fill them.

Before I know what's happening, I find myself submerged in the deafening noise of the new surroundings as I struggle to take it in. The fear that courses through me makes my stomach sink and I feel cold all over. At the forefront of my mind, I am suddenly immersed in a memory arising from a time I wish to stay forgotten. Suddenly, the sounds of gunfire could be heard resounding in the air around me.

"It's ok, come on out, come to Mummy," my mother whispered.

My mother's blood-encrusted hands reached toward me. In my attempt to drown out the sound of gunshots, I tried to hide in what appeared to be a cupboard, my hands covering my ears. In what appeared to be a cleaner's uniform, my mother had a patch across her heart that was sewn into the uniform. Blood soiled the front, and her skin was tainted in it.

"Come on, Ivy, I would like you to come to me," my mother said, and I didn't want to go with her, for some reason, she scared me but reluctantly I placed my hand in hers, and she pulled me out into the carnage. The memory fizzled and warped before I found myself breathing heavily as I tried to get my bearings. She was one of them. She really did do the horrible things she was accused of.

"Ivy, what is it?" Kyson asks, clutching me tighter against him while I tug on my hair, needing the pain to make it stop, to ground me back to the present.

"Ivy, you're scaring me. Speak to me," Kyson says as I descend into a panic attack. My lungs refuse to work as I try to suck in a breath when I suddenly feel the calling sweep over me. His deep purr emanates from him, forcing me to relax against him, and I let out a shaky breath, pressing closer and seeking it out instead of fighting against it.

"What happened?" he murmurs, but I shake my head, not wanting to remember and make the details clearer.

"She really did it, didn't she?" I whisper as tears blur my vision.

"Who?"

"My mother," I choke out, and he growls, his arms growing tighter, and I can feel the tremble of his arms as he grips me. I can sense he's trying to reign in his anger toward her and for me being hers.

"The patch triggered something?" he asks, unable to keep his anger from his voice, though his purring never stops, and I nod against his chest. He nods his head but says nothing instead, letting me calm down, his hand moving to rub my back soothingly.

"Come on, I will take you back to the room," he whispers.

I shake my head but Kyson presses the sharp points of his teeth against my shoulder. I shudder, but he seems to merely do it as if to tell me he is still there like I have somehow forgotten he is holding me.

"I will see if Gannon or Damian will take you for a walk then I have work to do. So, I can't right now," he whispers into my hair. "If they're busy; I will get someone to grab a pillow and blanket. You can rest on the couch until I'm done."

I chew my lip, suddenly embarrassed over my breakdown. I am meant to be avoiding the bond, not seeking it.

The window calls to me longingly, and I feel desperate to go outside. This room all of a sudden feels stuffy and closed in. "I won't run," I whisper before looking back at the king.

He watches me. "Ivy, I can't…"

"How are you going to trust me if you don't let me earn it?" I ask, and he pulls his lip between his teeth before pinching the bridge of his nose and sighing loudly.

"I will check in with Clarice every hour, I promise," I plead. He growls, not liking my idea, and I move to climb off him knowing he's going to refuse me when he pulls me back down, his hand grips my chin forcing my gaze to meet his.

"You'll check in every half an hour and if you are so much as a minute late. I will send the entire castle out to hunt you down," he warns, and excitement bubbles up within me at the thought of even a moment of freedom. He's letting me leave the room. I nod and move to climb off him when he once again holds me in place.

"I let you go by yourself. You will sleep in the bed with me?" he states, tilting my chin to the side and watching me. My guess is that he is trying to see if I am trying to deceive him.

"Promise me, I need sleep, and I can't with you sleeping on the goddamn couch," he says, and I pull away from him.

"I need an answer, Ivy, or you don't go," he says, waiting expectantly. I sigh, but I really want to get out of this room. Without him breathing down my neck, I need to breathe for a few minutes but most of all, I want to feel free, even if it is only momentarily, so I nod and agree to his request.

"Words, Ivy. I want to hear you say it," he tells me.

"I promise," I whisper, and he drags me closer, hugging me tightly like he is worried it will be the last time he sees me. His lips press to my temple and he sighs, letting me go.

"Then you can go; I will come to find you when I am done here," he says, and I get up off his lap. Moving toward the door, he speaks, "And Ivy." I stop looking back at him.

"Make sure you check in with Clarice."

"Yes, every half hour," I finish for him, and he nods, allowing me to leave. I quickly escape and head downstairs. Stepping outside, I sigh a breath of relief. Today it is pretty warm, and the sun feels nice on my cold skin. Looking around, Clarice is hanging the last sheet on the clothesline, however, Peter is nowhere to be found.

"Where did Peter go?" I ask her, and she jumps from not hearing me come up behind her.

"Gosh, my Queen, you gave me a fright," she says, clutching her hand that held two pegs to her chest.

"Sorry, is Peter around?" I ask.

"Down at the graveyard. Where is the King?" she asks, glancing around nervously. The entire castle is aware I am in lockdown and under strict guard, so it must have her worried seeing me without someone.

"He let me out, but I have to check up with you every half an hour," I tell her with a growl and she nods looking relieved.

"Right, well, Peter is busy. Although, I am sure he would love the company. Little shit tried to rope me into helping him," she chuckles. I nod, making my way down to the graveyard.

CHAPTER
THIRTY-FIVE

I VY

It takes me a good few minutes to spot Peter kneeling behind a huge headstone. Wandering over to him, he looks up when my shadow is cast over him.

"Ivy, I mean my Queen," he says, baring his neck to me.

"Ivy is fine," I tell him, and he lets out a breath.

"So can I help you with something?" he asks. I shrug, looking down at what he is doing. He is scrubbing and cleaning the headstones and removing the dead flowers.

"Want some help?" I ask.

He chews his lip before peering over the headstone and glancing at the castle. "Are you allowed?" he whispers, and I peer back over at the castle.

"Yes, I don't see why not," I shrug.

"Well, I am nearly done with this row. If you grab another bucket and brush, you'll also need a polishing rag," he says, showing me his tucked into his belt. Nodding, I turn and walk back toward the castle.

"In the laundry room, Ivy," he calls, and I nod, going in search of the cleaning supplies.

169

Retrieving what I need, I earn a few strange stares from those working in the laundry, but they say nothing or question me as I slip back out with everything. I make my way back to Peter, who is in the next row. He stands up, coming closer to me.

"Where do you want me?" I ask him, and he looks around.

"Um, well, you could start in the middle. Those are pretty old though and require more scrubbing, or there is the servant's cemetery over there," he says, pointing closest to the forest and castle. "Or the hunters and rebels' victims are the ones nearest the river."

"Hunters and rebels' victims?"

"Yes, most of those killed by rebel leaders Marissa and Darclay, Marissa was a rogue werewolf she killed the King's sister and that um, the royal family, they live, yeah I don't know hours out that-away," he says, pointing toward the forest. "Darclay, was the human head-hunter that recruited her," Peter rambles on, yet I am still stuck at the mention of my mother's name. Did Peter not know why the King kicked me out of the castle?

"How many are there?" I ask, looking out at the spanning field of graves.

"From the hunters? Though most kills came from Marissa, she would pretend to be a servant and then kill everyone while they were sleeping. Most of those are from her, about 211 last time I counted," he shrugs.

211! When I hear that all those lives had been lost, and because my mother was behind it all, I become sick to my stomach. I have to steady myself to keep from fainting.

"Yep, she was the worst Lycan serial killer in history," Peter says grimly.

"The King never got over it; he found his sister, and Marissa cut her unborn child out of her and mutilated him before stuffing him back in her womb. Well, that's what I heard anyway from Trey; he is one of the guards," he says, making me feel sick.

Peter then turns back to the grave he was cleaning and makes his way to the back. The first grave I come to belonged to a woman kneeling down. I set to work. When I finish hers, I move to the next and look across the rows; the weight of what my mother had done settles heavily on my shoulders.

I find it difficult to understand how the woman who raised and protected me could do such a thing to her own people. After turning back to the grave in front of me, I notice that it had the same last name as the woman's grave beside it. According to the birth and death date, it belonged to a child. Three months old, the child was barely given a chance to live. My heart breaks as I stare at the picture of the little angelic face on the headstone.

I had to accept the stark reality of my situation; I am the daughter of a serial killer. Bad blood runs through my veins. My hands are tainted by the blood of the woman who carried me. I scrub the grave and with all my might and clean it before moving on to the next and next. With each one, the pit of my stomach becomes deeper. The skin on my fingers is bleeding from the wind, and my hands are chapped from it. It is impossible for me to stop. I have to undo what she did to remove the taint she has marked on them. When I finish the row, I move on to the next and the next when suddenly feet stop beside me.

And I am caught off guard by a growl, and I forgot entirely that I hadn't checked in with Clarice. Looking around, I notice it is almost dark outside.

"My entire guard is out looking for you!" the King growls angrily. And I flinch at his words but don't stop, I need to clean them, need to fix what she did.

Kyson bends down, snatching the scrubbing brush from my hands. "Damn it, Ivy, look at your hands." Peering up at him, I snatch it back from him and turn back to the grave; *if I can just clean them all, it will undo it.* My mind is consumed with what she has done; I don't know what else to do, don't know how to take it back.

The King snatches the scrubbing brush and tosses it in the bucket. The water splashes outside the bucket and spills on me, and I see guards approaching.

"You didn't check in; Clarice is now in trouble for covering for you. Why are you out here? You disobeyed me," he snaps, bending down and gripping my arms. He shakes me.

Though, his actions don't affect me. Can't he see the blood on my hands? What she did? How it taints me, I need it off. I need to erase it, erase her. She doesn't deserve to be remembered, not after what she did. She was an imposter. The woman who raised me was a monster; I am the monster she gave life to.

"You're sunburnt; your skin is blistered," he hisses, trying to drag me toward the castle. I thrash, yanking out of his grip and staggering backward.

"Ivy!" he snaps, reaching for me as I grab the scrubbing brush. I can take it back; it will go away. I just need to clean them. His hand grips my arm, and the growl that leaves me makes him and everyone near me freeze.

"Ivy?" Kyson whispers, and I look up at him. How doesn't he see it? How can he stand looking at me when I am born of their blood shed?

"She killed them. I loved her, and she killed them. How could she love me and kill them?" I cry, my heart breaking at all the pain she has caused all these people. All the hurt from the years of torture made so much sense now. It was my punishment for being hers. Karma came back and took vengeance on Abbie and me. Everything that Abbie and I endured is because of what she did, because I am a monster created by a serial killer, and because I loved her when she didn't deserve love. I loved a monster, and I called her mom.

CHAPTER

THIRTY-SIX

KYSON

Clarice lied to me; she knew where Ivy was, but not once did Ivy check in like she was supposed to, which infuriates me.

"Where is she?" I snap at Clarice, and she seems to recoil in fear.

"Outside helping Peter," Clarice explains.

"I will deal with you when I get back," I say, turning toward my guards. "Fucking find her," I order them, and they take off.

"She isn't doing anything wrong, my King; she is only helping clean the graves," Clarice says in her defense. Hearing that only infuriates me further.

"You let the daughter of their killer, clean their graves. The disrespect, Clarice fucking think," I roar at her, and she narrows her eyes at me before pointing an accusing finger in my direction.

"You listen here Kyson, you may be King, but I have watched you grow, I helped fucking raise you, you do not speak to me like that." She jabs me in the chest with her finger. "That girl is not her mother and if you are too blind to see it, then you have no right being her mate," she snarls at me.

Clarice rarely gets angry at me but right now she is furious, so furious her canines have slipped out, as she fixes me with her glare. My fist smacks down on the bench beside us and she jumps but her glare doesn't waiver. This old woman is putting her foot out of line if she thinks she can speak to me this way.

"You are a bloody idiot. That girl has suffered enough. Stop punishing her for the crimes of her mother. She didn't kill Claire." Her words are like a physical blow, I growl at the mention of my sister's name, and I feel the urge to shift rush through every cell in my body, making my skin vibrate.

Turning on my heel, I walk out before I hurt the woman. She is right about helping raise me. Clarice was more my mother than my real one. She did most of the raising. She was my nanny since mum was always busy being Queen and ruling alongside Dad.

Walking outside, my men are all standing at the top of the grave-yard. Shoving past them, I growl when I don't see them grabbing her. Searching the rows, I find her at the very last one and stop beside her, I growl, and she looks up when I notice her hands. Her fingertips are bleeding, and she is covered in mud, the heat emanating off her skin I can feel even with the cool breeze. "My entire guard is out looking for you!" I growl angrily.

Taking the scrub brush from her hands, I snarl, "Damn it, Ivy, look at your hands." But she snatches it back from me, turning back to the grave. Snatching the scrubbing brush back, I toss it in the bucket. The water splashes against her, and I notice a few of the guards step closer. I glare at them, making them take a step back.

'Kyson!' Damian snarls through the mindlink.

'Quiet, you don't interfere when I am dealing with her,' I order back, ignoring his protests.

"You didn't check in; Clarice is now in trouble for covering for you. Why are you out here? You disobeyed me," I snap at her, bending down and gripping her arms. She turns to dead weight in my hands, so I shake her, her skin so hot it is making me angrier seeing how sunburnt she is.

"You're sunburnt; your skin is blistered," I growl at her. Trying to drag her toward the castle, but she starts thrashing and manages to yank out of my grip. "Ivy!" I snap at her disobedience, reaching for her about to toss her over my shoulder when Gannon and Damian move closer, and I growl at them.

"I'm not fucking hurting her, now step back," I order as she grabs the scrubbing brush and starts frantically scrubbing. She hiccups a sob, making me look at her.

"Ivy?" I whisper, and she looks up at me.

Ivy's eyes are bloodshot from crying, the whites now a deep shade of red. Tears streak down her cheeks, leaving tracks in the dirt and grime on her face. Her skin is sunburnt and blistered, her hands coated in dried blood. As she cries, her whole body shakes and her face contorts with grief.

However, it is her following words that make me realize something is wrong, I should have paid attention to the bond instead of my red-hot anger.

"She killed them. I loved her, and she killed them. How could she love me and kill them?" Ivy cries, looking at the graves before looking back at me. The scent of sweat and dirt mingles with the metallic tang of blood in the air. The smell of tears and anguish is also present, making the air heavy and suffocating. I swallow down the emotion that tries to choke me upon seeing her frantically scrub the skin off her fingers as she tries to clean the tombstones.

Clarice's words echo in my head. She is not her mother. Clarice is right. Her mother never shed tears over the lives she took. Ivy is not that sort of monster and the guilt on her face is proof of that. I don't know how to help her, looking at her like this, I can see the errors I made. Ivy is as much a victim as the rest of them, only she is a living one. She has to live with her mother's sins.

Kneeling down beside her, I grab her hands, dropping the scrubbing brush "You're not her," I whisper, looking into her cerulean blue eyes.

"I am, I am. She made me; can't you see?" Tears burn my eyes at seeing her so distraught as she holds her hands out to me like she can see their blood staining her.

"No, you aren't," I try to tell her, but she doesn't listen, rambling about having to take it back, that she needs to clean them, they need to be clean.

I look to Damian wanting to know what to do. He moves toward her before dropping beside her.

"My Queen, you need to come inside. It's not safe out here," Damian urges her, he tries to grab her arm but she growls at him and he puts his hands up.

"Please my Queen," he murmurs, trying to get her to go with him, but she doesn't move, intent on cleaning the other 50 or so graves in this row.

"Get me rag," I tell one of the guards.

"Sorry my King?" Dustin answers my request, and I look at him.

"I said get me rag," I tell him, taking the scrubbing brush from her fingers again and she reaches for it, her lips twisting into a snarl. I grip her wrist.

"Stop, I will clean it, but you need to stop," I whisper before sitting in front of the grave. I drag her closer, pulling her between my legs and grabbing the scrubbing brush that is almost down to the wood that holds it together.

Ivy has worn the bristles down from scrubbing and she tries to take it from me again, and I growl at her before locking my legs around her and using the calling to calm her. Though the moment I do she lashes out, hitting and clawing at me. I grunt as her hand comes in contact with my face, a furious growl leaves me, and Damian jumps to his feet when I pin her to the ground beneath me. Her chest rises and falls heavily and her eyes are glassy. She bucks beneath me, and I sigh heavily resting my head on her shoulder waiting for her to tire herself out beneath me.

"I will clean it, stop or I will force you inside," I warn her, and she stops thrashing. She breaks down beneath me, struggling to breathe through her gasping sobs. Seeing her like this breaks my heart, crushes the air from my lungs, and I pull back worried my weight on her will make her pass out as she has a panic attack. I sit up, pulling her into my lap and wrapping her legs around my waist to keep her off the hard ground before gripping her face in my hands.

"Breathe, Ivy," I urge, not wanting to use the calling on her, but if she doesn't breathe soon she'll give me no choice. "Breathe, I'll clean them, but I need you to breathe," I tell her, kissing her mouth. I pick up the scrubbing brush, letting my calling slip over her. I almost shatter and break down with her when I feel her press closer and take a gasping breath.

"Good girl," I whisper and she turns, watching me. She relaxes seeing me start scrubbing the tombstone. All of the guards have left us. "Take my shirt off," I tell her, but she is so out of it, she is barely able to follow instructions and I don't want to hurt by commanding her. I drop the brush and she reaches for it, but I grip her hands in one of mine. Using my other hand, I undo the buttons. She watches me, lulled by my calling as I remove it before draping it over. Letting her wrists go, I pull her arm through the sleeves before picking up the scrubbing brush.

A few minutes later, my guard returns with more buckets and scrubbing brushes. Dustin hands me a fresh scrubbing brush, taking his bucket to another grave when some of the kitchen staff also come out with Clarice, cleaning buckets in hand, and I grip Ivy's chin, forcing her to look at me.

"See, they will be cleaned," I tell her, pecking her lips, that are just as blistered as her skin. I turn her face so she can see all the guards and workers that have come to help.

"They aren't here for me, they're here for their Queen," I whisper to her.

"Where I should have been," I tell her, grabbing the scrubbing the fresh brush. It takes an hour for us to finish them but not one of my staff or guards stopped until we had cleaned every single one of them.

CHAPTER
THIRTY-SEVEN

K YSON

Ivy continues trying to help, but each time I just tuck her closer until, eventually, she gives up. Instead, she presses against my chest, listening to my calling for her and only moving when I pick her up and moved to the next gravestone. No one leaves until the last grave is cleaned. Only then did Ivy let me scoop her up in my arms to take her back to our quarters.

Climbing up the small hill, Clarice catches up to me. "I will make her something to eat," Clarice whispers as we walk up the hill through the graveyard. I nod to her and listen to Ivy hum the song that seems to comfort her. Over the last few days, I have heard her singing it or humming. She knows it word for word; she never gets a word wrong. The Kingdom's Anthem. I place her in her bedroom, telling Dustin to keep watch over her as I head across the castle to my old quarters.

I enter the room meant for the Princess Azalea. My sister worked so hard to set it up in the hopes we would find the missing girl. But we never did. She, like my sister and so many others, have long been dead.

Moving to the dresser, I pick up the silver jewelry box and open it. Removing the bracelet inside, I set it on the dresser before taking the small box back to the room, winding it up so Ivy can hear the song being played. Her song, the one she knows by heart. I wonder, briefly, if they used to place this to her at the orphanage.

When I walk into the room, I see her sitting huddled by the fire, shivering despite her skin being burned. I sit behind her, pulling her against me, placing the box in her hands, and opening the lid. The music starts, and she looks up at me, her brows furrowing before recognizing the tempo matched the song she sang.

"Where did you get this?" she asks, peering inside the box.

"Azalea's room," I answer, and she gasps, trying to pass it back, and I shake my head. "Have it, it's for you."

"No, no, take it," she says, placing it in my lap before standing and rushing off. I sigh, rubbing a hand down my face and quickly setting the box on the bookcase and going in search of her.

"Why would you give me that?" she sobs when I find her huddled under the clothes she had made a den out of.

"Because you like the song, and Azalea won't use it," I tell her, trying not to smile at her makeshift den. Knowing it is the werewolf side appearing suddenly, she frantically tries to place the clothes in order. Completely unaware, she continues building her den and has instinctively snuggled down inside it.

"You need a bath," I tell her while reaching for her, but she growls at me. Mumbling to herself and rearranging the clothes, she starts ripping more off the hangers.

"Bath now, then you can make your den on the bed; I am not sleeping on the floor," I tell her, and she stops looking at her hands and then looks around herself.

"I wasn't, I was..."

I can feel her confusion at her actions.

"You are, now come," I tell her, and she looks at the clothes she is shredding to pieces before blushing, having not realized. I know she deliberately fights her urges, and I swear she sometimes forgets I can feel her.

"Bath, then bed. Now come or do I need to make you?"

She seems confused, and I groan, grabbing her. Ivy snarls at me for removing her from her little sanctuary, biting into my arm and making me chuckle.

My laughter only enrages her as she bites me more brutally on the chest which makes me hiss at the sting. Her actions only amuse me, knowing she is acting on instinct and not of her conscious mind. She mauls me, her instincts taking over and eventually I gently pry Ivy's teeth from my arm, wincing at the pain. Blood trickles down my skin, staining my abs.

Ivy's eyes widen with panic as she realizes what she has done, her hands trembling as they reach out to touch the wound. I can see the struggle within her, the battle between her human self and the wild instincts of her wolf.

"Shh, it's alright," I say gently, cradling Ivy in my arms.

"I'm sorry," she whispers hoarsely, tears streaming down her face. "I don't want to hurt you."

I stroke her cheek, my thumb wiping away her tears. "I know you don't, Ivy." Panic and fear wash through the bond and I know she is worried about me punishing her.

"Deep breaths," I instruct softly, mirroring my words by taking slow, deliberate breaths myself. "In...and out."

We sit there together for what feels like an eternity, our breathing gradually synchronizing. The quietness of the room envelops us, broken only by the occasional sniffle from Ivy.

I manage to guide her towards the bathroom, careful not to exert too much force. The sound of running water fills the air as I fill the bathtub, adjusting the temperature to a soothing warmth. Ivy hesitates at the edge of the tub, her gaze fixed on the water as if it holds some hidden danger.

She won't let me bathe with her, so instead, I shower, watching her while she bathes. By the time she gets out, I can smell the food

Clarice had placed in the room. We dress quickly, and I have to lock the closet door to stop her from going back in there. "No, you promised me," I remind her, and she mutters something before she reluctantly climbs into bed.

Grabbing the tray, I set it between us though I am surprised when she picks up the raw meat, which I know Clarice had made for me, seeing as I am Lycan, and we prefer our meat raw. We can eat all sorts of foods, nothing off limits, but primarily I prefer raw meat. Lycan are carnivorous. We have adapted over time but some things always remain the same. Instinct isn't entirely gone despite the modern times.

However, I have never seen Ivy pick up raw meat. I watch her, finding it rather disturbing to see a werewolf eat it as they are part human. Lycans are more animal than person, and there was a time when we never used our human forms. It is only with the change in era and modern day technology and the human hysteria that we find ourselves more inclined to our human-looking side. At some point, it became safer and easier to blend in. Eventually and fortunately for us, humans forgot our existence and we became a mere myth.

So to see Ivy eating raw meat disturbs me, although I don't try to stop her. Yet, she is acting out of sorts, making me wonder if the calling has had some strange effect on her, putting some of my Lycan traits onto her. Nevertheless, I say nothing, just glad she is actually eating. Now I just have to wait for her to fall asleep to heal her a bit. She won't let me touch her more than slight brushes or when I manage to force her to accept my touch. However, I figure it best not to push my luck with her odd behavior and the meltdown earlier.

When Clarice knocks on the door, I grab the now-empty tray and walked over to the door, opening it, and gave it to her.

"Hungry, my King?" Clarice asks, and I peer back at Ivy, who is attacking my pillow like it is a threat in her sleep.

"No, Ivy was," I tell her, and she seems taken aback, pulling a funny face before looking in the door toward the bed.

"Maybe she is going into heat?" she asks though I can tell even she isn't sure.

"I thought?" Clarice doesn't finish and shakes her head. "Right, I will leave you to it. It has to be the heat only thing that makes sense," she murmurs, walking off and muttering to herself.

Shutting the door, I walk back over to the bed and climb in, thinking to myself. She has had no appetite for days. Yet at the prospect of raw meat, it seems she can't get enough.

My brows furrow as I glance down at her tucked into my side. Yet if she is going into heat, what does that mean for both of us when she won't let me touch her, and does that mean she will soon shift? The heat isn't just agony for a she-wolf, but with me being Lycan, I will go into it with her, which I have heard is just as painful. Lycan males react to pheromones, and it is maddening when we smell a heat ravaged female, but since she is my mate, it will be pure agony for me just like her until I knot her and if I don't it can become dangerous, the mate bond could turn lethal when she is in heat.

With so many thoughts running through my head, I struggle to sleep. Eventually, I am sucked into the oblivion of rest only to wake up to realize Ivy has shut the alarm off. Squinting at the brightness in the room, it must be late in the morning, and I sit up in a panic looking for her.

"Ivy?" I sing out, tossing the blanket back and heading for the bathroom. She isn't in there and I rip open the closet checking her den. Also not there.

She isn't in the room. With a growl, I search all the adjacent rooms before leaving it entirely, furious that she left it without telling me.

"Where is Ivy?" I ask the guard by the doors leading out.

"I haven't seen her, my King; I thought she was in her room with you; I only just came on shift," he answers.

I shake my head. How had she managed to slip past the guards once again?

"Find her," I snarl, and everyone in the corridors scatters taking off in search of her. I push out the front doors spotting Peter.

"Peter!" I call, seeing him come toward me up the path from the stables. He glances at me before looking away at my state of undress; I had my sleep shorts on, yet my chest is bare.

"Where is Ivy?" I demand and he turns pointing back the way he came.

"She's helping me in the stables," he says, and I growl, which makes him run off as I stalk toward the path fuming when panic rushes through the bond, and I start running.

THIRTY-EIGHT

IVY The morning light filtering in through the drapes wakes me up early. Kyson is snoring softly beside me and I sit up, he stirs in his sleep rolling toward me and I hold my breath. His heavy arm draped over my waist makes me glance down, and I quietly and slowly slip out from beneath the blanket and his arm.

Moving around the room, I find some clothes when his alarm sounds, my heart races as I run toward his phone, my fingers tapping the screen trying to shut it off.

I suck in a breath when the loud beeping stops, and my eyes dart to him on the bed. He has rolled but is thankfully still asleep. Setting the phone down, I carefully slip out the door before he can lock me away in the room or him. I'm sick of being cooped up inside all the time, it is driving me insane. How does he not see that his actions are driving me to the brink of insanity, his mood swings not helping in the slightest.

I am excited at the prospect of having a morning to myself, perhaps helping Clarice in the kitchens. I make my way down to the kitchens when Peter, the stable boy, enters and stops by the counters. He keeps shoving his fringe out of his green eyes as he wanders into the kitchens.

"Clarice, is Gannon or Dustin around? I need help moving the barrels from the shed into the barn."

"Barrels?" Clarice asks questionably, entering the room, and Peter sighs.

"Yeah, the empty wine barrels. Jamie wants me to cut them in half so he can make garden beds out of them, but I need to cut them and paint them first," he says with a huff, clearly not liking being given extra chores by the gardener.

"Do it in the shed," Clarice tells him with a shrug.

"Can't, there is not enough room; it's full of the furniture from the east wing," he whines.

"Well, you will have to go look for them. I have no idea where either of them..."

"I can help," I offer, cutting her off. Being outside sounded great, and Clarice hardly let me do anything to help besides peel potatoes, saying I shouldn't even be helping. However, with Abbie gone, I am constantly bored and I still haven't forgiven the King for marking me or healing me while I slept. I also hate that he used the calling on me to force me to submit the other night.

"The King will pitch a fit if he finds you in the stables working," Clarice says.

"Let him, I am helping Peter," I tell her, and Peter's eyes light up at the offer of help.

"Ivy, he will lose his mind if you get hurt," Clarice says, grabbing my hand gently.

"It's fine, Clarice; I will deal with the King if needed," I growl, grabbing Peter's arm and tugging him out the door.

"Are you sure, my Queen? I don't want you to get in trouble," Peter asks nervously as he sucks his lip between his teeth.

"Yes, I want to go outside anyway, I'm sick of watching people work and not letting me help," I tell him, dragging him through the castle. I know the king is still asleep, so I don't have to worry about him sending someone to look for me for a few hours anyway.

A few hours pass, and we manage to create enough room to drag the old wine barrels out, then we restack the shed, making it more accessible in the future. I watch as Peter cuts the wine barrels with a chainsaw by the stables. Peter won't let me try because he is too worried the King will be angry if he finds out, so I just watched. He does, however, let me help paint them.

When we finish, Peter heads up to see the gardener so he could let him know that we are just waiting for the paint to dry when I hear a loud squawking, which causes me to look toward the pier that extends over the lake from the stables.

My brows furrow at the noise when I hear it again, making me rise to my feet. Peering toward the peer the only thing I see moving is something flapping, so I suspect it is a bird.

I step cautiously onto the wooden pier and nervously glance at the blackened water beneath it as I move to the end. Upon reaching the end, I notice a beautiful swan flapping his wings frantically and squawking in the water as it tries to fly away. It appears to be caught in something, as every time it tries to take flight, it's pulled under once more. I move to help the poor, helpless creature.

I call out to Peter, but he is nowhere to be found. So I drop to my knees hoping to be able to reach it. Holding firmly onto the wooden pier with one hand, I reach my other hand out to grab the swan by the neck in an attempt to pull it closer. The bird seems to be caught in some netting or something. The creature shrieks and flaps its wings as it tries to free itself, and my fingertips graze the surface of its face and snapping beak. The bird flaps more frantically at my touch, causing its wing to become further stuck. I lean over more, attempting to save it once again before it gets dragged under. "Stop flapping," I growl at the silly swan.

I am in the process of grabbing the feathers of its back end when my weight and angle overbalance me. I scream, tumbling into the blackened water.

I frantically kick back to the surface, my arms flailing as I try to grip the pier has quickly become way out of reach. Panicking, I tangle myself in the mesh netting that the swan is trapped in and am pulled under. Water burns my nose and as I sputter for air.

When I breach the surface, I sputter and choke on the water as the swan flails frantically and takes off.

"Peter!" I rasp, screaming as loud as my burning throat allows.

"Peter!" I try to scream as my legs become more tangled. Desperately, I stretch my arm out to reach for the pier, only to be pulled further down.

I can feel myself being dragged under by the weight of what I am caught on. I choke on the water as it spills into my mouth, filling my lungs, and I know I am drowning. As my effort begins to die out, calm sweeps over me. It is an odd sensation. I know that I am dying, yet I feel an overwhelming sensation of peace fall over me and I sink further, the surface darkening when I hear a loud splash.

My eyes flutter as ripples in the water steal my attention and suddenly an arm wrapping tightly around my waist as I am dragged toward the surface.

The moment I breach the surface, the pain hits. Hands grip my waist, and I am hauled upright, gasping for breath, only to be ripped back under because my feet are still tangled in the netting. While I attempt to blink through the murky water, my eyes sting while someone untangles the mesh from around my legs. The moment we breach the surface, I panic, sputter, cough, and lock my legs around their waist.

As I shove him under, he coughs and splutters on the water, when a furious growl rips from his throat, and I am turned so I won't be able to push him beneath the surface again. Kyson wraps his arms across my chest and pulls my back to his chest.

"Calm down before you drown us both," he snaps at me while I suck in much-needed air. My lungs feel like they have been put through mincer-like razors slicing through my chest with each agonizing breath.

CHAPTER
THIRTY-NINE

I VY

As I struggle to catch my breath, I see guards running in our direction down the steep hill leading from the castle. I peer around frantically, still feeling disoriented and unsure if I'm completely out of the water.

"I'm going to turn you around. Don't push down on me," Kyson growls, and I can feel the movement of his legs behind me as he treads water. He turns me around, and my legs wrap around him, and he grabs them, pulling me up higher.

He sighs, pressing his head against mine, and my teeth chatter.

"What were you doing in the water when you can't swim!" he demands angrily.

"I was trying to help the swan!" I retort and he stares at me dumbfounded.

"Why would you risk your life for a fucking swan?" he demands, his grip tightening, a manifestation of his barely contained fury.

"The swan was tangled," I manage to say, my voice hoarse from coughing.

"You nearly drowned for a swan?" His voice is thick with disbelief and outrage.

"I slipped!" I retort, my fingers digging into his shoulder with a mix of fear and anger. He floats onto his back, effortlessly treading water. The guards on the hill, having halted their approach, still watch us intently until the king dismisses them with a wave. He growls, swimming further out into the lake, his movements fluid and confident.

"How can you not swim?" he mutters, more to himself than to me, shaking his head in disbelief.

As he moves further out, I reluctantly loosen my grip on him. "Just get me out of here if you're going to berate me! I nearly drowned, you don't need to be an asshole about it," I snap, my patience fraying.

He stops abruptly, his piercing gaze locking onto mine. "What did you just call me?" he growls, the dangerous edge in his voice sending a shiver down my spine.

I bite my lip, avoiding his gaze, but he's insistent, capturing my chin in his hand and forcing me to meet his eyes.

"Ivy," he says, a warning clear in his tone.

I swallow hard, indignancy replacing my fear. "I called you an asshole," I admit, my voice small. I sigh, rubbing my face. "Look, I'm sorry, it just slipped out" His eyes soften slightly but the hard lines don't disappear completely.

He stares at me for a moment before breaking silence, his voice an angry growl. "You do not speak to me like that, I am your King!" he snarls, his canines slipping out. My own anger rises, I scoff, a maniacal laugh in my tone.

"You are not my King. In fact, you're supposed to be my mate and all you do is fucking yell at me and order me around. You should have let me fucking drown if you were going to be a..." I grit my teeth when he growls. The man makes my blood boil, and tears spring in my eyes.

For a moment, we are locked in a silent battle of wills. Then, unexpectedly, his expression softens, the anger giving way to something more complex. A flicker of guilt passes over his features, and he sighs, the tension in his shoulders easing.

"I'm sorry," he murmurs, the words seemingly foreign to him. "I shouldn't have reacted that way."

His apology catches me off guard, and I stare at him in shock.

He pulls me closer, our bodies almost touching in the water, his muscles rippling under my hands. "Let me teach you to swim," he suggests, his voice gentle. I hesitate, then shake my head.

"You should know how to swim Ivy," he reminds me as he swims backward pulling me with him. I freak out when I am dragged on my stomach. My legs instantly wrap back around him and he sighs, moving upright again and treading water. His hands move to my thighs under my dress, rubbing gently.

"Unwrap your legs."

I shake my head, my legs gripping him tighter.

"Ivy," he urges.

"It's too late to teach me to swim, that's something kids learn," I tell him.

"Nonsense, now unwrap your legs. I won't let you drown, I'm right here," he says, his lips brushing my cheek gently.

"Please don't make me order you, you should know this, Ivy, let me teach you," he murmurs. Reluctantly, I untangle my legs from him, and he sighs. "Now put your arms around my neck," he orders, and I do as he says. He grips my waist tightly and kicks off, propelling us forward through the water. His arms encircle me, and he starts to move up and down, my legs dangling loose. As he moves against me, the fabric of my dress shifts slowly upwards, covering his chest.

"Relax," he murmurs in my ear, and I attempt to copy his movements. It doesn't work at first but gradually, I find the rhythm until I feel more comfortable. Kyson smiles down at me "See, you're doing great."

I blush, scarlet, as he continues teaching me how to swim while the sun beats down on us.

Despite my embarrassment and initial anger, it feels nice having him this close to me. Soft ripples stretch out around us

He guides my movements, his hands supportive under my body. "Kick your legs like this," he instructs, his tone patient and encouraging.

I mimic his movements, and to my surprise, I find myself floating. Laughter bubbles up inside me.

"Good girl, you're doing great," he praises, and there's a warmth in his words that makes my heart flutter unexpectedly. Kyson pulls me closer. Wrap your legs around me again for a second. I do as he says when he suddenly grabs my dress pulling up.

"Kyson!" I clutch it.

"No one can see you, but your dress is weighing you down," he murmurs, and I glance around to find the guards nowhere in sight. "See, I ordered them away," he tells me and I look at him. He peels the dress off before moving closer to the pier and tossing the dress on it. I try to cover my breasts.

"Move your hands, I've seen you naked, don't shy away from me," he murmurs.

Reluctantly, I drop them and he keeps his gaze trained on mine. He shows me how to move my arms, his hands guiding mine through the water. Our eyes often meet, and in those glances, I see a flicker of something tender, something that makes my breath catch.

As we continue, our proximity remains close, his body occasionally brushing against mine. Each touch sends a jolt of awareness through me, and I find myself increasingly conscious of him — not just as the king, but as a man.

Suddenly, Kyson takes my hand and tugs me towards him, pulling me onto his lap. I straddle his hips, feeling the hardness of his erection against my lower stomach. My eyes widen, but he doesn't let go, instead wrapping his arms around me. "Relax," he whispers.

His skin is warm against mine despite the cool water, and it sends shivers up my spine. Slowly, I relax into him, allowing myself to melt into his embrace as he teaches me how to synchronize my movements properly.

The water laps at us gently as we move together, and I feel the rhythm of our breathing begin to match. He leans in and kisses my forehead

He stops swimming and treads water, pulling me closer to him. My heart races as I look up at him with wide eyes. His eyes roam over my face, his fingers tracing the line of my jaw before cupping my cheek softly. "You're beautiful," he whispers, his voice low and deep.

His touch is firm but gentle at the same time; it's almost hypnotic how easily he guides me through each stroke as if we're one being moving together fluidly across the water's surface. We spend hours like this, just swimming when he suddenly pulls my hands from his shoulders when we are halfway to the other side. I freak out, kicking and trying to reach him as the king moves. He smiles before standing up.

I huff, thinking I am drowning when I realize the water here is only knee-deep, and my face heats at my idiocy. Kyson laughs at my embarrassed face, and I splash him.

"This side is shallow," he chuckles before bending down and grabbing me.

"You let me sleep in and left the room without me," he growls before sitting in the water and pulling me into his lap.

"You wouldn't let me go if I had," I say, to which he nods but says nothing. He grips my chin gently with his fingertips, tilting my face toward his. The calling washes over me, and I sigh instead of fighting against it as he leans closer, his lips molding around mine. Turning my face away, he growls before gripping my chin tighter and forcing my mouth open so he could kiss me. His tongue sweeps over my lip before he nibbles on my bottom one, becoming cranky when I don't answer his kiss.

"Stop fighting it," he snarls, breaking my soft skin when he bites a little harder. I wonder how he could stand to touch me after the horrible things my mother did. I wanted the bond before he broke it, and now I no longer feel worthy of it. The King sighs before pecking my lips.

"Why are you fighting the bond, it's driving me insane," he mutters more to himself than me.

"You broke our bond," I remind him.

"And I am trying to fix it, but you won't allow it," he snaps. "Don't pretend you can't feel it, I know you can," he warns, and I grip his shoulders to stand, only for him to pull me back down on him.

"Admit it," he tells me, and I glare at him. He watches me for a second.

"You can be so stubborn," he growls, and his hand moves to caress my ribs reminding me about my lack of clothes, his gaze roams down my skin heat under its intensity when his hand cups my breast gently making me gasp. "So beautiful," he murmurs, his thumb brushing over my hardened nipple.

"You tempt me then refuse me," he frowns at his words and I look away from him when he sighs, his lips press to my temple gently.

"We should head inside; I have meetings this afternoon," he whispers, and I nod. The King stands, picking me up with him, his hand caresses down my back gently as walks toward the pier. He picks up my dress, wrings it out before helping me pull it on, then walks me back toward the castle, and I shiver at the coldness of the breeze caressing my skin.

We make our way upstairs to our room, and I go to run a bath. Goosebumps cover my skin, and the cold starts to sink into my bones when the King comes up behind me.

"No, you shower with me," he says, gripping my hip. I go to protest when he grabs my hip tighter, tugging me back against him, his other hand going to my throat as he dips his face into the crook of my neck. He purrs. My eyes flutter shut before I shake my head, fighting against the urge to give in to him.

"You shower with me," he repeats before his lips cover mine, our tongues tangling, and his hand moves from neck to my breast as he squeezes it.

"Stop fighting the bond, Ivy. Let it reforge. Why do you keep fighting it?" he murmurs against my lips.

I resist the urge to scoff at him. How could he ask that? He shouldn't want the bond, not with me anyway. He growls, nipping at my lips. The calling washes over me like a tidal wave before I can resist it or struggle to stamp the urges down. I bite him, and he groans, my teeth raking down his flesh, and I know it is his doing, know he's using it against me. And I hate him for it.

"Don't fight me, and I won't use it," he mumbles, picking up my anger as I sink my teeth into his chest and bite him. Kyson moves, spinning me around and shoving me into the sink basin, his hands gripping my hips as he places me next to the sink.

The King presses himself between my thighs, his erection throbbing against me, and he groans while I try to shove him away. The calling grows more potent, and tears prick my eyes when he grips my hair as he tugs my head back. His tongue invades my mouth, and I moan into his mouth, the bond pulling to the surface as he forces it out.

A whimper escapes me as I tug him closer, my claws slipping free and scratching down his chest. Needing him, arousal floods into me, making my pussy clench. My entire body is buzzing from the bond in anticipation. His hand moves between my legs, and he rubs my throbbing core, my arousal spilling onto my thighs. All too soon, he pulls away, making me growl.

"You don't leave without telling me," he purrs, and I nod, anything to get his touch back. I reach for him, and he leans down and pecks my lips, the bond forcing my hands to his chest, needing his touch, wanting it, and craving him. He then pulls away and turns the shower on. I stare at his back as he removes his clothes, glaring at him that he riled me up and used the calling on me to force out the bond and then stop as soon as I answer it.

"In the shower," Kyson says while stepping under the water. I growl at him, stalking out of the bathroom and going to my closet. I hear him protest but ignore him, embarrassed that he tormented me that way, and I let him.

"Ivy, don't make me come get you," Kyson calls out, and I snarl before burrowing inside my den, seething at what he did. He will pay for that; he had caught me off guard. I won't let it happen again.

"Ivy!" he growls, and I reach up, locking the closet door.

CHAPTER
FORTY

K YSON

Ivy is driving me up the wall. I can't even kick the damn door down because I don't know if she is directly behind it or not. All night I wait, and damn, does she test my patience. I am back to swallowing the amber liquid, letting it scorch the back of my throat while I glare at the door.

I move off the bed and away from my stare off with the closet door separating us. I meander toward the small bar area in the corner, growling and muttering under my breath as I pour the last remnants from the bottle into my glass.

Her discomfort is beginning to make me nervous, her scent growing stronger as it permeates from under the door. Grabbing my glass, I move back toward the bed, pausing for a second by the bookshelf. My eyes move over the shelves before spotting the book we were reading before everything turned to shit. Moving the small jewelry box off the shelf, I accidentally drop it. The lid cracks open and the music starts playing. Bending down, I scoop the small box off the ground when I notice an engraving on the side of it. The inscription is small in the back corner of the tiny box.

Azalea. I. Landeena.

12.3.2004

Love Mum & Dad.

My brows furrow, and I glance over at the door. Ivy and Azalea share the same birthday. Shaking my head, I place the box back before looking back at the door and grabbing the book off the shelf before moving to sit by the door, and she growls, sensing my presence. I open it up to where the ribbon lay between the pages before reading aloud. Her growls and snarls quiet, and after about five minutes, I hear her move within the confines of her closet and makeshift den.

I know she's cozy, yet I can also sense her discomfort at being there. It is a weird sensation to feel from her. Almost as if it is her safe place, but also a place that torments her. Her emotions fluctuate between peace and panic, and I know she is claustrophobic. I have witnessed her distress not only through the bond when she made her den the last time, but also saw it for myself. Yet as much as she hates the closet, it is almost as if she fears the outside world past the door or maybe just me, which makes me shift uncomfortably.

Eventually, all noises stop inside the closet, and I can hear her heart pounding as she draws nearer to listen to what I'm saying. My purr reverberates around the room, echoing off the walls as I call her to come to me. Her anger and fear amplify as she fights an invisible war within herself. As she fights against my calling, I tone it down a little, giving her the choice to fight it or answer it, while still encouraging her to come to me. However, reading simultaneously is also a little tricky trying to maintain both tasks. Coughing, I take a sip of my drink, resting my head back against the wall.

"If you come out, I will read to you," I tell her. She doesn't answer straight away. When she does, it isn't the answer I am hoping for.

"No, you will use the bond against me," she growls.

"You are my bond Ivy," I tell her, turning my head to look at the door handle. I twist it, but she still hasn't unlocked it.

"Don't you want the bond?" I ask her, wondering how she can

fight so hard against it and refuse me when I am hers as much as she is mine.

"You broke it," she says, and the sadness through the bond stings me.

"And I am trying to fix it," I reply, closing my eyes as I lean my head back.

"It wasn't just yours to break," she states.

"And I said I am trying to fix it," I repeat.

"And what if I don't want you to?"

"It's not up to you; I told you already. You are mine; I meant that Ivy, I won't let you go again," I tell her, becoming annoyed that she dares to challenge our bond. I don't understand what she wants. She wanted the bond. I broke it, and now I am trying to fix it. What more does she want from me? I can't go and take everything I did back.

"Until you find something else to hate me for or I do something you don't like, then you will cast me aside because you can, and there is nothing I can do about it," she murmurs. "You hurt me," she whispers so softly I nearly missed it.

"I didn't mean to break your hand, Ivy; I didn't know it was there," I snap at her. I bloody healed it, for god sake.

"I'm not talking about my hand, Kyson. I know you didn't do that on purpose."

I growl, annoyed, shaking my head.

"You think broken bones hurt? Scratches, wounds that refuse to heal for months on end. They hurt, but they also mend when the skin closes over. After that you're left with a scar, a distant memory of what was once painful. Yet that hurt ends," she pauses, and I pick up my glass, draining the last of it about to break the handle and drag her out, tired of playing these games of hide and seek. Standing, I go to grab the handle when she speaks again.

"Do you have any idea how humiliating it is to allow yourself to trust someone, let them see every dark ugly piece of you only for them to throw it in your face?"

I paused, wondering what she is on about now.

"Are you going to finish, or are you going to make me guess?" I ask her, gripping the door handle; the metal creases as my grip tightens around the brass knob.

"I trusted you; I allowed myself to love you despite knowing better than to get my hopes up."

She takes a moment's pause, perhaps waiting for me to answer. When I don't, she continues.

"Mrs. Daley taught me to know my place, and you made me believe I could find that with you. That I was free to choose that place." Her words sting. I know I messed up but I never would've thought she'd compare me to Mrs. Daley, the woman who tormented her for years.

"Freedom. My version of freedom for years was death. I was ready to die on that podium that day, ready to be set free. I was convinced it would be better than the life handed to us. Then you showed me another sort of freedom."

I take my hand off the door handle, figuring it's better to let her finish.

"I realized I was never living. We were already dead, and then you gave us our names back, and our lives back, for a while anyway. Then just as quickly as you gave it to me, you took it away. The ultimate puppet master with a god complex that I can't compete against."

"Ivy," I say, her name coming out as a choked whimper.

"No, Kyson. You took it, you made me wish for freedom again. I wished that you would have left me to die that day; it would have been a more humane thing to do than give me hope only to show me how foolish it was to have it in the first place."

My heart twists painfully in my chest as I feel the truth behind the words she speaks.

"Now that is pain, and nothing haunts me more than knowing you have the power to send me back to a place that the only freedom I will long for is death."

I bite my tongue and swallow, feeling guilty. "I made a mistake. I blamed you because you were there to blame, not because you did anything wrong. I see that now," I tell her.

"I get why you hate me Kyson; I am the by-product, the spinoff version of my mother..."

"You are not your mother," I tell her, cutting her words off. That much, I am sure of. Ivy laughs, and my brows furrow.

"My mother was a monster. Therefore, I am."

"No, you were just her last victim, only you survived to live with what she took from you," I tell her. She falls quiet. Yet, I mean what I'm saying and only wish she could see that.

"You have your freedom with me, Ivy," I tell her.

"No, you give the illusion of freedom, Kyson. You give false promises, you built me up, only to then show me how beneath you I truly am."

"No, Ivy, that is not what I am doing, just open the door please," I beg, a note of desperation in my voice.

"I should have died on that podium; at least it would have been quick and final. Instead, you showed me the glimpse of what living could be, teasing me with a hope I'd have rather not known. I'd rather have died without ever longing for something I'd never truly have."

"And what is that Ivy?" I dare to ask.

"Happiness, you let me taste it, let me put all of mine into you, only to show me how easily you could take it away."

"That was never my intention, I was blinded by my anger Ivy. I don't want to take your freedom," I tell her, pressing my forehead against the door.

"Prove it," she murmurs. I sigh, wanting her to come out, to stop ignoring me because it is driving me insane. It takes every fiber of my being to ignore my own instincts to drag her out, kicking and screaming and forcing her to submit to the bond.

I sit back down and let her be, instead, picking up the book and continuing to read to her. She falls quiet, and after a few chapters, I hear the door unlock, making me look at it before the handle twists. Her scent wafts to me as the door cracks open. Before I can muffle it, the calling slips out, my purr resounding yet not forcing her, leaving her choice, just enough to coax her out if she chooses. Letting her know I mean no harm, so I let it be instead of stifling the sound. I hear her bones cracking from lying on the hard ground and feel the ache to go to the comfy bed.

Glancing up at her, I see she has an armful of my clothes, her werewolf side reappearing stronger no matter how much she fights against it. At least she has changed out of the wet clothes and is now wearing one of my shirts. The bond is reforging and solidifying despite her attempts to ignore it.

"You can take them to the bed, or you could let me sleep next to you," I tell her, and she walks part way to the bed before stopping and glancing between the bed and me like she is fighting against what she knows she needs and wants. Her urges are all over the place. I remain still as much as it kills me to do so.

"You won't use the calling on me, I mean no more than you are now?" she asks, and I can feel her uncertainty. I wouldn't tell her this, but I also know she hates the calling as much as she likes it. Mostly because she doesn't understand it. Sure, she sees the barbaric side of it, but doesn't realize that more often than not, I can't even control it myself. It's a natural instinct to soothe your mate when they're distressed. The bond forces it, drawing off her energy. Sure, there are plenty of ways to abuse it but at base, it's instinctual.

"No, but I can't help it sometimes. It reacts to your emotions," I tell her. Ivy chews her lip and nods once before moving toward the bed again. She climbs in, dragging my pile of clothes with her to burrow down in. I sigh before turning the next page, expecting to sleep on the couch when she speaks.

"You can sleep in the bed," she says, and my eyes flit to hers. I can sense her heart rate picking up. My skin ripples as I stand, feeling a surge of excitement that she's finally letting me close to her. Grabbing the book, I crawl in beside her and reopen it, ready to keep reading. Ivy moves closer, her claws scraping down my ribs as she wiggles closer, to see the tiny pictures in the corners of the pages. Fighting the urge to drag her on top of me, I continue reading, content enough with her beside me.

CHAPTER
FORTY-ONE

I VY

I awake to whispers reaching my ears. Groggily rolling over, I look toward Kyson who is standing by the door. Beta Damian's scent wafts to me, so I know he must be in the room. Stretching, my back cracks as I yawn. That was the best sleep I had had in days, waking up and feeling rested. Sitting up, I notice the King has the jewelry box in his hands, and I tilt my head better to listen to what they are speaking about.

"Find me anything on Azalea, everything you can find," Kyson says to Damian, his tone urgent and serious. I feel my brows pinch together, wondering what he wants with a child who has ben long dead. . My stomach drops, wondering what he's trying to dig up. *Is he looking for more reasons to hate me?* I wonder.

"Something isn't right, and she..." Kyson shakes his head. "Something doesn't add up," he tells Beta Damian, looking over his shoulder at me. Beta Damian takes the box from him.

"I'll see what I can find out," Damian tells him, and the King nods before shutting the door. He turns to face me before wandering over to the coffee table and retrieving a tray of food and placing it on my lap. I stare down at the steak and salad before he grabs his own tray and comes to sit by me.

"What was that about?" I ask casually as he takes his seat.

"I need him to look into something, eat your lunch," he says before cutting into his steak. His steak is bleeding while mine looks a bit more well done. My mouth salivates hungrily, my belly rumbling. Though I am a little shocked to learn, it is already the middle of the day. I cut into my steak and pop a piece into my mouth. The hunger instantly dies down, no longer wanting to eat as I force myself to chew and swallow. The King watches me curiously as I try not to be rude and spit the meat out onto the plate. Forcing it down is like trying to swallow an apple whole as it lodges in my throat.

"Can I call Abbie?" I ask him, and he nods.

"After you eat," he says, inclining his head toward the plate. I scrunch my nose up at it. Ever since finding out he is my mate; I swear my taste buds have changed. Stuff I usually like no longer holds any appeal to me. Everything *feels* different, yet I still haven't shifted. It makes me wonder if all these changes were really for the better.

"I'm not hungry," I say, placing the plate on the bedside table, and I move to get up. Kyson growls in response, cutting a piece of his own steak before offering the fork to me, holding it to my lips. The same thing happens; my mouth waters instantly, making me wonder why his food smells different. It is hardly cooked, if you could call it cooked at all, more like seared on either side and practically raw. Yet I open my mouth and almost moan at the taste, my appetite coming back despite tasting the blood filling my mouth as I chew. *How odd,* I think. I had *never* enjoyed raw meat in the past.

Reaching for my plate, the King places it on his lap before giving me his. "Eat," he says, tapping my plate with the fork. My brows furrow as I look at the plate. Kyson also looks rather disgusted by my own well-done steak, but says nothing other than encouraging me to keep eating. .

"All of it," the King says when he finishes his, leaving only the salad. The steak is huge, and I am struggling to eat the entire thing after getting through half of it. I force another mouthful down, my stomach full but my tastebuds savoring the taste. I watch the King pull his phone from his pocket and scroll through it.

"I can't eat anymore," I say while trying to cut through another. Kyson looks up from his screen before staring at the half-eaten steak and sighs.

"You hardly ate anything yesterday. Eat half of it, and then you can call her," he says and I glare at him. A growl emanates from me, and he arches an eyebrow at me.

"Ivy!"

"I will eat two more pieces. I can't eat much more. You will make me sick," I snap at him.

"Three."

"One!" I retort and he sighs.

"Fine, two more mouthfuls then," he growls, turning his attention back to the phone. I quickly eat, wanting to speak to Abbie. It feels like a lifetime ago since I heard her voice, the longest we've ever gone without speaking. When I finish, I snatch the phone from his grip. He growls at me but takes my plate, setting it back on the tray and placing it out the door before coming back to sit by me, looking over my shoulder as I scroll through the letter A's. Yet some of the names have similar spelling which confused me.

"No, back up," the King says, clicking on her name for me. "You can video call her."

"What's that?" I ask, listening to the phone ring. He takes it from me, pressing a button, and the screen changes, and I can see myself on the screen.

"Now, you will be able to see her if she can figure out how to turn her camera on. Gannon did show her, so hopefully she remembers," Kyson says. The phone rings, and I glance at Kyson, who sits up. He dials her number again, sitting up before passing it back to me.

When she doesn't answer again, he takes the phone from me, leaning against the headboard. He opens something else on his phone and types away. I peer over to see what he is doing, watching as he types quickly.

"I messaged her mate," Kyson says, before patting the spot between his legs, wanting me to sit there.

"What did you say?" I ask him.

"Come, I will show you," he says, and I roll my eyes but crawl into his lap. He presses his lips to my shoulder and pulls up his messages.

FORTY-TWO

IVY

"I need to teach you how to read. Try and read that," he says, and I peer at the screen in concentration. I recognize Abbie's name this time, and I recognize the letter's but can't make sense of how they fit together.

"I can tell Abbie's name," I answer, my face heating up that I am unable to do something that was so basic to others.

"Why. Isn't. Abbie. Answering. Her. Phone." Kyson says, pointing to the words. Kyson leans forward before reaching into his bedside drawer and pulling out a bigger phone.

"This is a tablet, like my phone, but bigger," he says before scrolling through it. "I had some reading apps put on it for you. It will help you identify different words. Kind of like a game. I want you to use this when you aren't doing anything but it also has a voice to text," he says, opening an app. He clicks on the little microphone picture in the center of the screen before speaking into the tablet.

"Kyson loves Ivy," he says, and the words he spoke flash across the screen before reciting them back to him in a robot voice.

"You can also type words into it, and it will read them to you.

Copy the text on my phone into it," he says, bringing up a small keypad on the screen. He hands me his phone, and I place the tablet on my lap before copying the letters when Kyson leans over my shoulder to peer at the screen.

"You need to put spaces between the words," he murmurs, his breath warm on my neck as it fans over me. I shiver involuntarily, and he purrs softly at my reaction.

"I don't know how," I tell him before he hits a long blank button on the keypad.

"That one. Now redo it," he says, deleting everything I just painstakingly typed into the screen. Remembering to use the space button this time, I type his text message again into the tablet. When I finish, Kyson presses the speech button, and the phone reads out what I wrote, and I smile that it said what Kyson read from his text message.

"Good, you will get the hang of it, and I will read to you at night, so you should pick it up quickly with some help." I glance at the bookshelf, since he finished reading *Treasure Island* last night. I am eager for him to read me another book.

His phone vibrates in my hand, and I glance at the small screen. "He is going to mindlink her to get her phone. He said he isn't with her right now, but they have the mindlink now that he has marked her," Kyson tells me, and I nod before typing his new message into the tablet to read it to me again while he watches behind me. A few minutes later, another message comes through.

"What does it say?" I ask him.

"Says to try her now," he answers before pulling me back against him and fiddling with his phone. It starts ringing, and he turns the camera thing on, and my face pops up on the screen along with the King's chest behind me. It rings a few times before she answers.

"Finally, you called," she squeals excitedly, though her face never pops up on the screen. Kyson has to talk her through how to do it before finally I get to see her. She cries excitedly, waving to me and gushing about how much she misses me.

"Where are you? You look like you're outside?" I ask her, looking at the scenery behind her.

"At the cabin, I was hanging out washing and didn't hear my phone. Plus, I ran out of credit. I have been trying to reach you for days; I have been so worried about you. Kade said the King caught you before you could get to the bridge," she says.

"And someone could have told me how to hang up, too. I rang the castle phone, but it went to some message machine and ate all my credit," she explains.

"Your mate hasn't put credit on it for you?" Kyson asks her over my shoulder. She squints at the screen, and her eyes widen. "Sorry, my King. I didn't see you in the background," she says, becoming a little nervous now she realized he is behind me.

"It's fine, Abbie; I'm not angry with you," Kyson tells her, and she chews her fingernail and nods but doesn't say much, knowing he is behind me. I sigh.

"So, do you like it there?" I ask her, and she shrugs.

"Yeah, it's not bad. He comes during the day, but it has been two days since I saw him last. He says he is always busy with work and sleeps there sometimes."

Kyson growls behind me, and I peek over my shoulder at him, but he shakes his head, and his hand goes to my stomach, tugging me back against him.

"What about the people in his pack? Do you like them? Did you make any friends?"

"I haven't met any of them yet, he said soon, but I need to stay inside first. He thinks I will go into heat soon because I keep getting the worst stomach cramps. I ask him to take me to see a pack doctor because I don't think it is that. My chest feels really tight, and it hurts. I actually thought I was having a heart attack last night. It's not just my stomach, and I feel fine on days when he does come here," Abbie says while she moves around. The King growls again, and I peer over at him, wondering why he is becoming so angry. After all, he gave me permission to talk to her.

"I like it other than that, but I am hoping he will take me to visit you soon. He promised I could," she tells me, and excitement bubbles in my stomach at the idea of seeing her.

"If he can't, Abbie, I will send Gannon to come and pick you up to bring you here," Kyson tells her.

"Really? I never got to say goodbye to Gannon; he walked off," she says excitedly, although I notice her face fall when she mentions Gannon's name.

"Yes, if he can't bring you here, I will send Gannon. I will put your phone on my plan, so you don't run out of credit too. That way, you can call Ivy whenever you like," Kyson tells her.

"Oh, oh, I hear a car. I think he is here." Abbie babbles excitedly. "I love you, but I have to go," she says.

"Love you too," I tell her.

"More than life," she says.

"More than life," I reply before she hangs up. With a sigh, I hand the phone back to him, and he glares at it.

"Everything okay?" I ask him, wondering why he is angry.

"Yes, it will be," he says, kissing my shoulder.

"I need to go speak with Gannon," he says abruptly, and I hop up, wanting to get out of the room myself.

"What are you doing?" the king asks when I also climb off the bed.

"Going to help Peter," I tell him.

"No, you aren't leaving...." he pauses before pinching the bridge of his nose.

"Just stay away from the water and take Dustin with you, please," he adds, coming over to me. He presses his lips to my forehead before taking my chin in his hands, gently forcing me to look up at him.

"Don't wander off," he says, and I nod. Not like I have anywhere to go anyway.

CHAPTER
FORTY-THREE

KYSON

I feel somewhat sick knowing Ivy isn't beside me where I can touch her and feel her warmth. So I resolve to stalk through the halls searching for Gannon, who oddly isn't answering the mindlink. Every cell in my body calls out to her, telling me to go back to my mate and covet her away from the rest of the world. However, I have to remember Ivy doesn't want that. At least not yet. I'm not even sure she wants me in any capacity, not after the heartache I caused her. One thing is becoming more evident to me, though. Her instincts are growing stronger, and I know she will soon shift. It is inevitable, and I am just waiting for it to happen.

'Where are you?' Damian rushes through the mindlink, making me halt my steps in the middle of the corridor.

'Looking for Gannon, I need to speak to him about Abbie,' I tell him, jogging down the steps toward his room.

'He's with me. Come to the office; it's important,'" Damian says, cutting off the link abruptly. I growl, turning on my heel and stalking toward the front of the castle to my office. Pushing it open, I see a messy scene before me. Damian has boxes of files scattered all over

the floor. Dustin is also rummaging through paperwork, and I spot Gannon passed out drunk in a chair by the window. The smell of liquor hangs heavily in the air, and it is so unlike Gannon to get himself into this sort of state. Clicking my tongue, I turn my attention to Damian and Dustin just as Dustin hands Damian what appeared to be a picture.

"Here's another one."

"How the fuck did we not figure this out?" Damian mutters under his breath. He suddenly runs his arm over my desk, swiping everything off it, and it crashes to the floor as he and Dustin start setting out documents and pictures.

"Marissa isn't her mother; you were right," Damian says, a grave expression on his face.

Concerned and confused, I walk to the table. *What have they gotten themselves into now?* I wonder. *Is this an elaborate ruse to get me to go easier on Ivy?*

"The man pretending to be Ivy's father, Jason Clenton, was King Garret and Queen Tatiana's gardener. Marissa was a staff member inside the castle, but everyone assumed she was a cleaner or cook. We could never find any documentation of what position she applied for," Damian says, his eyes manic, while sliding a document over to me.

"Okay, but did you find anything on Azalea?" I ask him, still unsure what to make of this situation.

"That's just it. Azalea never existed in any files: we don't even have her birth certificate, but we have this," Dustin says, handing me an application form for a job. I glance over it, noting Jason's name on top of the document.

"For a gardener position?" I ask, shaking my head, wondering what this was supposed to mean.

"Look in the notes, down the bottom and the date. We were so busy looking at Marissa's files, we never thought to check anyone else's, assuming they were killed when she opened the gates for the hunters. My eyes scan over the document to see some handwritten notes by the King and Queen.

The applicant has a partner wishing to apply for a nanny position. It then lists Marissa's name and her mobile number. It's dated three days after Azalea was born. Dustin hands me another document, which I recognize as our old staff application. Inside are her identity documents, a criminal history which appears squeaky clean, but down the bottom was a part saying: *Applicant admits she has a seven-year-old child and can't work weekends as her babysitter works on Saturdays and Sundays.* I glanced at her records, catching note of the start date. So, she applied to work for our family years after Garret and Tatiana? My eyes look up to Damian's and Dustin's. "Abbie's parents had to be watching the woman's daughter, right?" Damian nods.

"Azalea would have been seven when Marissa started working here. Nine, when my sister died, which wasn't long before Ivy ended up in the orphanage." I tell him, glancing back down at the paperwork.

"Yes, she worked for the King and Queen for two years. Azalea would have been two when she went missing, which matches everything else; your sister was killed eight years later, making Azalea ten at the time. *AND* we found something else," says Damian, his eyes wide with madness.

He hands me an aged but elegant notebook. I feel annoyed. Can he just tell me what he's on about?

"Why are you giving me a book?" I ask.

"It's a diary," says Damian. "And it belonged to the Queen."

. "Where did you get this?" I ask him.

"When we visited the kingdom with Ivy, we found it in a shoebox in the shed. They were mainly working diaries with appointments, and that was stuffed down the bottom. Dustin and I found it today when we looked through the box."

"My eyes scan the page, and I gasp. A picture of a small child sitting on the Queen's lap eating a strawberry from her mother's fingertips has been crammed between the pages. I see Marissa standing nearby in the background, watching them in her uniform. Those cold eyes send shivers up and down my spine. "That was taken two days before the attack; look at the date. More importantly, look at the name," Damian says.

Azalea Ivy-Rose Landeena, 4-years old.

The large office suddenly feels small and stuffy. My head grows warm as I grapple with this new information. Could Ivy, the rogue girl from the orphanage, be Princess Azalea, the royal heir and my royal match who was taken as a baby? A girl who had been presumed dead for over a decade? I start to panic. Does this mean I damaged our bond, potentially permanently, over this mistake? How did I not put the pieces together?

"Ivy... is Azalea," I mutter "Are you positive?" I ask, wanting to be 100% sure I had the right information. However, like a dark veil being lifted, everything starts to become crystal clear. So many things click into place... her instincts... her eyes. How could I be so *stupid?* I want to hit myself, hit *something.* We assumed she was a werewolf because that's what Ivy thought she was, what she was listed in the orphanage, and what her kidnapper parents were.

"One way to be 100% positive, though I am positive, Ivy is Azalea. Check this out...," says Damian, pointing to the following line in the diary, which lists Azalea's meal plan, her feed times, and routine. Along with identifying characteristics, height, weight measurements, as well as a birthmark. According to the diary, there was a strawberry-shaped birthmark on her inner left thigh along the crease at the apex of her legs. My brows furrow, trying to remember if I noticed any mark on her there, but I wasn't really paying attention when I had my face down there, too busy enjoying the noise she made and the taste of her flesh.

"In the back of the diary were some things the Queen listed, complaints she had warned to her husband about Marissa," Dustin says, turning the diary over and upside down before opening the back page.

"Marissa was warned numerous times for calling Azalea Ivy instead of using her first name. She was also whipped three times on separate occasions when she was caught telling Azalea to call her mummy," Dustin continues, pointing out the different notations made inside the diary.

"Ivy's Lycan. She's fucking royalty!" I murmur, horrified. Some part of me hopes that we're wrong while longing to be right. On one hand, she would no longer be tied to that evil woman. On the other, things would get a whole hell of a lot more complicated.

"What have I done?" I whisper. Damian folds his arms, watching me before rubbing his chin. Dustin falls back in his chair and scrubs both hands down his face.

"We will work it out. She'll forgive you," Damian says, and I shake my head.

"I blamed her!" I roar, punching the desk. The wood creaks and groans, splitting down the middle whilst I try to rein control over myself.

"She'll forgive you, Kyson. You aren't the only one to blame. We all should have figured it out," Damian says and Dustin nods, putting his head down.

"She is a Lycan. I could have killed her by tossing her aside, Damian. She could have fucking died! Lycan bonds are sacred, but that explains why she never shifted. It explains so much and I could have killed her. Lycan's need their bonds!" I yell at him.

"You didn't know! You just need to get her to mark you, and it will be fine. Ivy being a Lycan, can go into heat any day now, Kyson, and she will mark you, which will reforge the bond completely. She won't be able to help herself. You said it yourself, that the bond wasn't completely severed for you, so it couldn't have been for her either, you never outright rejected her, luckily! Only werewolves can reject their mates, us doing so can kill us or turn us savage! You can still fix this my King. Once she marks you there is no way for her to break the bond, not without hurting herself anyway," Damian says, trying to reason.

"Your words are making it worse, Damian. She would have been in agony. No wonder she fretted the way she did," I say, dropping into my chair and placing my head in my hands.

"You can't take back what you did, but you can make it up to her, Kyson," he replies, but I don't see how that would be possible.

"She barely lets me touch her!" I snap at him.

"Yet she is acting on instinct mostly these last couple of days. It is only a matter of time before she shifts," Damian says, and I sigh before looking up at him and shaking my head.

"If she doesn't mark me beforehand, her shift will be excruciating since I put the stress on our bond. She would already be weakened," I scoff, shaking my head at how badly I fucked everything up. Damian and Dustin say nothing, knowing I am right. What could they say other than I fucked up? Now I just had to hope she would forgive me for it. They tried to warn me. Everyone tried to warn me.

We are in the middle of packing everything up when a sudden realization strikes me as I glance at Dustin. "Wait, you should be with Ivy. She wanted to leave the room earlier," I tell him, and his head snaps up.

"You could have told me, shit, she is probably wondering why I am not around," Dustin says, getting to go in search of her. I shake my head.

"It's fine; I can feel she is fine. She must still be in the room," I breathe.

"I suppose I should go see if I can find this birthmark before I tell her, that is if she lets me touch her," I huff before walking out of my office to go in search of her.

CHAPTER
FORTY-FOUR

K YSON
Anxiety fills me as I approach our room, wondering if he managed to sneak out without a guard. However, I am surprised to walk in and find her sitting on the floor in front of the fireplace. One of my books is open on the floor beside her and the tablet is in her hand. Her tongue is poking out the side adorably as she presses her fingers to the touch screen before holding the tablet up to listen to the words.

Once she is done, she sets the tablet down to do the following sentence. I stop behind her, and she doesn't look up until my shadow blocks out the heat from the fireplace. Only then do I realize she is shivering, and goosebumps cover her skin. I bend down and pick up my book, and she sighs. "I was going to put it back," she says, her teeth chattering. *Pride and Prejudice*. I hand it back to her, and she takes it.

"You can touch whatever you like, Az." I pause, almost calling her Azalea. "Whatever you want, just ask Ivy. What's mine is yours," I tell her, and she nods, taking the book from me and finding her page.

"I thought you wanted to go for a walk?" I ask her, sitting down behind her and propping my arm on my knee. I lean back against the armchair, trying to figure out how to ask her if I can not only look between her legs but also tell her she isn't the daughter of a monster. Before she can answer, though, Clarice opens the door, bringing in our dinner.

"What chapter did you get to, my Queen?" Clarice asks her, bringing her tray over and setting it on the coffee table.

"Only page eight," Ivy says with a frown.

"You'll be able to read by yourself in no time," Clarice nods.

I do notice that Ivy doesn't bat an eyelash at Clarice using her title. It's almost as if she had come to accept it. Ivy thanks her, and I see how she subtly sniffs the air before frowning when she realizes the meat is what I consider to be burned or ruined. I swap our plates, handing her mine.

"Can you ask the kitchen staff to prepare Ivy's meals the same way as mine from now on?" I ask Clarice.

"From now on, my King," she says, her eyes flicking to Ivy, who is typing away again.

"Yes, Clarice," I tell her, and she glances between the both of us.

"And you're sure, my King?" Clarice asks, and I sigh. News clearly travels fast. I haven't been here five minutes, and the entire castle is now aware. *Would it kill my guard to have a little discretion?* I think, annoyed, realizing I have no choice but to tell her tonight.

"Positive," I nod at her.

"Very well, my King. Enjoy your book, Ivy," Clarice tells her, but Ivy isn't even paying attention, too busy typing into the device. Clarice smiles before leaving. I eat, watching Ivy let her food get cold before taking the tablet from her.

"Eat first. Your food is going cold," I tell her, and she growls. Ivy folds the corner of the page and shuts the book. I internally cringe. My biggest pet peeve is folded book pages, and it's a first edition, making it even more cringe-worthy. I remain quiet, knowing if I say anything, she won't understand. It'll take some time before she realizes the importance of first editions.

218

Ivy picks up her knife and starts cutting her meat, devouring her food hungrily. She shivers, her entire body shuddering from it. Her teeth are chattering, yet her skin is flushed like she is overheating. I reach over her, touching her head to find her skin blistering hot, and the moment my hand comes in contact with her skin, she sighs, pressing against it. Yet her scent hasn't changed, so it couldn't be her going into heat, her pheromones aren't strong enough for it to be heat. I move my hand off her head, and she shivers again before going back to her food.

"Did you find Gannon?" she asks. I nod, watching her. She's eating like she hasn't been fed in weeks, and I remember I was the same way before I shifted.

"Yes, I did. What did you do today?" I ask her.

"Nothing, I couldn't find Dustin, then I got distracted with the tablet and tried to read the book," she says, shrugging. Ivy went back to her food, only slowing down when she was nearly finished. She chews slowly, exceptionally slowly, and her face pales before she jumps up, running for the bathroom.

"Ivy?" I call, setting my plate aside when I hear her gag. Rushing into the bathroom, I find her head in the toilet bowl as she throws up.

"You alright?" I ask, grabbing her hair as she continues to be sick. She eventually falls backward on her butt.

"Must be the stupid fruit salad, been feeling sick since eating it," she groans, clutching her stomach before laying on the cool tiles. I flush the toilet and move to turn the shower on.

"The fruit salad?" I ask.

"Yeah, I think some of the fruit is off; it tasted funny?"

I nod, gripping her shoulders and sitting her upright. "I don't think it's the fruit salad; I think you may be going to shift soon," I tell her.

"I can't shift; I would have already," she murmurs.

"Well, I would say that is wrong; you are just a late bloomer since I hurt our bond," I tell her, peeling off her sweater.

"I don't want to shift; I don't want to shift without Abbie!" she says, sitting upright. Her face threatens panic. I grip her shoulders, stopping her from getting to her feet.

"I am right here with you, Ivy," I tell her, but she pushes my hands away.

"No, I want Abbie."

I grit my teeth and look away. It hurts me deeply to know she'd rather be with Abbie, but I can't blame her. Taking a deep breath and willing myself to remain calm, I face her, cupping her face in my hands. "Abbie isn't here, but I am. So calm down. You won't be alone," I tell her, but her eyes brim with tears as she starts hyperventilating, evidently experiencing another panic attack. Her breathing turns rapid and shallow.

"No, No," she shakes her head.

"Shh Ivy, calm down. Let's just get you in the shower first," I tell her, but every time I go to remove more of her clothes, she slaps my hands and tell me not to touch her.

Unclipping her bra, she growls at me. "Get out!" she snaps.

"Ivy?"

"Get out, this is your fault, now get out!" she screams at me. Her eyes blaze brightly, almost glowing as she continues to panic. I chew the inside of my lip, knowing it is just the shift bringing on her sudden change in emotions. It truly brings out our monstrous side. Yet I can feel her resentment towards me and hurt that I am the reason she is delayed.

FORTY-FIVE

K YSON
"I won't touch you then, okay, but I am staying. You're
not shifting on your own," I tell her, fighting the urge to stifle her
worry by using the bond and calling. She looks away from me.

"I said get out," she whispers, wiping a stray tear. My heart
pinches at her defeat and I know she blames me for this; I blame
myself.

"I will find you some clothes," I tell her, getting up off the floor
and walking out. I find her some of my clothes and set them on the
bed before standing by the bathroom door and listening.

I am only met with silence and the sound of the running of the
water. I knock on the door, but she doesn't answer.

"Ivy, I am going to come in, okay," I call out to her. " I need to
make sure you're safe." I wait, but she doesn't answer, so I gently
push the door open to find her clothes scattered on the floor and her
sitting in the bottom of the shower directly under the water. Her skin
looks red from how hot she had turned up the shower temperature.

"Ivy?" I ask, crouching beside her just outside the shower spray.
She turns her head to the side, and I notice her eyes glowing. Why

couldn't her shift wait one more day so I could explain? Now is probably the worst time to tell her something that will no doubt make her feel more emotional than she already is. The best I can do is walk her through the changes so she feels less scared.

"It's so cold," she murmurs, and I nod.

"Yes, then you will be hot, then cold again," I tell her, and she nods, tucking her face back into her knees. I look at the window, click my tongue, and shake my head. There is no moon high in the sky tonight.

"Come on, we can lay in front of the fireplace; I will move all the bedding over there," I tell her, holding out my hand to her. She lifts her head and looks at it.

"There is no moon tonight," she says, and I press my lips in line that she has noticed. I nod my head.

"I will be right by your side. I'm not going anywhere, but I do need to ask a favor you probably won't like," I tell her. Ivy looks at my hand before sighing.

"What is it?"

"Let's get you dry first," I tell her. Her eyebrows pinch together before she takes my hand, and I pull her to her feet. She wraps a towel around shivering, naked body. Though her teeth are chattering, she still looks flushed. I hand her one of my shirts, and she dries herself. As she dresses, I move the furniture in front of the fireplace before dragging the mattress and blankets over. I turn to face her to see her hunched over while rummaging through the drawer for underwear. Her other hand is clutching her stomach.

"Ivy," I call out to her. Ivy looks over at me before retrieving a pair and slipping them on. She walks over, lying down closest to the fire and tugging the duvet over herself. I grab her book, bring it over and kneel on the mattress beside her.

"You should try to sleep while you can before the pain becomes too much; I can read to you if you like."

She rolls over to face me. "If that was supposed to make me feel better, it didn't," she says but yawns. I chuckle, placing the book on the pillow.

"Have you got any birthmarks?" I ask her, and she yawns again before she nods.

"Yes, on my leg, next to...," she pauses. "It looks like a smudge," she says.

"Can I see it?"

"What? No," she says, rolling herself tighter in her blanket. "Why?" she says, glaring at me.

"I won't do anything, I promise, I just want to see it, to confirm something."

"Something like what?" she demands, her eyes narrowing.

"Your identity."

She snorts and rolls her eyes. "Great, what now, is my father the boogeyman or grim reaper?" she scoffs.

I take a deep breath. I guess it's now or never. "No, Ivy. I believe your father was the King."

Ivy stares at me, her expression hard to read. Then, she laughs coldly. "That isn't funny, Kyson."

"I know it isn't funny because if I am right and you are the King's daughter, that also means Marissa wasn't your mother, and you are the stolen princess from the Kingdom of Landeena," I tell her.

She stares at me in shock before shaking her head. "No, Marissa is my mother," she replies though she seems confused, less sure.

"We believe Marissa was your nanny, and she took you when she killed your parents. The royal baby Azalea was never found. I didn't believe it myself but Ivy... it all makes sense. The timeline, your birthmark, everything. "

Her eyes widen and then narrow as she looks at me with a cold rage. "Is this some trick? Are you really that cruel to think doing something like this would be funny? Is this some punishment of yours?" she chokes out, tears brimming and spilling over and down her cheeks. Her lip quivers uncontrollably and I can feel through the bond she honestly believes I am saying this to hurt her more. She doesn't trust me at all, and my stomach sinks at the thought.

"I know I fucked up, but please, Ivy, just let me check. I swear I won't ask for anything else; I just have to be sure; I wouldn't have told you if I didn't believe it were true," I plead with her.

"Yet you were quick to believe I am the daughter of a monster?" she jeers.

I sigh and nod. "I was angry, and what I did was wrong, but please, Ivy. I just want to be certain."

"Well, you will find out when I shift tonight then, won't you?"

"That's why I need to know; if you're Lycan Ivy, I could have killed you when I ignored our bond, which could affect your shift. The fact you are shifting makes this dire. Lycan are more sensitive to the bond, our souls are tied to each other once marked. So please, I know you don't want me touching you, but I need to see because if you are, I want to be prepared if you don't shift properly."

Ivy blinks, dumbfounded by the news, her mouth opens and closes a few times as if she is trying to think of something to say. The shock and confusion is clear on her flushed face.

"I believe you may be a Lycan and not a werewolf," I repeat letting my words settle over her.

"Excuse me? Any more terrible news you want to give me tonight, Kyson?" she snaps before groaning and hunching over in pain.

I tug her to me, pulling her onto my lap rolled in her blanket. She whimpers, and her entire body shudders for a few moments before relaxing while I rub her back. Suddenly, Ivy lurches forward in my arms, tripping as she tangles in the blanket. She gets to her feet racing for the bathroom to throw up once again.

FORTY-SIX

KYSON

I scramble to my feet, following Ivy into the bathroom. Her skin feels clammy as she ambles to the sink basin to rinse her and brush her teeth. Leaning on the door frame, I watch her wet her face before wetting the back of her neck. She stops beside me when she goes to leave, and I step aside, letting her pass. By the time she gets back to the bed in front of the fireplace, her teeth are chattering once more. Goosebumps cover every inch of flesh as she huddles beneath the blanket.

As she rests, I can see her mind churning. I can feel it, feel her confusion yet also curiosity and fear of knowing the truth. Her pain writhes through the bond, the cramping, nausea. Seeing her struggle selfishly makes me glad that I don't have to experience it myself again. It's just the initial shift, the body preparing itself. A Lycan's first shift always sticks with you; it is excruciating. Hers would be made worse by my sabotaging of the bond.

"It makes no sense," she murmurs, barely audible even to my ears. I roll on my side, peeling the blanket back. She is bundled up like a Lycan burrito.

225

"What doesn't?" I ask her.

"If it were true, why would she take me? Why not kill me?"

"Unfortunately, not everything makes sense, Ivy, and I don't think I want to make sense of that woman's mind; if it made sense, we would be like her if we shared her mindset," I answer.

Ivy sighs, and her big cerulean blue eyes peer up at me. "And if you're wrong?"

"I'm not. I was the first time; I am sure this time, Ivy," I answer.

"But if you are?"

"Then nothing, you're still my mate, and you are not your mother," I tell her. She snuggles down in the blanket, only her nose up peeking out from the blanket.

"My body heat will help regulate your temperature. The bond calls for it now. It recognizes me, Ivy. Don't suffer just because I was a prick. You have me and the bond; use it. I won't force you to do anything unless you ask me to," I tell her.

"Why would I ask you to?" she says, like I am absurd.

"The calling, Ivy. I know you don't like me using it, but there is a reason male Lycans are gifted with it."

"Yeah, to rape women," she says with a roll of her eyes. She is half correct. It is barbaric when viewed from that perspective. But it gets a bad rap because of that.

"I would never rape you. Do you think that little of me?"

"I don't think much of you when you use it to get what you want," she says, and I sigh.

"It's not used just for getting you to submit. It helps calm the bond. Calm your bond to me, Ivy. Yes, it can be used in a sense as an aphrodisiac or to calm you, which is my only intention to calm our bond, and to forge it as you go through this change," I tell her.

She clicks her tongue, and her eyes flit away as she shudders and her teeth clatter.

"If you mark me, you would be able to feel me better. Once the bond is forged for Lycans, we can even get a sense of each other's thoughts. It goes beyond just feeling each other's emotions."

"How so?" she asks.

"I can tell when you're hurt, like your hand. For example, mine hurt too. I can feel your curiosity to know if I am right about you being Azalea. Yet your apprehension at also knowing, I can tell that I scare you," I admit before swallowing.

"But I haven't marked you?"

"No, but I have marked you. Once you mark me, there is nothing you would be able to hide from me, Ivy, I will feel and sense everything when it comes to you, but that goes both ways. You will also feel everything I feel."

If she doesn't mark me, she'll cetainly be in for a long night. However, I doubt my ability to convince her. "Marking me will strengthen you," I tell her in a last-ditch effort.

"I don't want strength, Kyson; I am sick of being strong. Sick of biting my tongue, sick of answering to someone, sick of the mold everyone puts me in. I'm tired. Strength? Strength isn't physical; it's enduring. Enduring of everything when all you want to do is nothing but crumble and let it go; it becomes too heavy. Abbie and I were each other's strength, each fighting to hold on for the other; I don't need strength, Kyson. I need peace," she says with an exasperated sigh.

"More than my life?" I whisper to her, and she nods. I've always been curious about what it means to them.

"Yes, nothing means I love you more than my heart is still beating for you; we stopped living for ourselves. Instead, we lived for each other. You go, I go, so you keep fighting because you can't bear the thought of leaving the other behind," Ivy answers.

"Like a pact?"

"Yes. We made it when we were fifteen."

"What happened when you were fifteen?"

"Abbie went missing.," Ivy says, glancing down at her fingers. .

"One day, she didn't come up from the cellar," she whispers so softly I almost miss it. But, I can hear the anguish in her voice making me wonder what was so bad in the cellar. What depravity did Mrs. Daley inflict on them to get this response from the bond?

"What's in the cellar, Ivy," I ask, not sure I truly want to know. The feeling through the bond alone is making me queasy.

"She was supposed to be cleaning the mop buckets, so I looked for her." Ivy's lips quiver, and she picks at the blanket wrapped around her.

"I found her in the cellar, her tunic torn, her thighs covered in blood. Abbie was standing on a chair with a rope around her neck. She wouldn't tell me what happened, but I knew. I should have known when he went missing too." Ivy wipes a tear that slides down her cheek. "He hurt her, there.... There was so much blood."

I swallow thickly, a lump forming in my throat, terrified at the thought of two fifteen-year-old girls going through this.

"She was taking too long. Abbie told me to leave, but I grabbed the other chair and climbed up beside her and loosened the noose, wrapping it around my neck too," Ivy answers, her eyes getting a faraway expression like she's trapped in some memory. The fear through the bond makes me clench my jaw. That pack still has so much to answer for.

"I told her 'more than my life.' Mine wasn't worth living either if she wasn't in it, that we would go together because her life was worth more than mine."

"And she got down?" I ask, the calling slipping out at her distress, and she lifts her eyes to mine as it washes over her. "Helping?" I ask her, and she sighs but nods. "So obviously, she didn't kill herself," I continue, wanting to know what happened as much as it sickens me. It helps distract her from the fact she would be shifting any time now.

"No."

My brows furrow at her words in confusion. She moves her hair behind her shoulder showing me the back of her neck and behind her ear. A white scar travels across her neck and behind her ear. I had seen it before but never really paid much attention to it. I know she is self conscious about the scars that lace her skin, and I just figured it was another inflicted by the whip.

"We both jumped, but the rope didn't hold our weight," Ivy says, and my stomach drops before Ivy fixes her hair, covering the scars back up.

"Abbie has a scar behind her left ear where the rope cut into her. Instead of death, we both got a headache when our heads collided," Ivy chuckles.

How could she laugh at something so horrific, like it is nothing. The fact that she can laugh speaks enough for what those two girls endured.

"And that's how it started?" I ask. Ivy shrugs.

"Afterward, Mrs. Daley started calling for us to cook dinner. Abbie didn't want to go up, so I helped clean her up. I swapped her tunic for mine, and we went to cook dinner," Ivy says, pulling her face from the blanket so I can see her a little better.

"I got 12 lashes for that ruined tunic, but what it cost Abbie was worse. Mrs. Daley didn't just give her scars that day, she broke her soul. So for Abbie, I wore it. Then we cooked dinner. Later that day, I saw Mrs. Daley get paid by the butcher who hurt Abbie."

"The butcher?"

"He delivered meat to the orphanage," says Ivy, shuddering and wiping a stray tear from her eye "After that, where Abbie went, I went, where I went, she went, more than my life. If she were to endure it, I would too," Ivy says.

I need to get Abbie away from Alpha Kade. The poor girl has endured enough. I now worry once she realizes he is married, it will truly destroy her. I now understand why the pair of them are so close. They are dependent on each other. I chew my lip; Mrs. Daley is lucky to be alive. She will never walk again after the lashes she received, yet that is even too kind. She won't be left breathing when I send Gannon back for her and God help the butcher when Gannon learns his name.

Silence eventually falls over both of us. She doesn't even fight against me using the calling. Yet as the night drags on and her pain gets worse, she moves closer before letting me under the blanket with her. Her legs kick as her pain intensifies, and I wonder why it was taking forever. It isn't until the early morning hours that I struggle to handle seeing her like that as she rolls and turns over, trying to get comfortable.

"Ivy?" I call to her as she rolls over, moving closer to the fire. Her eyes blaze brightly like jewels, her pupils fully dilated with a silver hue through them. She groans, kicking off the blankets, her skin heating. I can tell she's nearly started shifting, recalling my own burning sensation I experienced during my shift.

CHAPTER
FORTY-SEVEN

K YSON
   "Make it stop, make it stop," she cries as her cries turn
into scream. I hear her back cracking. Gripping her arms, I yank her
on top of me. Her skin is so hot that it's burning me. Her feet scratch
down my legs.

   "Ivy, let me help," I tell her. She screams in pain, her spine
breaking and realigning beneath my palms. I tug off the shirt that's
restricting her movement. Ivy pants, her nails digging into my chest,
and I feel her feet changing, her toenails turning to claws as they
rake down my flesh, tearing me to pieces and making me hiss. Yet I
don't let her go, my pain is nothing compared to what she feels.

   "Ivy, let me help!" I repeat. She writhes but nods desperately.

   "Please, please Kyson, make it stop," she begs, her hands
clutching my chest and abs. Desperate to relieve her pain, I flood
her with the calling just as her fingers break, her claws sinking
deeply into my chest like hooks. My blood runs down my side. At
this rate, she will bleed me out if I remain in this flimsy skin-suit.
The sound of her femur breaking, and her scream will always haunt
me. I unleash the full weight of my calling on her, my hands

brushing her hair while her claws tear chunks off me. "I'm right here, you're okay. You'll be okay," I whisper, soothing her the best I can.

Ivy pants, whimpering in pain. I turn her head so her ear is flat against my chest so she can listen to my heartbeat and feel the vibration of the calling. She calms some but is still in agony when her claws dig in deeper, and I can feel them grating across bone. They are that deep. Gritting my teeth I remind myself she's not doing it on purpose and pull her hands off my chest.

Her claws are definitely longer than a werewolf's claws. Blood gushes out of me where she gets me and she sniffs the air and panics.

"I'm hurting you," she whimpers.

"I'm fine, but I'm going to shift so you can't rip me to pieces," I whisper, pressing my lips to her head.

"Can I shift Ivy? You can't freak out on me when I'm in that form, I'll hunt you," I warn her and she hesitantly nods, I drag her up my body higher then I shift beneath her, my bones breaking quickly and just in time before she clenches her hands, her claws raking down my chest, only this skin is more durable. My hand moves up and down her back as I try to calm her down when the door opens. I know everyone is worried; her screams are deafening.

"Get out!" I order at whoever it is, and the door quickly shuts just as her bones start breaking again. The shift is going back and forth, prolonging her transformation, and I can't get her to mark me; she is entirely out of her mind with the pain.

"Shh, breathe, Ivy," I whisper, hugging her close, using my temperature to bring hers down as I absorb what I can through the bond.

"Kill me, kill me," she begs, and I shake my head, hugging her closer as tears slip down my cheeks knowing my stupidity is half the blame for this.

"Please, just kill me," she cries.

"I can make you shift, Ivy but it will hurt like hell; it would be quick," I tell her as her spine ridges against my hand and her legs lengthen, her feet touching mine, fur spreading along her naked flesh as she sobs.

"Just make it stop," she cries, and I clutch her face in my hands, tilting her face up toward mine. I gasp at the sight of her eyes. There is no doubt she is my Azalea. Her eyes remain that deep cerulean blue I could get lost in. A trait only Landeena's have, their unique bloodline dating back to the Moon Goddess herself. They are more than royals; they hold power of which Lycans can't even dream. Her eyes are a marker of that bloodline, leaving not a shadow of doubt in me in who it is I hold in my arms.

Ivy is more than my mate, she is existence itself, she has no idea the powers she'll one day possess once she comes into herself.

"I will make it stop, love," I tell her as tears spill down her cheeks. I can't let her remain like this longer than necessary when I can command her to shift and force it. I hate that I have to but she deserves better, this is my fault and fast is better than hours of her screams.

I flood her with the calling, numbing her best I can before tilting her face up to me, she doesn't fight me as I partially shift back and kiss her, instead kissing me back almost as if she needs the distraction from the pain, her lips maul mine, her tears spilling down her cheeks and dripping on me.

"That's it baby, I got you, don't fight the calling pull on it, give it to me," I whisper when another scream breaks past her full lips. I kiss her fiercely cutting her screams off. She clutches me tightly when I use my command. "Forgive me baby, but you need to shift," whisper against her lips.

"Shift!" I command. Her lips part, and her face reddens as if she is choking before every bone breaks simultaneously.

Suddenly, fur ripples over her body, replacing her soft skin. Clawed hands replace her petite ones, and the sound is horrendous as she shifts in my arms. Her scream chills me to the bone, but within seconds, she is lying on my chest, only she isn't Ivy. Her fur is a deep, gunmetal gray with an almost-blue hue. Her eyes are glowing like sapphire jewels as I turn her face in my hands to mine to look at her. A sob escapes my lips when I see the Landeena bloodline eyes staring back at me.

The Landeenas all share one quality. Their eyes remain the same color, blending into their natural eye color while most Lycan eyes bleed black. Ivy turns her head to look at her hand, turning it over to find it isn't a paw but long claws slipping from her elongated fingertips. Her eyes then dart to me, in shock at the realization of her true identity.

"I am a Lycan?" she murmurs, flexing her fingers before tilting her head at the sound of her voice in this form. I chuckle, tears streaking down my face as I play with her ear sticking upright on her head. A purr leaves me as I pull her higher, burying my face in her neck.

"You're home, Azalea," I whisper to her, sitting upright, and pulling her in my lap so she can see herself, her long bushy tail wagging from side to side, and I grab it, showing her and she takes it with two hands tugging on it than she giggles. She lets it go, looking down at herself and gasping.

"I'm not hers," she sobs, and I know she means Marissa's. Relief must be washing over her, but also sadness that her life was all a lie.

"No, you are the missing Princess. Azalea Ivy-Rose Landeena. Queen of the Landeena Kingdom, and my Queen of Valkyrie. You are so much more than any of us can possibly fathom," I whisper to her while running my nose across her face, her fur tickling my nose as I try to stop my emotions from choking me.

"More?" she asks, and I feel her confusion but I am scared of her realizing what and who she truly is, what she represents, for she is more than my mate, my Queen. She is my very existence, and the existence of the Lycan race.

"You were My Lost Lycan Luna," I tell her with a chuckle, hugging her tighter and purring.

"Now you're my Found Lycan Luna."

About the Author

Join my Facebook group to connect with me
https://www.facebook.com/jessicahall91

Enjoy all of my series
https://www.amazon.com/Jessica-Hall/e/B09TSM8RZ7

FB: Jessica Hall Author Page
Website: jessicahallauthor.com
Insta: Jessica.hall.author
Goodreads: Jessica_Hall

Also by Jessica Hall

Authors I Recommend

Jane Knight

Want books with an immersive story that sucks you in until you're left wanting more? Queen of spice, Jane Knight has got you covered with her mix of paranormal and contemporary romance stories. She's a master of heat, but not all of her characters are nice. They're dark and controlling and not afraid to take their mates over their knees for a good spanking that will leave you just as shaken as the leading ladies. Or if you'd prefer the daddy-do type, she writes those too just so they can tell you that you are a good girl before growling in you ear. Her writing is dark and erotic. Her reverse-harems will leave you craving more and the kinks will have you wondering if you'll call the safe word or keep going for that happily every after.]

Follow her on facebook.com/janeknightwrites

Check out her books on https://www.amazon.com/stores/Jane-Knight/author/B08B1M8WD8

Moonlight Muse

Looking for a storyline that will have you on the edge of your seat? The spice levels are high with a plot that will keep you flipping to the next page and ready for more. You won't be disappointed with Moonlight Muse.

Her women as sassy and her men are possessive alpha-holes with high tensions and tons of steam. She'll draw you into her taboo tales, breaking your heart before giving you the happily ever after.

Follow her on facebook.com/author.moonlight.muse

Check out her books on https://www.amazon.com/stores/Moonlight-Muse/author/B0B1CKZFHQ

Made in the USA
Monee, IL
01 August 2024